Fired Up

Other Books by Anna Durand

Lachlan in a Kilt (The Ballachulish Trilogy, Book One)
Aidan in a Kilt (The Ballachulish Trilogy, Book Two)
Rory in a Kilt (The Ballachulish Trilogy, Book Three)
The American Wives Club (A Hot Brits/Hot Scots/Au Naturel Crossover Book)
Brit vs. Scot (A Hot Brits/Hot Scots/Au Naturel Crossover Book)
Dangerous in a Kilt (Hot Scots, Book One)
Wicked in a Kilt (Hot Scots, Book Two)
Scandalous in a Kilt (Hot Scots, Book Three)
The MacTaggart Brothers Trilogy (Hot Scots, Books 1-3)
Gift-Wrapped in a Kilt (Hot Scots, Book Four)
Notorious in a Kilt (Hot Scots, Book Five)
Insatiable in a Kilt (Hot Scots, Book Six)
Lethal in a Kilt (Hot Scots, Book Seven)
Irresistible in a Kilt (Hot Scots, Book Eight)
Devastating in a Kilt (Hot Scots, Book Nine)
Spellbound in a Kilt (Hot Scots, Book Ten)
Relentless in a Kilt (Hot Scots, Book Eleven)
One Hot Chance (Hot Brits, Book One)
One Hot Roomie (Hot Brits, Book Two)
One Hot Crush (Hot Brits, Book Three)
The Dixon Brothers Trilogy (Hot Brits, Books 1-3)
One Hot Escape (Hot Brits, Book Four)
One Hot Rumor (Hot Brits, Book Five)
One Hot Christmas (Hot Brits, Book Six)
Natural Passion (Au Naturel Trilogy, Book One)
Natural Impulse (Au Naturel Trilogy, Book Two)
Natural Satisfaction (Au Naturel Trilogy, Book Three)
Echo Power (Echo Power Trilogy, Book One)
The Mortal Falls (Undercover Elementals, Book One)
The Mortal Fires (Undercover Elementals, Book Two)
The Mortal Tempest (Undercover Elementals, Book Three)
The Janusite Trilogy (Undercover Elementals, Books 1-3)
Obsidian Hunger (Undercover Elementals, Book Four)
Unbidden Hunger (Undercover Elementals, Book Five)
Willpower (Psychic Crossroads, Book One)
Intuition (Psychic Crossroads, Book Two)
Kinetic (Psychic Crossroads, Book Three)
Passion Never Dies: The Complete Reborn Series

ANNA DURAND

FIRED UP

Copyright © 2017 by Lisa A. Shiel
All rights reserved.

The characters and events in this book are fictional. No portion of this book may be copied, reproduced, or transmitted in any form or by any means, electronic or otherwise, including recording, photocopying, or inclusion in any information storage and retrieval system, without the express written permission of the publisher and author, except for brief excerpts quoted in published reviews.

ISBN: 978-1-934631-90-4 (pbk.)
ISBN: 978-1-934631-91-1 (ebook)
ISBN: 978-0-9746553-9-0 (audiobook)
Library of Congress Control Number: 2017949230

Manufactured in the United States.

Jacobsville Books
www.JacobsvilleBooks.com

Publisher's Cataloging-in-Publication Data
provided by Five Rainbows Cataloging Services

Names: Durand, Anna.
Title: Fired up / Anna Durand.
Description: Marietta, OH : Jacobsville Books, 2017.
Identifiers: LCCN2017949230 | ISBN 978-1-934631-90-4 (pbk.) | ISBN 978-1-934631-91-1 (ebook) | 978-0-9746553-9-0 (audiobook)
Subjects: LCSH: Best friends--Fiction. | Fire fighters--Fiction. | Man-woman relationships--Fiction. | Chicago (Ill.)--Fiction. | Romance fiction. | BISAC: FICTION / Romance / Contemporary. | FICTION / Romance / Firefighters | GSAFD: Love stories.
Classification: LCC PS3604.U724 F57 2017 (print) | LCC PS3604.U724 (ebook) | DDC 813/.6--dc23.

Chapter One

Mel Thompson wandered down the darkened hallway, clutching the hand of her best friend, Kaya Makino. The bass-heavy music pulsed louder with each step she took toward their destination—Dance Ardor, Chicago's newest and hottest underground club. Her two best friends had conspired to drag her into this mysterious place, hidden inside an abandoned warehouse, to cheer her up on her birthday. She loved them for it, but this kind of venue wasn't her thing.

Kaya tugged her hand and Mel realized she'd stopped moving. A few yards ahead, the cramped entryway opened into the club. Mel took a deep breath, exhaled slowly, and trailed her friend out into the unknown.

The beat of the sensual, electronic music throbbed into her body. The club existed in a deep twilight, penetrated by strobe lights of such intense purple and red they provoked thoughts of jewels—amethyst and garnet—melted into mist. The colors stroked across the dance floor, merging and dividing, sliding over the polished black floor and the writhing shapes of couples.

Straight ahead, steps descended to the dance floor, but Kaya led her down the platform that ringed the space. Men and women, in couples and in groups, gathered around high tables, seated on stool chairs upholstered in plum velvet. Kaya located an empty table and hauled Mel toward it. They hopped up onto the high seats. Mel hooked the heels of her shoes on a rung of the stool, rather than let her feet dangle six inches above the floor. The plum-colored tabletop glistened in the strobing light.

Mel rubbed her temples. Her eyes ached with the first pangs of a headache, thanks to the pounding music. Why did she ever agree to this? Because Kaya and Adam, the two people she adored most in the world, coaxed her into it. She should at least try to enjoy it, if only to keep from disappointing them. She resisted the urge to hustle for the exit and instead draped one arm over the table, letting the other rest casually on her lap.

Kaya grinned at her. "Cool, huh?"

She shouted to be heard above the din.

Mel reciprocating Kaya's grin. She couldn't *not* reciprocate, faced with the girl's infectious glee. But then the music intensified, pounding through her skull, and she asked, "Couldn't we go to a nice restaurant instead? Someplace quiet."

Kaya rolled her dark, almond-shaped eyes. "I'm glad you dumped Devon, but come on. You've got to start having fun again." She waved at Mel's outfit. "You are way too hot to keep hiding in your apartment brooding about a loser you never even loved."

Ouch. But it was true. She wasted two years on Devon McCallister. Now she'd declared a moratorium on dating, though she hadn't shared her decision with her friends yet. They'd been too excited about tonight. About getting her "out there" again.

"You look amazing," Kaya said. "The new dress is perfect."

"Thanks. I love yours too."

She glanced down at herself. Her halter dress, sky blue with a plunging neckline, accentuated all her best features and set off her blue eyes. She'd worn high heels, a rare occasion for her—nothing close to Kaya's stilettos, but tall enough to make her feel sexy and daring after so long either trapped in business suits or lounging in sweats and T-shirts. Compared to Kaya, Mel was a geek. Her friend had mastered slinky, with her super-short, strapless dress in a deep green that complemented her exotic, golden complexion and those skyscraper stilettos. Jeez, it was a miracle the girl could keep upright in those shoes. They boosted her five-foot-four frame into supermodel height.

Kaya tossed her long, raven hair and loose curls over her shoulders. She narrowed her eyes on Mel, her lips pursing. "I'm under orders to make sure you have fun. I think I should get overtime pay for this job."

Mel groaned, though she doubted her friend heard it. "I appreciate the sentiment, but you guys know I hate clubs. And this is my birthday, after all."

"Adam made me pinky swear not to let you be a wallflower."

Great. Her first best friend coerced her second best friend into dragging her to a night club (which she hated), on her birthday (which she hated). Shouldn't she at least get to choose her own instrument of annual torture?

"It's weird," Kaya said, giving her friend an odd look, "but you seem way happier since you ditched Devon."

And she was. Mel had wasted two years of her life on a relationship she'd never really wanted. Devon been a "catch," according to every other woman in Chicago—an intelligent, successful lawyer equipped with an arsenal of charm. Mel had succumbed to the charm, discovering too late the handsome exterior concealed a slimy worm underneath. Discovering he'd cheated, repeatedly, had freed her. The need to control the tack of her own life, her allergic reaction to change, those were the reasons she'd stayed with Devon. Idiotic reasons. Wimpy reasons.

Some smart, independent woman you turned out to be.

Thus, her moratorium. It had nothing to do with Devon, not directly. Still, if her friends had known about her new life plan, they would've dragged her to a psychologist's office instead of a night club. She would make them understand, eventually.

A pink-haired waitress toddled up carrying a tray of objects Mel couldn't make out. The girl proffered the tray to them. "It's mask night, ladies. Pick one, they're free."

Masks? Mel glanced at the dancers and suddenly noticed they were all wearing them. This just got better every second.

Kaya snagged a glittery purple mask with a scarlet feather sticking out of the top, lowering it over her eyes. She beamed, then nodded toward the tray. Strictly to avoid being pestered, Mel snatched up a red mask and donned it. The plastic scratched on her cheeks.

Her ears ached from the noise and her stomach grumbled for some nachos and beer, but she'd settle for a margarita and peanuts at the bar. Kaya would never allow her to run off. *Stop whining, your friends love you and this is their goofy way of showing it.*

She could do the grin-and-bear-it thing. For her friends. And who knew, she might actually pull off having some fun in the process.

The glitter on Kaya's mask sparkled in the oscillating lights as she wagged her head in time to the music. Mel smiled.

"What do you think?" Kaya petted the feather. The mask highlighted her lovely eyes and the red feather set off amber flecks in her deep-brown irises.

"Gorgeous, as usual."

Kaya's cheeks dimpled. She flung a hand out to cover Mel's, giving it a light squeeze. "I've missed you, honey. We haven't hung out in forever."

"I know, sorry." Mel adjusted her mask, but it still scraped a little. Watching her friend bounce in her seat, waving her arms and swaying to the beat, she resisted a stab of envy. Once, years ago, she'd relished every chance to cut loose with her friends, but no more. She'd forgotten how. Work had become her sole purpose, her obsession.

Her shoes pinched her toes. Mel wriggled them, finding a measure of relief. "Where's Adam?"

Kaya shrugged, scanning the club. "He should be here by now. But he is a hottie, and kind of a player, so maybe a girl nabbed him for a dance."

The player comment Mel understood. Adam loved the ladies and shied away from any commitment beyond a few weeks. The hottie part...Well, she'd never admit it aloud, but she wasn't unaware of his good looks and muscular physique. No woman with a pulse could be. Like all the firefighters she'd met, Adam worked out to stay in condition for the job.

Once in a while, when she and Adam were sitting side by side on her sofa, just hanging out watching a Cubs game on TV, her gaze drifted to those rippling muscles. Her stomach would do a funny little flip-flop, and she'd wonder fleetingly how it would feel to have that body wrapped around hers. Then she'd remember it was Adam and give herself a mental slap—or two, or three. To think of him *that* way was weird. She'd known him all her life. Adam was...Adam.

So, where the blazes was he?

A waiter stopped by to take their drink orders. Kaya insisted on champagne "for the birthday girl, whether she likes it or not." By the time the bottle and three glasses arrived, Mel craved the false bliss alcohol granted. Was she getting tipsy? *Nah.* The dancers gyrating, the suggestive wall paintings, it all stirred in her a need she'd suppressed for too long, one she would not indulge. Not with Adam, for sure.

The waiter popped open the bottle and poured the drinks. Champagne fizzed inside the flutes, its golden color enlivened by the rainbow lights.

Mel grabbed her glass and guzzled half of it. The bubbles tingled on her tongue and in her throat.

Kaya sipped her glass, then bent forward. "On a scale of one to ten, how miserable are you?"

"Not at all." Uncomfortable, yes. Miserable, no.

A slim, dark-haired man sashayed up to Kaya's side of the table. He wore a lionesque mask, complete with whiskers. Flashing a charming grin, he offered a hand to her. "May I have this dance, my lady?"

The old-fashioned sweetness of his query teased a grin from Mel—and from Kaya. Her head bobbed in response, her hair bounced around her face. She took his hand, hopped off the stool, and wandered out onto the floor with her masked prince. Even with her stilettos, her head barely reached the guy's neck, but neither of them seemed to care.

Mel peeled off her mask, sighing, and plucked her phone out of her purse. She tapped the screen to speed-dial Adam's cell. Voicemail picked up the call. She disconnected without leaving a message. The music would've drowned out her voice, anyway. She switched to texting, punching out a short message to him.

Where are you? she typed. Teenagers might like using silly abbreviations, but a thirty-year-old woman should use full words, in her opinion.

Seconds ticked by on the clock on her phone. Then: *Delayed. Flat tire.*

Fantastic. As she started to type a response, another message popped up from Adam.

How's the club?

She tapped out four letters: *LOUD.*

It's a dance club, dummy.

Before she could enter a scathing retort, another text from him appeared. The man texted faster than anyone else on earth and watching his thumbs fly across the screen often entranced her. That he could maintain a conversation with her while texting someone else left her in awe of his focus and dexterity.

She smiled at the new message: *I love you, but you really need to remember how to have fun.*

Often his comments to her began with *I love you but.* He might say "I love you, but sometimes you're such an idiot" or "I love you, but you have terrible taste in guys." Adam knew her far too well to worry about offending her.

Her thumbs cramped up after she typed out her reply: *You've thrown me to the wolves here, buster. I'm about to flee.*

A strange shiver raised the hairs on the back of her neck. She glanced around the club, gripped by a certainty Adam was nearby. He wasn't, of course. She shook off the ridiculous idea, as her phone chimed and a new text appeared onscreen.

I'm coming, Adam said. *Wait for me.*

Patience had never been her strong suit. Fidgeting in her seat, she replied: *Good thing you're cute or I'd friend-dump you.*

The second after she sent the message, awareness of what she'd said whisked a chill over her skin. The phrase had sounded a bit too much like flirting. God, the champagne was getting to her. Adam would know she hadn't meant it that way.

His response came back: *Cute? Woman-speak for hot. That means you think I'm...*

Oh. Dear. God. She tried to compose a reply explaining away what she'd said, but her mind went blank. She stared at the screen as the clock turned over another minute.

Adam fired off another text: *Just wait for me. Please.*

Thank heaven, he was letting her off the hook. She answered, *Okay... for now.*

Have FUN.

They signed off and she tucked the phone back in her purse. A flat tire? How long would that take to fix? She drummed her nails on the table. A draft was chilling her exposed back and the ache in her feet had spread into her ankles. She yearned for a pair of sneakers, a T-shirt, and relaxed fit jeans.

To distract herself, she surveyed the dance floor. One couple caught her attention with their thrusting movements, passionate kissing, and hungry hands pawing at each other. She fidgeted, averting her eyes.

A figure separated from the throng on the dance floor, heading straight for her. A black mask, accented with swirling gold lines, covered everything except his mouth and eyes. A long-sleeve black shirt hugged his muscular torso and dark blue jeans displayed the rest of his assets to best advantage. Mel raked her gaze up and down that body, triggering a shiver in her own flesh. He couldn't be coming to see *her*.

The man stopped at her table, next to Kaya's empty stool. His sensuous lips curved into a decadent smile as he held out one large, masculine hand.

She touched a hand to her face and searched the crowd for Kaya, but her friend was nowhere in sight.

The man wiggled his fingers in a come-hither gesture. The top two buttons of shirt hung undone, revealing a tantalizing glimpse of toned flesh. Her mouth watered at the sight of him.

Have fun, her friends admonished. *Oh what the hell*. It was her birthday, and what harm could come from one dance with a sexy stranger?

She slid off the stool and settled her hand in his.

The warmth of his skin simmered into her, his fingers curled around hers. He lured her away from the table, out onto the heart of the dance floor. The frenetic music died away, replaced by a slow and sensual song with a beat that pulsated through her entire body. The strobe lights winked off, and in the crimson glow of the remaining lights, the stranger drew her into his arms.

Both his hands settled on her hips, urging her to sway. She took hold of his upper arms. Her stomach fluttered, her skin tingled, every nerve electrified.

He tugged her closer. His hips rocked with hers, his hands ensuring she stayed in rhythm. She tilted her head up to study his eyes, but the dim lighting concealed them. His hands drifted to the small of her back. The muscles of his arms flexed under her hands, driven by the motion of their hips. The music sifted into her, consuming her senses until nothing existed except the two of them, joined in mutual want. She surrendered to the moment, wrapping her arms around his neck, her body pressed into him. Her lips inches from his, she inhaled his breaths, savoring the scent of brandy.

She longed to slip her tongue into his mouth and relish the heady flavor. Her cheeks flamed at the thought, but desire blossomed inside her, torrid and delicious.

As their bodies mirrored the rhythm of the song, her mind blanked, her focus devoured by his mouth, his hard body, the whispering of his breaths on her cheek. He skimmed his hands up her back, fingertips dancing along her spine. Her skin tingled in their wake and a hungry ache burgeoned between her thighs.

His lips brushed across her cheek to her ear. He captured her lobe between his teeth and suckled lightly.

A soft moan vibrated her vocal chords, but the music drowned it out.

His lips trailed back over her cheek, pausing at the corner of her mouth. He dropped one arm to her waist. His other hand dove into her hair to cradle the back of her head and ease it backward.

Their gazes converged as the light struck his eyes. The irises, brown as dark caramel, scorched into hers. A thought struggled to surface in her mind, only to plummet into the depths again when his mouth shifted to hover over hers. His chest heaved and her own breathing grew shallow and fast. Need throbbed between her damp thighs.

He released her so abruptly she stumbled backward a step.

Then he whirled and stalked away, vanishing into the crowd.

Chapter Two

Mel stood there for a minute, or two, or three. A bubble encased her, shutting out the world and time. She'd permitted a stranger to touch her. Hell, she wrapped herself around him, all but begging him to…

What? Take her right there on the dance floor?

Christ. She'd lost her mind.

The slow song faded, as a frenetic beat superseded it. Dazed, she wandered back to the table. Her body thrummed. Her thoughts whirled. She clambered onto her stool and clutched her empty champagne flute. Too much alcohol, that was it. The bubbly carbonated her brain and rendered her a mute, overheated puddle of desperation. *Her.* The control freak.

This was why she rarely drank and never overindulged.

If a girl couldn't cut loose on her thirtieth birthday, when could she? Besides, tomorrow she'd start on her new life path, the one without men or romance—or steamy encounters. The stranger had revved her up and abandoned her, clearly having lost interest after one dance. Anyone who got her that revved up was dangerous, a threat to her sanity and her dignity. The epitome of why she needed a break from men.

With one exception.

Adam would've stopped her from making a fool of herself. She glanced around the club, but still saw no hint of him. The third stool was tucked under the table and the third champagne flute sat unused. Her number one best friend wouldn't ditch her, not on her birthday.

Not ever. Adam was, if anything, dependable.

He'd told her she'd forgotten how to have fun and, hard as it was to admit, she knew he'd made an accurate assessment. Her days of horsing around with Adam and his brothers had ended three years ago, when she'd committed to expanding her business at any cost, which had turned out to mean working fourteen hours a day, seven days a week. She missed hanging out with the Caras boys, who treated her like their little sister. Well, all of them except Adam. He'd never treated her like a sister, but more like a princess he was sworn to protect. As they both matured into adulthood, their relationship had matured too, though into what, she couldn't figure out. Best friends, always.

Kaya stumbled off the dance floor toward their table. Her companion, Mr. Dark and Charming, clasped her elbow to aid her. Kaya might've been a touch inebriated, but mostly her sky-high heels hindered her normal grace. The gentleman grasped her waist, in a chaste manner, to hoist her onto her stool. She giggled, pecking a kiss on his cheek. He grinned—a disarming, boyish expression—whispered something in her ear, and departed.

Mel arched an eyebrow at her friend, grateful for any distraction from the lust lingering in her body. "Prince Charming?"

Kaya shrugged. "Too early to tell. But he's cute *and* sweet." She swigged the last two mouthfuls of champagne from her glass. "And boy oh boy, can he dance."

"He's very chivalrous."

"I know." Kaya giggled again. Her grin morphed into a sly smile and, with the hand holding her glass, she pointed at Mel. "I saw you doing the temptation tango with some hottie. Who is he?"

"No clue."

"He was totally into you."

"Sorry to disappoint, but he ditched me without so much as a thank-you."

Kaya leaned back, finger tapping on the champagne flute, a teasing glint in her eyes. "I've never seen you dance like that with anybody, especially not dull Devon."

"He wasn't dull." Her ex relished control almost as much as she did, which explained why they fought so often. It was the wrong kind of passion, though.

"But you had fun, right?" Kaya's hopeful expression infected her voice too. "Slinking it up with the mysterious hunk in black?"

"Sure. It was nice." Her skin sizzled at the memory, but Kaya didn't need to hear about that.

A knowing smile spread Kaya's red-painted lips. "You're all flushed, like you just—"

"It was a dance," Mel told her. "It meant nothing."

Except it had meant something. Exactly what, she didn't know. Like Kaya said, never in her life had Mel done the bump-and-grind with anyone, outside of her dreams. Her breakup with Devon must've affected her in a weird way, making her a little bit nuts. Or it was the champagne. Or maybe thinking about Adam all night—

No. The champagne, for sure.

She grabbed her half-full glass and swigged another mouthful. The fizz shimmied down her throat, exciting, enticing, her thirst for it out of character.

Just like her bump-and-grind with the dancer.

Kaya poured more champagne into Mel's glass.

Mel took the bottle from her friend's hand. "I'll be wanting more."

Once Adam got here, she'd feel like herself again. Until then, she'd forbid her wanton mind from thinking about the stranger. That was the idea, anyway. The more she drank, though, the more her body softened—along with her inhibitions. God, it felt incredible to release her tension and float on a cloud of fizzing bubbles, carried away by everything she'd held inside for two years.

Adam. His name rippled through her like a wave of heated air. Her alcohol-liberated mind had no qualms about envisioning his rippling muscles, his sinfully full lips, his caramel eyes, those strong hands. On her skin. On her breasts.

She splashed more champagne into her glass.

Adam Caras barreled out of the club into the parking lot. At his car, he stumbled to a halt, one hand clamped around the door handle. What in hell had possessed him? He released the handle and flipped around to sag against the car, dropping his head into his hands.

Dammit. He hadn't meant to—

What had he meant to do, then? Dance with Mel. Entice her into seeing him as a man, instead of the little boy she grew up with, dependable Adam.

He rubbed his hands on his chest, on the black shirt he'd bought yesterday, determined to wear something new, just for Mel. The clothes he reserved for charming a woman into his bed seemed inappropriate for this task. Mel deserved better. She wasn't some girl he might enjoy for a few weeks. Despite what Kaya and Mel—and yeah, every woman he'd ever dated—believed about him, he was not afraid of commitment. None of his lovers inspired the slightest thought of commitment, for one simple reason that he hadn't realized until exactly six weeks after Mel hooked up with the schmuck of the century, Devon McCallister. It was then, as if the universe had a sick sense of humor, when his epiphany struck.

He was in love with Mel.

Two years of waiting for her to wise up nearly killed him. At last, she'd dumped the bastard. She seemed fine about the breakup, happier than she'd been for a long time. Adam had given her three weeks, the most agonizing weeks of his life, to readjust to the single life. He couldn't wait anymore.

He was an ass for doing this, but she'd left him no choice. Every time he tried to ask her out on a real date, she misunderstood his intentions. They'd wind up munching burgers and chili fries with Kaya, rather than holding hands while sharing a candlelight dinner. He had to admit he sucked at dating, more accustomed to seducing than wooing, so maybe he screwed up the asking-out bit. He had a bigger problem, though.

Mel couldn't *see* him.

An ad in the newspaper, announcing mask night at Dance Ardor, sparked the idea. Sparked his lust was more like it. With Devon gone, he glimpsed his opening and he had no intention of letting it slam shut on him.

With Kaya's help, though she knew nothing about his true motivations, he coaxed Mel into spending her birthday at this club. He asked Kaya to escort her here, giving him one chance to test his theory that if she saw him as a man, she'd want him as intensely as he wanted her.

He'd arrived at the club early, put on a mask to conceal most of his face, and waited for her to show.

When she strolled into the club, the sight of her knocked the breath out of him and clenched his entire body. The silky blue fabric of her dress clung to her form, its flared hem swishing around her thighs as she sashayed into view. Her high heels made her shapely legs look even more delectable and the loose fall of her chestnut hair caressed her shoulders. Right then, a fantasy had crashed into his mind—burying his face in that glistening hair, breathing in her sweet scent, while one hand cupped her ass and the other kneaded her breast.

Here, now, paralyzed in the parking lot, the erotic image consumed him once more. A long-repressed carnal need strained to break out of him. *Shit.* He had to get a grip, somehow, before he traipsed back into the club and saw her again, in that dress. How could he look at her without flashing back to their dance? To her body molded to his. Her hair grazing his face. The sensual rhythm of her hips swaying against his. He'd teetered on the verge of kissing her, at long last, the blood rushing to his groin, and he recognized any second he'd go hard and she'd freak out. He resorted to the only option his hormone-drenched brain could muster.

He ran.

At least he'd uncovered the truth. She did want him, Adam the man. He needed to show her the truth without ruining their relationship. He could not lose her, but he couldn't keep up this friendship farce for much longer either. *Tell her it was you she danced with*, the logical part of his brain urged. But a cold, wrenching fear overrode his good sense. The longer he waited to tell her, the worse it would be. He knew this, but he couldn't shake the fear. Losing Mel would be like cutting out his own heart.

Ripping the car door open, he snatched his gym bag off the passenger seat. The zipper made a loud *scritch* when he yanked it open. Cold autumn air zinged on his skin as he tore off the black shirt, tossing it into the car along with the mask. From the bag, he dug out a looser-fitting shirt—sky blue, to match Mel's dress—and pulled it on. He'd had no clue what her new dress looked like, but Kaya mentioned the color yesterday.

After all these years, he hoped Mel had been given enough time to acclimate to him. Trouble was, she *had* acclimated. In the wrong way. If they'd met for the first time tonight, he could flirt with her, let his gaze reveal his hunger for that creamy skin and those slender lips, and charm the hell out of her. Adam Caras knew how to win over a lady. He'd taken enough women into his bed to realize the opposite sex liked him. And he liked them.

But he loved only one woman. And she was oblivious.

Shirt buttoned, he hurled the gym bag into the car and slammed the door. His body still burned for her. He pulled in a ragged breath, then another, gulping in deep lungfuls of air until his physical response to her waned. His mind reeled with hot, wet visions of their bodies entangled. He dragged in more deep breaths, bracing himself with both hands on the car, and committed to a decision.

For the rest of tonight, he had to act like normal. Good old Adam, the asexual best friend.

He groaned, head drooping. This would be painful, but he could pull it off. Mel never needed to know what he'd done tonight. His deceit was in the past, a dumb-ass stunt he'd rather forget. He'd concentrate on accomplishing one task, possibly the most terrifying feat he'd ever set his sights on in his life.

Asking his best friend out on a date.

He'd been too vague before. Tonight, he'd leave no room for misunderstanding. If she said no…*Don't think that way. Make her see you.*

Seducing her he could manage, no problem. Convincing her they belonged together? He had zero experience with that.

Adam marched into the club, straight to the table where Mel and Kaya sat, leaning toward each other and laughing. He straightened, studiously avoided looking at Mel's bare back, and said, "There's my birthday girl."

Mel flew off the stool, spinning around so fast her left heel skidded. Her body catapulted forward, aimed straight for the polished black floor. Adam caught her, sweeping her off her feet in the most literal way, her body pinned to his and her face within kissing distance. His hands were flat on her exposed back, just like when they'd danced. The blood rushed to his groin.

He pushed her away.

She patted her delicate hands on his chest. "I've never actually thrown myself at a guy before. Lucky it was you, since you're not the least inclined to take advantage of me."

He choked on a breath, sputtering as Mel scrunched her eyebrows.

"You okay?" she asked.

"Fine."

He'd deceived her again. No way was he okay. After holding her so tight against him, after caressing her skin and tasting her flesh, he would never be okay, not until he'd earned her heart and ravished her body.

Mel hugged him, her supple, full breasts mashed into his chest.

He stifled a groan. If he had to wait any longer to have her, it just might kill him. One way or another, tonight he would finagle a way to get her alone and ask her out.

Operation Get the Girl was in play.

Chapter Three

Pinned to Adam's body, for the briefest moment, Mel experienced a bizarre rush of deja vu. Probably because she'd been daydreaming—evening dreaming?—about him for about fifteen minutes. A small, sober part of her brain had warned against giving in to those taboo fantasies, but the champagne had silenced that annoying, controlling whiner.

He deposited her on her feet, slapped her arm lightly, and targeted her with his trademark smirk. His gaze flitted to the table for an instant. "How much champagne have you had, Mel?"

"As much as I want. Turning thirty demands alcohol."

He squinted at her. "Are you drunk?"

She snorted, rolling her eyes. "Of course not."

Maybe a little tipsy, but certainly not drunk. Mel Thompon did not get soused.

Kaya, still perched on her stool, chimed in. "Mel had a steamy dance with a masked hottie."

Adam's smirk faltered for a heartbeat, the lapse gone before she could decipher it. Sometimes he baffled her. Considering their lifelong friendship, it amazed her that he still could. Everyone concealed a few secrets, she supposed. *I certainly do.*

Kaya observed them with an odd expression, something akin to concern tinged with excitement. One side of her mouth crimped as she squinted at Adam's legs and feet. Kaya's attention seemed to unnerve him, but Mel had trouble figuring out why.

"Ignore her," Mel said, casting Kaya a dirty look. "She exaggerates."

Kaya stuck her tongue out at Mel. "I do not. You were practically doing it on the dance floor."

Adam's expression went stony. "Let's sit down."

"Yes, sir." Mel saluted.

With a shake of his head and a flicker of a smile, Adam cupped her elbow to guide her back to her stool. He sat—or rather, considering his height, leaned—on the third stool. Kaya decanted champagne into all three flutes and raised hers for a toast.

"Happy birthday to our favorite lady. Even if she is over the hill."

"Hey!" Mel feigned a scowl.

Kaya tossed her hair over her shoulder. "Kidding, Mel. Here's to your still-climbing-that-hill, totally-hot-and-amazing self."

Mel clinked glasses with Kaya. As her flute touched Adam's, his brown eyes locked on hers. "Happy birthday."

Despite the necessity of raising his voice to be heard over the music, he spoke those two simple words with a quiet intensity. His eyes smoldered. An odd shiver shimmied through her.

Sheesh. What was wrong with her? Adam was the same guy he'd been her whole life. Sweet, loyal, considerate, rarely bossy. His eyes didn't smolder. They were the same as ever, deep brown flecked with amber. The coruscating lights ignited those flecks, lending his eyes a preternatural glow.

It was the lighting, nothing more. That and her uncharacteristic dance with a complete stranger. And the champagne. God, she was losing it to-night.

She clapped her glass down on the table. *No more alcohol for you, missy.*

Adam's full lips twisted into a near scowl. He averted his eyes, rubbing his hands on his blue jeans. The long-sleeve blue shirt he wore matched her dress and hugged his trim waist in a flattering cut. He tugged at the open collar, his mouth warping again.

"You okay?" she asked.

He gave her a tight smile and nodded.

She folded her arms over her chest.

"I'm fine," he shouted, with more volume than necessary. Raking a hand through his black hair, he shook his head. "This place is loud."

She grinned. "See. I'm always right."

"Can we go someplace else?"

"Yes, let's." Her temples ached, her ears too.

The dark-and-mysterious stranger Kaya had danced with sauntered up to their table. He plucked the mask off his eyes and beamed a wide, sexy smile at Kaya. He held out his hand. "I'm Taj. May I buy you a drink?"

"I'm Kaya, and I'd love to but—" She set her champagne flute on the table and threw Mel a sidelong, pleading look.

Mel waved her hand. "Go. Adam will take care of me."

Kaya's knowing smile returned. "I bet he will."

Adam glanced from Mel to Kaya. "You're both drunk. I'm taking you home."

Kaya sniffed, chin raised. "I am perfectly sober."

The faint slur in her voice contradicted her declaration.

"Come on," Mel said, clasping Kaya's hand. "We can't leave you here."

"Maybe your friends are right," Taj said. He kissed her hand. "May I have my lady's phone number?"

Giggling, Kaya pulled a business card out of her purse. Mel glimpsed the logo of her company, Claddagh Web Design, on the card and knew the lettering beneath it spelled out Kaya's official title, executive assistant. Mel had met Kaya a little over a year ago, when she interviewed her now-friend for the job.

Kaya handed the card to Taj. "Call me at work, honey."

Taj bowed and left.

Mel slid off her stool. The hem of her dress rode up, exposing half of her right thigh, and fluttered down when she straightened, both feet on the floor. Adam's eyes were riveted to her leg. He didn't like her dress. That must be why he was gaping at her leg. She hadn't worn anything this sexy in…ever.

She prodded his arm. "I'd like to get the hell out of here."

He jumped, shaking his head and blinking rapidly before he nodded. "I'll drive you home, but first we'll drop off Kaya."

Their conversation ended there. Adam led her and Kaya out of the club, across the parking lot, to his car. Kaya settled into the backseat beside a rectangular shape concealed under a flannel shirt.

Kaya peeked beneath the shirt. A sloppy grin split her face right before she collapsed against her seat. When Adam opened the passenger door for Mel, she paused to lay one hand on his arm.

"I haven't had my cake yet." She slanted in close, as she'd done so many times before. "Did you buy me a present?"

"Yes." He stared into the backseat, swallowing visibly. "I've got your cake too. We can have a private party at your apartment."

"Sounds good." She pecked his cheek.

He flinched.

"Adam, are you sure you're okay?"

"Get in the car." He made a pained face and added, "Please."

She got in. Her dress caught on the velvety fabric of the seat, sliding up again to reveal a portion of her thigh. She tugged it down but caught a glimpse of Adam's strange expression. He seemed to be breathing hard too. Maybe he'd had a bad day at work. A severe fire that rattled him. Today was his day off, though.

If he wouldn't talk soon, she'd start the interrogation.

He bent down to grumble, "Buckle your seatbelt."

She obeyed, mostly because she'd been about to buckle up anyway. Adam shut the door, hustled around to the other side, and climbed inside without saying a word or so much as glancing sideways at her. He yanked the door shut. Once they were out on the road, he swerved into the right lane with a tad too much force.

Kaya let out a sharp shriek.

Mel gripped her arm rest and the center console as she eyed him askance. "Adam? You okay?"

He shifted in his seat, wincing faintly. "Fine."

When his gaze flicked to her dress, he winced again and veered his focus back to the road.

The night just kept getting weirder.

Adam lodged the cake box under one arm and helped Mel into her apartment, his other arm around her back, her silky bare skin a tantalizing torment. He'd intended to ask her out tonight, but then she went and got drunk.

Mel. Drunk.

In his entire life, he had never seen her like this. Even before the last few years—when Mel grew to covet control, of herself and of any situation—she would drink only in moderation. She might sip some beer or champagne if the occasion called for it, but nothing more.

How much did she drink while he was changing his shirt in the parking lot? She hadn't seemed drunk when they danced. But then, the feel of her warm, alluring body pressed against him had shattered his every thought. Maybe he overlooked the signs. Except she wasn't slurring her words or stumbling around like stoned people usually did. Only the faint flush in her cheeks gave away the fact she'd had too much to drink. Otherwise, she seemed just…free.

Adam set the cake box on the table by the door.

Mel pushed away from him, making a beeline to the sofa. He reached for her, but she batted away his hands.

"I'm fine," she said. "You can go."

Leave her like this? *Uh-uh.* What if Devon stopped by to pester her about taking him back? What if she was more wasted than she seemed and decided a walk would clear her head, only to stumble out into traffic? Every worst-case scenario plagued him as she ambled toward the sofa, hips swaying.

Mel planted her butt on the sofa's back and angled toward him, her sapphire eyes hooded. Her tongue darted out to moisten her lips. "Kiss me."

His heart thudded. "What?"

"Kiss. Me." She skated her hands up his chest and around his neck, kneading his nape. "You want to. I want to. So do it."

"You must be smashed."

"No." She slid her butt off the sofa. Her high heels brought her up to his level, her mouth dangerously close to his. "I know exactly what I'm doing."

She sounded normal, except for the part where she was telling him to kiss her. His hands were still on her shoulders, inches from her naked back. He wanted her, but not like this. "I don't want to kiss you."

Not while she was drunk, anyway.

The fact he'd had sex only a handful of times in the past two years, and none at all in the last ten months, did not improve his willpower. The fact he'd spent two years secretly worshiping and lusting for Mel made things even worse. *Get a grip, man, you can't let it happen like this.* He felt like a bastard, getting turned on by his drunk best friend, but his dick had a mind of its own.

"Mmmm." She ran her tongue across his bottom lip. "I think you do. Want to kiss me."

Her tongue sneaked between his lips, questing, teasing.

The breath burst out of him. Heat flashed through him from head to toe and his entire body went rigid at the whisper of her breath on his skin. If this went on much longer, he might lose it and do something they'd both regret.

He scooped her up in his arms and carried her into the bedroom.

When he set her on her feet, her mouth curved in a sensual smile. "This is better. Right to the point."

"I'm putting you to bed, Mel."

"Ahhh, yes. Perfect."

She lifted her hands to his chest, but he snagged her wrists before she made contact. Pouting, she shuffled backward. Her flushed cheeks and creamy skin made her look so good he longed to taste her, everywhere. It was the alcohol reddening her cheeks. He had to remember that. There would be another time for this, for them. He thrust a hand into his hair, sucking in a deep breath. Patience, he needed some fucking patience.

Mel clasped her hands behind her neck, rolled her shoulders back, and moaned. Her hands skimmed down her throat. Her fingers brushed over her breasts and she cupped them in her palms, her thumbs rubbing the nipples through her dress.

Had she been like this with Devon? With any of her boyfriends? The thought made his jaw tighten and his gut twist.

While she glided her hands over her hips and down her thighs, he focused all his self-control on *not* looking at her, despite the peripheral—totally accidental—glimpses he got. He searched the room for a nightie, ransacking drawers and knocking over a laundry hamper in his haste. She must have a nightie. Something sensible, no doubt. An oversize T-shirt. Or maybe a simple cotton sleep shirt.

What if she sleeps naked? What then? His heart pounded, cold sweat broke out on his brow. Maybe he should run. Fast.

Instead, he turned toward her. "Where's your—"

His words choked off as his gaze fell on *her*. Mel swayed her hips in a languid, fluid rhythm that made her dress swish around her thighs. Knees bent, she threw her head back, so into her dancing her eyes had drifted shut and her lips had parted. Her delicate hands roved up and down her spread thighs.

Adam lost his breath. He stared at her writhing body, at her lush breasts and milky thighs. *Snap out of it.* He shook his head, fists and jaw clenched. Where the hell did women keep their nighties? Under the pillow had been a popular place for the ones he'd known. He prayed Mel kept hers there or he was a dead man.

On his way to the bed, he veered around her, somehow managing not to touch or glance at her, even sideways, despite her body hovering inches from him.

She hummed softly, her sultry voice caressing his senses.

At the side of the bed, he froze. She was humming the song they'd danced to at the club, an exotic number with a flowing melody that conjured images of bodies entangled. *Don't look, don't you do it.*

He hurled the pillow aside. There, on the pale pink sheets, lay a satin nightie with spaghetti straps. He hooked one forefinger under each strap and lifted. The garment unfurled beneath his hands. Short. Plunging neckline. Lace panels over the breasts and lace trim on the hem.

Oh hell no. He could not see Mel in this. He dropped the nightie and spun around.

Mel had snuck up behind him, a playful smile on her lips.

"Uh," he said, his brain locked up. "We've gotta find you something to wear to bed."

"I can sleep naked."

"No you can't." The words were strangled on a failed breath.

She unfastened the straps of her halter dress.

He seized her hands. "Stop."

Those luscious lips of hers grazed his. "I've always wanted to be naked for you."

She's drunk, she doesn't mean what she's saying. His erection had a different opinion. He was a complete ass for getting turned on. How could he get aroused by her drunken seduction? He must be a worse bastard than he'd thought.

"Not like this, Mel." He tied the halter straps as best he could and snagged her hands before she could try again. "Stand here and don't move a muscle. Okay?"

She nodded, biting her lip.

He dropped her hands and stalked toward the dresser. His hands shook as he hunted for an appropriate substitute for her scandalous nightie. Nothing had prepared him for that…that…thing under her pillow.

After a minute or two that dragged like hours, he dug up a big T-shirt emblazoned with the Chicago Cubs logo. She liked to wear baggie T-shirts sometimes.

He whipped the shirt out of the drawer and stomped over to her. She wet her lips. He swallowed, shoved the T-shirt at her, and growled, "Put this on."

She reached for her halter straps again.

"No-no-no." He grabbed her hands and jerked them down to her sides. She pursed her lips. Laser-focused on the task at hand, he yanked the T-shirt down over her head, then worked her arms through the short sleeves. When he'd finished, the knot securing her halter straps poked out from under the T-shirt's neck.

"You're no fun," Mel said.

"I can live with that." One day, he'd show her all the ways they could have fun together—naked. He tugged the T-shirt down to its full length, halfway down her thighs. The scent of her arousal teased his senses, musky and sweet and heady.

Mel raked her fingers through his hair. "Let the Arsonist come out and play."

"Don't call me that."

"What is it your firefighter friends say?" She tapped her lip as if thinking hard, then she raised one finger, her face alight. "You can set a woman's libido on fire with one scorching look. They call it remote detonation."

He never used to mind the nickname his buddies gave him, but since he'd recognized his feelings for Mel, he hated being called the Arsonist. Like he was a criminal destroying women, using them as fuel for his explosive lust. He enjoyed women, and sex, but he always treated his lovers with respect. He did not want Mel thinking of him as some kind of sex maniac.

And yet here he was, tempted by a tipsy woman. Maybe the guys were right. He did have a criminal lurking inside him, the kind of cretin who might take advantage of his best friend.

Mel thrust her fingers into his hair again, the delicate tips massaging his scalp. A groan vibrated in his chest. Just his luck. The woman he adored but who had no clue about his feelings, the one who played the serious businesswoman the rest of the time, turned into a vixen after tossing back too much champagne.

Rising, he unfastened her halter straps. She couldn't very well sleep with her dress on under her T-shirt. Yeah, sure, that was why decided to help her out of the dress. It *was* the reason, dammit.

"Kick your shoes off," he told her. "Then slip off the dress."

"Sure thing."

Adam held up a finger. "Do not remove the T-shirt or pull it up or anything like that. Keep your underwear on."

Her lips twisted into a semi-frown. She rolled her eyes, but stuck to his orders, kicking her shoes off and shimmying out of the dress.

Adam cleared his throat. The air must've been dry, because his throat had turned scratchy and his mouth had gone parched.

Dressed in her new, much less sexy nightie, Mel swept her hands down and back up, indicating her outfit. "Okay?"

"Yeah." He clapped his hands on her shoulders and rotated her toward the bed. "Now get in and go to sleep."

"Unh," she whined. "Too hot to sleep."

The air conditioning hummed, but sweat dribbled down his temples. Alcohol heated her up. He had no excuse, except for the effort of resisting the irresistible, the thing he shouldn't want right now. He tossed back the covers. "In."

Mel leaned over the bed and crawled onto it. Her hips swayed with the motion. The T-shirt rode up just enough to reveal a glimpse of her black lace panties. The black lace thong exposed the soft curves of her behind.

He slapped her ass. "Lie down."

She fell onto the bed, wriggling on her back, arms stretched above her head. "Join me?"

"Not this time." He pulled the sheet over her, but left the blanket lumped at her feet. She'd said she was hot and he decided to take her at her word. He leaned a little closer, keeping a good three feet between them. "Comfy?"

She responded with a throaty purr and an arching stretch that jutted her breasts up. Despite his every urge, he refused to compound his one smallish mistake into several enormous ones.

"Good night, Mel."

She grabbed a handful of his shirt and pulled him closer, the scent of her light, flowery perfume surrounding him. In a sleepy voice, she replied, "Sure you don't wanna come to bed?"

A bead of cold sweat slithered down his temple. "I'm sure."

"Okay. Night, Adam." She rolled over, her back to him. "If you change your mind…"

"Sleep," he all but snarled.

He shut off the light and retreated into the living room. Though he tugged off his boots and settled onto the sofa, he knew he wouldn't sleep. The Arsonist had almost violated his number-one rule. Never take advantage of a woman, for any reason. Didn't matter that he suffered from years of pent-up desires. Didn't matter that she hadn't seemed all that drunk. Didn't even matter he'd resisted her. All that did matter was, like the player everyone assumed he was, he'd almost succumbed.

Nope, no sleep for him.

And he deserved this torment. Putting on a mask and tricking her into a spicy dance at the club made him both a coward and a cretin. Wanting Mel in her current condition made him the worst kind of sleaze. This was his punishment.

He covered his face with his hands, a hard lump in his gut. Mel might never realize she'd danced with him at the club, but if she remembered this catastrophe in the morning, he might lose her anyway.

Adam punched the sofa pillow, flipping onto his side.

Soon he would make up for his mistakes with her, mistakes he'd never made with any other woman. Soon Mel would admit what she could show only when alcohol demolished her inhibitions. Soon they would be together, despite his shitty judgment. And once he had her in his arms, for real, he'd never let her go.

When he did fall asleep, in the pre-dawn hours, he dreamed of Mel in a slinky blue dress, ensconced in his arms, their hips locked in an erotic dance.

Chapter Four

Mel crept out of the bedroom and down the hallway, her socked feet dragging across the wood floor. On the living room threshold, she hesitated, wringing her hands. Last night...

Her heart thumped. Oh God, last night she'd thrown herself at Adam. Had she really untied the straps of her halter dress to bare herself to him? She squeezed her eyes shut. Oh yes, she had done that. Still, she must've imagined writhing around on the bed? The memory of it rushed through her mind, exciting her body all over again even as she cringed at her behavior.

Yet she had gotten tipsy on purpose, aware of the effect it might have on her inhibitions. At the time, she'd longed for the freedom of loosening her iron grip on her desires. Once the alcohol had kicked in, she'd given in to those deep-seated, long-repressed cravings for...Adam.

Both hands on her burning cheeks, she shut her eyes and sent out a fervent prayer nothing else happened that she *didn't* remember. She scuffled out into the living room, her gaze passing over the floor-to-ceiling windows and their view over the tops of modern buildings toward the blue stripe of Lake Michigan. The vista, her favorite part of her apartment, failed to captivate her today. Instead, she became fixated on the pair of brown leather boots with metal buckles that sat by the sofa and the two decorative pillows piled at one end of the sofa, the top pillow indented in the shape of a human head.

Adam's boots. Adam's head. He must've slept on the sofa, ever the gentleman looking out for his best friend. If his boots were still here, that meant *he* was here.

One hand flew to her chest, where a pang started behind her ribs. How on earth could she face him after last night? Acid burned up her throat, souring her tongue. She glanced down at the yoga pants and form-fitting T-shirt she'd slipped on after crawling out of bed a few minutes ago. Maybe she should change into baggier clothes, something less attractive.

Oh for heaven's sake, it was Adam, not some lecherous creep. If he'd wanted to take advantage of her, he could've done it last night. Instead, he'd escaped her bedroom as fast as he could, no doubt embarrassed by her wanton behavior. Despite his aversion to commitment, Adam treated women with respect.

But where was he? Not in the living room, or the open kitchen.

Mel wandered through the living room, down the short hallway to the bathroom, and froze. The soft, lulling sound of the shower running emanated from the bathroom. The door was closed. Though she couldn't see inside the room, her mind went wild filling in the scene. On the other side, mere feet away, Adam stood in the shower naked and wet, surrounded by steam.

The water shut off. Paralyzed, she stared at the door.

Wet, nude, muscular Adam. Right there. On the other side. Her hand floated up to the door knob, her finger curled around the cool metal. Hot, wet Adam.

The door swung open, the knob jerked out of her hand.

Adam's gaze swept over the length of her. "Good morning."

"Morning," she croaked.

"How do you feel?" he asked, squinting at her.

"Fine."

He reached for her arm, but she shrugged away from his touch. The thought of his skin on hers ricocheted memories through her mind—Adam carrying her into the bedroom, her commanding him to kiss her, his stern refusal, her slithering across the bed like a porn star. Her cheeks flamed. Worst of all, she'd expressed a fervent desire to strip for him—and nearly demonstrated it. The heat in her cheeks rushed over her whole face, her ears, even her scalp.

Adam sighed, dropping his hand. "You remember, don't you?"

She hugged herself, unable to meet his gaze. "Um, yeah."

Her focus landed on his chest. Droplets of heated water drizzled down his chiseled torso to dip beneath his towel—the only piece of cloth on his body. The towel, sized for her, strained to encircle his hips. Her heartbeat accelerated at the sight of a bulge under the fabric. Last night, he'd been aroused. Very aroused. She'd seen the hard lump inside his pants and the shameless part of her had longed to thrust her hand under the waistband and fondle him.

"You were drunk," Adam said in a matter-of-fact tone. "That gives you a pass for what you said and did."

She tore her gaze away from his crotch and somehow, with an effort that made her stomach lurch, managed to look him in the eye. Well, the corner of his eye. The trouble was, she knew she hadn't been inebriated enough to earn a pass for anything she'd done last night. The champagne unchained a desire she'd sublimated and locked away in the deepest corner of her psyche. She no longer had the luxury of denying she harbored those feelings, but she could chain them up again. With five padlocks. Each welded shut.

"Hey." Adam hooked a finger under her chin, lifting it to level their gazes. "What's wrong?"

"Nothing." *Liar.* She forced a smile. If he wasn't going to bring up her behavior, she'd repress the memory of it. "I do not need a babysitter, so you can leave. I'm sure your *femme du jour* is waiting for your call."

"How's your head?"

"A-okay. No headache, no nausea, my mind is clear as a bell." She almost wished it weren't, so she wouldn't have to recall last night.

"You seem okay," he said.

"Because I am." She shooed him away with her hands. "Go on home."

Folding his arms over his broad, gorgeous chest, he shook his head. "No. We need to talk."

"You'd leave the *femme du jour* out in the cold?"

"Stop with the stupid French words."

"It means woman of the day."

"Yeah, I got the gist of it." He scrunched up his face and cocked one hip.

The bulge protruded more and she could not wrench her gaze away from it. He was bigger than Devon. She swerved her head sideways, shutting her eyes. She meant taller, not—not—*that* kind of bigger.

She raised her eyes to the heavens. If her late father was watching over her, she prayed he'd averted his attention for the past twelve hours or so.

Mel rolled back her shoulders and nailed her gaze to Adam's. "I don't need a babysitter, which means you—"

"Not leaving." He pushed past her, headed for the laundry room.

She hurried after him. "Where are your clothes?"

"In the dryer."

"Why?"

"Because they were wet after I washed them."

"How did they get dirty?" she asked. He'd looked spic and span at the club, and from what she remembered of after, he'd been dirt-free in her bedroom. She tried to shove her hands in her pockets, but the damn yoga pants didn't have any. *Don't think about last night, don't think about it, don't you do it.*

She sidled along the wall, keeping a distance between them.

"Couldn't sleep," he said, pausing at the laundry room door. "So, I brewed up some of your herbal tea, the stuff that's supposed to make you sleepy, but then I spilled it all over myself."

"You're not burned, are you?"

"No." He walked into the laundry room and yanked the dryer door open, huffing out a breath as he plunged his hands inside to retrieve his clothes. While he lumped them in his arms, he threw her a sidelong glance. "Unless you want to see me without this towel, Mel, you better leave."

Adam without the towel? Molten desire erupted inside her, spreading down between her thighs, triggering a dampness there. *Shit.*

He watched her and his lips parted, his tongue tracing the inner edge of his lower lip.

She could do nothing except stare at his chest, at the beads of moisture still clinging to his skin.

Adam dropped his clothes and sauntered toward her, stopping close enough the scent of his aftershave tantalized her with hints of cedar and spice. He planted his hands on the wall at either side of her shoulders, dipping his head down to whisper in her ear. "You're looking at me like you did last night. Like you want to lick me from head to toe."

Her clitoris pulsed, as if he'd caressed her there. She could almost feel his fingers on her. It didn't help that his voice had lowered to a deep, sensuous rumble. A bit too breathless for her peace of mind, she said, "Don't be ridiculous."

"Last night you wanted me to kiss you. Practically begged me."

His lips quivered on her earlobe, the sensation rippling through her all the way down to her core. "It was a mistake."

"But you knew what you were doing."

"Unfortunately."

He shifted his body closer, though not quite near enough for his muscles, or any other part of him, to brush against her. "You still want me to kiss you. I can feel it."

She tried for a sarcastic laugh, but it came out as a piglike snort.

"Damn," he said, "you really know how to turn a guy on."

Mel latched onto a slender thread of screwy logic, anxious to end this. "That's right, I'm not at all sexy without a glass or two of champagne in me. The old, boring control freak is back and she's here to stay."

"You're not a freak." He closed his lips around her earlobe, suckling, flicking his tongue across it. "And I'm hot for you no matter what noises you make. Snort like a pig, bark like a dog, I don't care."

"Gee, what a flattering portrait of me." *Oh damn.* Her voice was still too breathless for convincing sarcasm. Her gaze flittered over his face and his smooth, clean skin. "How did you shave? You weren't planning to stay the night."

"I used your razor." He ran his hand up and down his jaw, his gaze traveling down to her legs. "Next time you shave, you'll think of me. Maybe you'll even feel me on your skin."

Oh great. Now she *would* think of him next time—every time—she used that razor, the one that had kissed his skin.

Adam slid a hand down her arm to her waist, curving it around her hip. He covered her ear with his mouth, injecting his voice straight into her. "In the shower, I was imagining you in there with me. Wet. Naked. Rubbing up against me. I pretended I was fucking you instead of my hand."

Her pulse raced so fast and hard her head grew light. And of course, a vision exploded in her mind, of Adam stroking himself in the shower, grunting and groaning and throwing his head back as he climaxed.

While fantasizing about her.

No man had ever confessed to such a thing before. His statement would've struck her with the same power whether he'd made it up or really had done it. Moments ago. Fifteen feet from this spot. Her bra suddenly felt tight. Her nipples shot rigid, straining against the fabric.

His hand on her hip glided down, cupping her ass. "I'm going to kiss you. Now. If you don't want it, walk away."

Moving his head, he forced her to tip her head back to see him as he ran his tongue across his front teeth, back and forth, back and forth, and for a heart-stopping second she wondered if he was imagining exploring her with that tongue.

"Adam—"

"Leave, or I'm kissing you."

She ought to leave. Part of her wanted to. But a far more powerful part craved his mouth like she'd never craved anything in her life. Since she must've already wrecked their friendship with her antics last night, what harm could it do to enjoy a taste? *Screwy logic again and you know it.*

To hell with logic. She could indulge in one kiss before she enacted her new life plan. They could still be friends afterward. One kiss, nothing more.

Adam brushed his lips across hers, the barest contact, but it robbed her of breath. Her eyes fluttered shut and her body came alive, every nerve excited, every hair taut. He traced the seam of her lips with his tongue, so delicately, and she couldn't stop her lips from parting for him, pleading for him to take her mouth. And oh, she burned for him to do exactly that.

His tongue stole inside her mouth, stroking over hers, lingering with each silken caress, teasing her into responding. Still, he kept the pace languid, tormenting her with every lap, exploring her mouth as if he planned on spending days just kissing her. His hand massaged her ass, and as his fingers kneaded harder and faster, his tongue thrust hotter and stronger, propelling her need to dizzying heights.

She flattened her palms on his six-pack abs, dragging them down to the towel. Slipping her fingertips between the terrycloth and his skin, she tugged on the towel to urge him closer—or maybe to dislodge the towel. His tongue was driving her mad, driving out reason, until she had no clue what she was doing.

With both hands, he grasped her hips and dragged her into him, his erection trapped between their bodies. He rocked it against her. She yearned to enact one of her secret fantasies, to close her hand around his cock and pump until he had no choice but to take her right here, right now.

No. She didn't want that. She couldn't. Could she?

He pulled back, studying her.

"Adam, this was…" She shook her head, biting down on her lip. "A gigantic mistake."

She spun around and raced out of the laundry room.

Adam scrambled to get his clothes on and hurried after Mel. He hadn't meant to freak her out. Ever since last night, his number-one goal had been to ease her out of friendship and into something more, without pushing her toward sex. But when he opened the bathroom door, she couldn't take her eyes off of his chest—until she caught sight of his dick, pushing against the towel. Then he couldn't take his eyes off of her, with those flushed cheeks, her heaving breasts, the way her tongue darted out to wet her lips.

She wanted him. And heaven help him, he couldn't stop himself from teasing her. He relished her reactions, because they turned him on and fried his brain like a power surge. He hadn't meant to kiss her, not at first. Everything snowballed, though, until savoring her lips and her mouth became inevitable.

Yeah, sure. Making out with Mel was destiny. Not pure lust originating from his throbbing cock, but cosmic intervention.

So full of shit.

Adam halted at the entrance to the living room. Mel stood at the massive windows, facing away from him, staring out at the view. Her living room measured twice the size of his living room and kitchen put together, but then, he lived on a firefighter's salary and she earned a tidy sum from her web design business, all because she worked her ass off seven days a week. The sweet girl who made wisecracks and played practical jokes on him had turned into a driven workaholic. It had all gotten worse after she hooked up with Devon. He'd asked her once why she didn't move in with Devon, since the schmuck kept asking her to do it. Mel had replied that she needed to maintain her independence. Her control was what she'd really meant.

That was Mel. Always in motion. Always in control.

Except last night. And a few minutes ago.

Watching her now, her body tense and her arms wrapped around herself, Adam had an almost overwhelming urge to pull her into his arms. The morning sun ignited bronze highlights in her chestnut hair and, as she turned toward him, the light shimmered on her sapphire blue eyes. She was beautiful, but more than her body, he admired her intelligence and determination. She'd built her business from scratch, working long hours to mold it into a successful enterprise that boasted ten employees.

His throat constricted. What on earth made him think a woman of her caliber could love a Casanova like him?

Adam hauled in a deep breath, and as he exhaled, he reined in his passions with all the willpower he could muster. Slow and easy, that was the ticket with Mel. He hoped. Adam Caras knew how to seduce a woman into bed, but seducing one into a committed relationship...

He shoved both hands into his hair. Before he could quash it, a groan escaped him.

Mel's brows hiked up, a question in her eyes.

He swallowed the lump in his throat. "I'm sorry I pushed. With the kissing thing. Are you okay?"

For a moment, she just looked at him. Her gaze wandered down to his legs and her eyes narrowed, her brows furrowed. That was a lot like the way Kaya had looked at him in the club, and he had the same eerie feeling the woman studying him knew what he'd done last night. The mask. The dance.

Mel shook her head, as if shedding a ridiculous thought. Her eyes focused on his face. "I've known you my whole life. For as long as I can remember, you've been my best friend. What are we supposed to do? Our friendship is wrecked."

"Friendships change." He scratched his neck, shrugging. For some reason, his heart began to pound. "We can have a different kind of relationship."

"A relationship with you is out of the question."

Her words struck him like a physical blow and he flinched. Out of the question? She'd get involved with a prick like Devon, but Adam was out of the question?

"How can you say that?" he asked, moving toward her, reaching out to touch her arm. He pulled his hand away, clenching his fingers. "What's going on with you, Mel?"

She drew in a long breath and exhaled slowly. Her shoulders sagged. She folded her arms over her lush breasts, her expression far too calm.

He knew this Mel. Self-contained. Distant. She retreated into herself whenever she couldn't handle what was going on in her life. It couldn't just be about him and the kiss. Something else had her on edge, something she wouldn't tell him.

"I have to go to work," she said.

He went cold, his mouth dry. "It's Saturday."

"You know I work weekends, nights, whatever it takes."

"Stop being a workaholic for five minutes." He dared to touch her then, settling his hands on her shoulders. "Don't you want your birthday present?"

Mel wrinkled her nose, her blue eyes glittering with humor. "Not sure. What is it?"

"Wouldn't be a surprise if I told you. What are you afraid of?"

"You did once give me a farting pillow."

"I was twelve. Relax, I've outgrown that phase." He jerked a hand in the direction of the sofa. "Sit."

Those small-but-alluring lips of hers puckered. She dropped her arms so quickly her breasts jiggled. "Why?"

"Come on, Mel. Trust me and sit down."

She marched to the sofa, her glistening hair flouncing around her neck. Her bare feet padded across the carpet, inexorably drawing his attention to her adorable little toes with their pink-painted nails. He followed her to the sofa while he drank in the delicate curves of her ankles and thighs, his gaze tracking up her legs and over the swell of her hips. He would've risked anything, even destroying their friendship, to strip her naked and run his mouth up her legs to savor the taste of her flesh, until he found her sweet spot.

"Adam, are you sick?"

Her voice yanked him out of the fantasy. His jeans had gotten tighter in the crotch all of a sudden. Yeah, big mystery why.

Mel flopped down on the sofa. Hair flounced. Breasts jiggled.

"Not sick," he said, and grasped the back of his neck. "Stay there."

"Aye-aye, captain." She crossed one leg over the other.

Hunger rushed through him. He'd kept his desires in check for two whole fucking years, but a man could take only so much before he cracked. It was his own fault, he knew. That stupid dance last night had driven him half mad and Mel's attempt at seduction had amped up his libido even more, but the kiss this morning had pushed him to the brink. A light breeze could tip him over the edge.

Oh, he was sick all right. Sick to death of pretending he hadn't burned to make love to her for two years. Why hadn't he realized his own feelings until five minutes after Devon McCallister swooped in? He supposed he and Mel had known each other too long, grown too close as friends, and they couldn't see beyond that, couldn't acknowledge their deeper feelings.

Except he'd acknowledged them at last. And he remembered exactly when his epiphany hit.

Mel had been at a yoga class and he showed up to take her to lunch, as they'd planned. Devon hated her spending any time with her friends, especially Adam. Maybe the jerk recognized the bond between Adam and Mel. Either way, Adam hadn't given a damn what Devon liked or didn't like. He kept spending time with Mel.

That day, he'd arrived a little early and her class wasn't quite over yet. He'd waited in the hallway, near a picture window that overlooked the yoga studio. Through the glass, he spotted her. She wore tight sweatpants and a tank top, her hair gathered up in a ponytail high on her head. Her bra lifted her breasts, the inner slopes exposed.

As he watched her bend and stretch her lithe body into various poses, something happened to him. He couldn't stop watching her. He couldn't stop his gaze from tracing the lines of her slender legs up to her voluptuous hips. Then she stretched her arms high over her head and her shirt rode up. The sight of her smooth, flat abdomen shot a bolt of heat lightning through him. His gaze darted up to her breasts, sliding up her torso to her delicate neck and those earlobes that begged to be nibbled and sucked.

He'd gone hard right there in the hallway of the yoga studio.

"You're catatonic again."

His focus reeled back from the past and zeroed in on present-day Mel seated on the sofa. Her knees bent, legs tipped on their sides, one hip elevated. One hand stroked her thigh. Those gorgeous blue eyes, bright and rich and sparkling, studied him with faint amusement.

Adam cleared his throat. "I'll be right back. Stay put."

When he came back a few minutes later, he carried a layer cake on a cardboard platter balanced on one hand, and a small gift-wrapped box in the other. A plastic shopping bag, its handles hooked around one wrist, rustled as he moved toward Mel.

She smiled and warmth spread through his chest. A different kind of warmth. Something triggered by a deep, aching longing. Not for her body, but for her. He loved this woman. He'd realized that a few minutes after his libido overwhelmed him at the yoga studio, when a single thought popped into his brain.

Devon gets to touch her. But I'm the one who loves her.

In that moment, a weight had slammed into his chest and a wave of cold had doused his lust. He realized their relationship had changed in gradual, subtle ways over the years. Every time he'd admired her body, every time he'd imagined kissing her, every time his heart hurt thinking of her with someone else, he'd passed it off as nothing—until his epiphany in the yoga studio woke him up to the new reality.

They were more than friends and had been for a long time.

Back in the here and now, he set the cake on the coffee table in front of Mel.

She leaned forward, rubbing her palms together as she oohed at the confection. "Is that red velvet?"

"Of course. It's your favorite."

"You know me so well." She inhaled deeply, eyes half closing, and moaned with pleasure. "It smells wonderful."

Why did she have to go and do that? He tried to steel himself against her sex appeal. Yeah right, that'd work. He blew out the breath he'd forgotten he was holding and concentrated on his task. From the shopping bag, he produced two plates and two forks, a knife, and napkins emblazoned with "Happy Birthday." He placed them on the table. The gift in his hand, he settled onto the sofa beside her, a good two feet away from her, so as not to spook her or torture himself any more than necessary.

Adam cleared his throat, averting his gaze from her enraptured admiration of the cake. "Kaya said you two had a party of your own at lunch yesterday. I hope you're not caked out."

"Oh no." Her voice had gone throaty, her eyes glossy. "Can't have too much cake on your birthday. Or the morning after your birthday." She straightened and her eyes flicked down to the gift in his hand, then back up to his face. "Cake or present first?"

"The birthday girl gets whatever she wants."

Mel smiled again and his heart stuttered. "Anything?"

She purred the single word, her lips sliding into a teasing curl.

First, she freaked out over a kiss. Now, she flirted with him. He was so far gone, he didn't even care if she confused the hell out of him. "For you, Mel, anything."

Despite what she'd said about a relationship being out of the question—a relationship *with him*—he couldn't help feeling like he still had a chance with her. A chance at more. Trouble was, he'd never had a real relationship. After his screw-ups last night, maybe he didn't deserve her. But he needed her. For the first time ever, he wanted more than sex with a woman. He wanted something real and permanent.

Mel believed they couldn't have a real relationship. It was "out of the question."

And he no clue how to change her mind. Talking about feelings? He sucked at that, had no experience with it—especially with a woman. Not just any woman either, but the only one he'd ever really needed, the only one he'd ever loved. No wonder he floundered every time he tried with her. Maybe if he started with the physical, showed her how good they could be in bed, then the rest would fall into place. Yeah, he sucked at romance. But he had a talent, one he'd honed for his entire adult life. He knew how to pleasure a woman.

After her display last night and their mind-blowing kiss this morning, he had all the proof he needed that she wanted him as much as he wanted her. He latched onto that thought, onto the hope, and contemplated the many ways he might, slowly and delicately, seduce his best friend.

Chapter Five

Mel reached for the gift, fingers wriggling. "Present first. Gimme."

In the wake of the laundry room incident, she'd been about to bolt and hide out in her office all weekend to avoid the fallout. One whiff of red velvet cake and the anxiety evaporated, replaced by a girlish glee at the prospect of pigging out on dessert and ripping open a present. She could almost forget about the Adam issue. How she slurped a teensy bit too much champagne and threw herself at him. How she not only let him kiss her, but actively kissed him back.

What on earth had come over her? Their friendship meant more to her than a moment's pleasure.

Adam handed her the small box, wrapped in sparkly pink paper with a tiny pink bow perched on top. Adam sat a couple feet away, body rigid, one hand on his knee with his fingers tapping. He was still peeved about her rejecting him. She knew it. He'd seemed to take it the exact wrong way when she told him a relationship with him was out of the question. It wasn't about him, not really. She'd made her decision before her birthday.

At the thought of sharing her decision with Adam, her stomach burned with acid. How could he ever understand? She needed a lifestyle change, one that would make no sense to a man like him.

"You planning to open that present this year?"

"Uh-huh," she mumbled, turning the little box over in her hand.

She ripped the wrappings off her present and froze. The little jewelry box fit inside her palm. She ran her fingers over the velvet covering. Jewelry? Adam Caras did not give jewelry to anyone, ever. He'd once told her that, with his lovers, he preferred less expensive gifts free of any implications of long-term romantic intentions, things like flowers or scarves. His mom had never cared for jewelry and his brothers would've clobbered him if he gifted them with earrings. With Mel, he chose more practical gifts, often pretty blouses that fit her to a tee and complemented both her figure and her complexion. Adam knew how to dress a woman. But never, ever did he give her jewelry.

"It's not a bomb, Mel," Adam said. "Open the frigging thing."

She opened the frigging thing, flipping up the lid. There, nestled in satin, lay a pair of drop earrings ornamented with delicately engraved, silver-colored metal. The stones at their centers glistened a deep red. She danced a finger over one stone. "Are these rubies?"

"Yeah." He flexed his fingers over his thigh once, twice, three times. "Your birthstone."

Her eyes stung. She suddenly realized she'd stopped blinking. Urging her lids to function, she stared down at the beautiful earrings.

"That's white gold," he said.

Her mouth went dry and her jaw dropped. "White gold? Rubies? Adam, you shouldn't have bought these. They're way too expensive."

"You're worth it."

"But—" She struggled for the right words, but her brain had taken a coffee break. "I…uh…Adam, you can't give me expensive jewelry."

"Why not?" He aimed a confounded look at her.

"You just can't." She clapped the box shut and set it on the table. "If my ex-boyfriend wouldn't give me jewelry, you absolutely should not either. It's inappropriate."

Devon had preferred to gift her with kitchen gadgets or monogrammed towels. And funnily enough, she hadn't fallen head over heels for him.

The skin between Adam's eyebrows wrinkled. He shook his head, lips parted. "You're being ridiculous, Mel. It's your thirtieth birthday and I wanted to get you a special present, that's all."

She was being a bitch. An ungrateful, stupid bitch. Why did these earrings drive a spike of fear into her heart? She plucked up the box and opened it again, studying the rubies and shimmering white gold. A special present for her thirtieth birthday. Her gaze flitted to the cake. Red velvet, her favorite. Rubies, her birthstone. No one except her mom and Kaya paid this much attention to selecting gifts for her, but even they didn't know her the way Adam did.

"They're earrings, not shackles," Adam said gruffly. "Take them or don't, your choice."

His irritation stemmed, she knew, not simply from her confusion over the earrings. She'd led him on—unintentionally, but still—and he had a perfect right to get testy about it.

The stones felt cool and smooth under her fingertip, the facets hard junctures in the flawless surface. She glanced up at Adam. The sky-blue shirt, the same one he'd worn last night, lent him a mysterious air and the cut of it accentuated his muscular torso. His black slacks fit snugly, the fabric stretched taut over his groin, putting his assets on full display.

She blinked rapidly, her focus locked on his *assets*.

For a second, earlier, she'd entertained the crazy notion Adam had been the dancer who inflamed her body last night. Insane, of course.

Mel swallowed hard, unable to tear her gaze away from the lump inside his pants.

Adam huffed out a breath. "Now what's wrong? If you hate the earrings that much—"

"No." Mel uncrossed her legs and pressed her thighs together, but the heavy ache between them refused to let up. "I'm sorry for acting so weird. Forgive me?"

One corner of his mouth twisted downward, but she recognized he was edgy about something else, not the earrings. She'd gotten him wound up and left him hanging.

"I love the earrings and of course I want them." She reached out to lay her hand on his, on his thigh. "Thank you, Adam. The earrings and the cake, it's all very thoughtful and sweet."

The tension evacuated his body on a rush of breath. His lips formed a small smile.

She added, "You are an incredible friend. I don't know what I'd do without you."

His smile wavered, but only for a second, and then his lips curved up again. "You'll never have to find out. I'll always be here for you, Mel."

"I know." She withdrew her hand. Did she know? Last night had unleashed a forbidden desire in her, one that scared the living daylights out of her. Sex would ruin everything. Not that she wanted sex with Adam. Sure, she had enjoyed the odd, fleeting thought about him in that way. Thoughts of his muscles, his strong hands, his lips that had tasted even better than she ever imagined. Sometimes, when she was alone in her bedroom, Adam inspired more than daydreams. That she had surrendered to those...other things as often as she had made her cringe inside. It also got her a little hot, recalling those nights. Kissing him had only intensified her taboo thoughts, until she couldn't escape them anymore.

So stop thinking about it. Problem solved. Except she couldn't stop. Not anymore.

Yes, she damn well could. Mel Thompson had a knack for repressing her feelings.

Adam settled one arm on the sofa's back. "Birthday girl cuts the cake."

She picked up the knife. Out of the corner of her eye, she caught him watching her with the same odd intensity he'd displayed back in the club, different from the way he'd looked at her earlier in the laundry room, when lust had seized them both. No, this look was more personal, more…something.

He leaned back into the corner of the sofa and bent one leg, hooking his ankle over the opposite thigh. His bent knee brushed her leg, sending an odd tingle through her.

The plastic knife slipped from her grasp, clattering onto the table. "Look, I'm sorry I gave you the wrong impression."

"About what?"

"Us. What we are."

"I know what we are." His lips slid into a suggestive smile. "We're consenting adults."

She snatched up the knife, slashing it into the cake. "I meant what we are to each other. We're friends, nothing more. Last night, I let myself give in to a crazy fantasy. And this morning was a fluke."

"A fluke?" He laughed and ran a hand over his mouth as if struggling to quell his amusement. "What we did this morning, that was real. You wanted me and I wanted you."

Mel grabbed a paper plate and dumped the slice of cake onto it, refusing to glance at him. "It was temporary insanity."

Adam leaned closer, draping his arm over the sofa behind her shoulders, his breaths fanning over her cheek. "Desire is nothing to be ashamed of. It's natural."

"I'm not ashamed." Staring at the slice of cake on its pink paper plate, she gnawed on her lower lip. Her skin sizzled with an awareness of him, of his nearness and his easy sensuality, and of his attention centered exclusively on her.

"Mel, why did you get drunk last night?"

"I was tipsy, not drunk." Why had she done it? Because letting the alcohol soften her inhibitions had felt wonderful. Because the masked dancer had reminded her of Adam, which was weird. Because after the dance, she couldn't stop thinking about Adam in a very non-friend way. Maybe she'd wanted the champagne to fuel her with liquid courage, so she could do the things she'd never had the nerve to do before. Adam didn't need to know that, but she had to answer his question with something honest. "I liked feeling out of control for a while. When I decided to expand my business, I got a little control-freaky, kind of obsessed with work. It left no room for anything else. The champagne helped me cut loose a bit."

"I can think of more gratifying ways to lose control."

His voice dripped innuendo, oozing through her veins like warm honey, dribbling down, down, down until the heat inundated her most intimate places.

Turning thirty had messed with her head, which explained everything. No matter how much her body disagreed, she would nip this bizarre attraction to Adam in the bud. Hell, she'd better shred the bud and chuck the remnants into a volcano.

Without moving his arm off the sofa, Adam picked up the plate and a fork, setting the plate on her lap. He speared the fork's tines into the cake's dark, succulent flesh. "You haven't tried your cake."

He all but purred the words into her ear, his lips fluttering over the shell.

Suddenly, she was speechless. Breathless. Entranced by the bite of cake on the pink fork.

Adam lifted the fork to her lips. "Taste it. You know you want to."

Was this how he behaved with his lovers? If she were brutally honest with herself, she'd always been a bit jealous of those women, the ones who got to know a part of Adam she never could—the Arsonist side of his personality. Not long after he became a firefighter, his colleagues gave him the nickname, and though she'd known about it for years, never before had she considered all that it implied. Never before had she experienced this side of him.

It was…so damn hot.

Adam bounced the fork before her lips, his mouth still at her ear. "Go on. Give in to the craving, Mel."

Heart pounding, she parted her lips.

As he slid the fork onto her tongue, she closed her lips around the cool, moist cake. He withdrew the fork little by little.

For a second, she let the confection lie on her tongue, the decadent sweetness and slight tang of it spreading through her mouth. When she began to chew, the creaminess of the frosting melded with the cake, swirling into a flavor so rich and satisfying she moaned.

Beside her, Adam shifted his weight with a sharp intake of breath.

Swallowing the cake, she glanced at him.

His smoky eyes blazed into her, melting her from the inside out until she sagged back against the sofa, into his waiting arm.

Adam speared another bite of cake, raising it to his mouth. Opening his lips, he took the food into his mouth. As he slid the fork out between his closed lips, he devoured the cake with slow, sensuous movements, his eyes never wavering from hers.

She swallowed, her throat tight.

Breaking off another piece of cake with the fork, he brought it to her mouth.

"Ew, Adam." She shooed his hand away. "You slobbered all over that fork. It's unsanitary."

He grinned, chuckling softly. "I've had my tongue in your mouth and you're worried about sharing a fork?"

Just like that, a memory barreled through her. His lips on her mouth. His tongue gliding over hers. The flavor of him, that indefinable essence of Adam, penetrating deep.

"What are you really afraid of?" he asked, returning the plate and fork to the table.

"I need my best friend, not—"

"A lover?" He settled a hand on her thigh, his fingers tracing circles, the sensation teasing her skin through the thin fabric of her pants. "We'll still be friends, no matter what."

His fingers, the feather-light pressure of them, it tormented her in the most exquisite way. But she had to be honest with him. "I've never understood what the fuss is about."

"The fuss?"

"I've never been impressed with sex. It's nothing special."

His mouth fell open. "Nothing special?"

"Don't get me wrong, it's nice and all." She shrugged. "But it's far from spectacular."

Adam gaped at her as if she'd suggested every man on earth should get neutered. After a few seconds, though, he regained his composure. "I'm guessing the guys you've been with didn't care about your pleasure."

"I don't know." She flattened her hands on the sofa, drumming her fingers, considering how to respond. "I like the intimacy of it, the closeness, but the rest is highly overrated. Not worth the fuss people make about it."

With one finger on her chin, he turned her face toward him. "I can show you why people like fucking."

Heat rushed through her, quickening her breaths. "For heaven's sake, Adam, do you have to be so crude?"

"You've heard me say 'fuck' before and you didn't mind." He stroked his finger along her jaw, up to her mouth, over her lips. "I don't think you're offended. I think you're turned on."

Adam bent his head down, his mouth descending toward hers.

His phone rang.

Cursing under his breath, he whipped the phone out of his pants pocket and scrutinized the screen. "Shit, it's my dad. He never calls so early in the day. I have to take this."

At least his phone call gave her time to stuff her inappropriate thoughts into a nice, tight box in the back of her mind, padlocked behind a reinforced steel door. Yes, Mel Thompson knew how to hold things inside—no matter how much it hurt.

As he answered his phone with a gruff hello, he held up one hand in a *stay put* gesture.

She pulled her knees up to her chest, arms belted around them. For Adam, she'd risk any amount of pain, even the agony of unsatisfied lust, because losing his friendship would destroy her. And she tried really, really hard not to consider why.

"Hey, Dad, what's up?" Adam aimed for nonchalance in his voice, though he kept his gaze pinned to Mel. To her profile. Because she was staring blankly at the bookcase across the room. He'd been about to kiss her again, to begin the slow and delicate process of seducing her, when his phone rang, shattering the mood.

Now Mel was retreating again. He did not understand why her attraction to him scared her so much. Of course, he'd had two years to adjust and she recognized her feelings only last night.

"Adam?" His father sounded groggy and tired. "I, uh, need a ride home. Can you come?"

Robert Caras did not call for help without a damn good reason. Adam gripped the phone tighter. "Where are you?"

"The hospital."

Adam went cold. He struggled to keep the panic off his face, to stop Mel from worrying, but she was still fixated on the other side of the room. With incredible effort, he managed a calm tone. "What's going on, Dad?"

"Look, it's kinda embarrassing, okay?" The elder Caras paused and Adam heard a faint exhalation. "I was brought here in an ambulance. I thought it was my heart but seems like it was just a panic attack."

"Dad." Adam's pitch and volume hiked up a notch. He took long, slow breaths to calm himself. Yeah, that worked. "You should've called me earlier."

"Please don't tell anybody about this. You gotta swear, Adam."

He groaned at his father's request.

Mel glanced at him, her brows knitted in an adorable, if concerned, way. He longed to pull her into his arms and soothe her worries, along with his own, but he had to focus on his dad. Something was up, but his father wouldn't tell him over the phone. Adam sensed that in his wary tone. "Dad, I'm with Mel."

His father said nothing for a couple seconds. "Don't tell her. Please. I'm okay, I'll explain everything when you pick me up, but you gotta keep this to yourself." He paused, and Adam could picture his father rubbing his forehead. "That's why I called you, Adam. Of all my boys, you're the one who can handle this and keep it secret."

Handle what? He couldn't ask, not with Mel watching him, wondering. He practically heard the gears turning behind those blue eyes, inside her keen mind. "Sure, Dad, I can come help you with a flat tire."

Twice in the past twelve hours he'd lied to Mel. What had he turned into lately? At least this lie was for family, for a good cause—he hoped. If it turned out his dad got snookered by a telephone scam artist and lost his life savings, triggering the panic attack, he'd rethink things. But no. Robert Caras, tough ex-cop, would never fall for a phone scam.

"Thanks, Adam," his dad said. "I'm at Mercy Hospital."

"I'm on my way." Adam tucked the phone in his pocket. Meeting Mel's sharp gaze, he said, "I have to go."

She squinted at him. "I thought your dad was a long-time member of Triple A."

"Yeah but, um..." *Shit*. Here came another lie. "He accidentally let it lapse. Besides, he's only a few miles away. It's faster if I go."

She hopped to her feet. "I'll come with you. Haven't see your dad in over a month."

"No." It came out too harsh, too loud. Wincing, he pushed up off the sofa. "Mel, I'm sorry."

She braced her hands on her hips, fingers tapping.

He took hold of her upper arms. "We need to talk, about a lot of things, but I have to go and I don't know how long it'll take." He glanced at the uneaten cake on the table, a remnant of what had almost been. What would be, soon. Just not today. "If I'm not back in an hour, assume I'm not coming back today. I'm on duty tomorrow, which means I won't see you until Monday. We'll talk then for sure."

"Uh-huh."

He kissed her forehead. "Happy birthday."

Adam rushed out of the apartment, abandoning the only woman he'd ever loved, to take care of the only father he'd ever have. The man who taught him about integrity and honesty. If his dad had any idea how much his oldest son had messed up recently, he would've walked the ten miles home.

By the time Adam got to his car, he was clenching his jaw, his thoughts whirling around his dad's call. Panic attack? *Bullshit*. It'd take a hell of a lot to make his father panic about anything. Ten minutes later, after violating a slew of traffic laws, he veered into a parking space at the hospital, jumped out of the car, and slammed the door. He sprinted for the entrance and stopped with a jolt, tripping over his own feet.

His dad slumped on a bench outside the automatic glass doors, his head bowed. He clutched his hands on his lap. Dressed in flannel lounge pants and a plain white T-shirt, with half-laced sneakers, he looked like he'd crawled out of bed minutes ago. His gray hair was rumpled too.

Adam crossed the distance in two big strides. "Dad."

Robert Caras lifted his head, his bloodshot eyes focusing in on his son. "Thanks for coming. You didn't tell Mel, did you?"

"No, you said not to." Adam perched on the bench's edge beside his father. "What is going on, Dad?"

"You're the level-headed one." His father scratched his head. "Jack's a worrier, he'd get an ulcer the second I told him, and Rick would think he needs to fix me. Plus, he's on duty today and you know he's stressed about his first month as a firefighter. Toby has Sonya to worry about, what with the twins on the way. We can't say a word to them, or anyone."

A cold weight lodged in Adam's chest. He grasped his knees, his gaze never leaving his dad's face.

"It's not the kinda thing guys talk about." Dad rubbed his neck, his jaw, his forehead. "In my day, nobody woulda mentioned it. Doctors woulda said here, this is what you gotta do. These days, they won't tell you what to do. They say it's your decision. But how the hell should I know? I'm no doctor. Times like this, I almost wish your ma was here."

"She moved to California ten years ago and married somebody else."

His father gazed wistfully at nothing in particular.

Things must've gotten really bad for his tough-guy dad to wish his ex-wife was here. Their split had been amicable, but still.

Adam wrestled against the urge to badger the truth out of his father. "Tell me. I can handle it, whatever it is."

Dad nodded, his eyes bleary. "It's my prostate. I got cancer."

Chapter Six

For an hour and forty minutes, Mel paced the length of the living room, barefoot, until she was too tired to walk anymore. Then she retrieved a hoodie from her bedroom, shrugging into it as she curled up on the sofa, in the corner, her knees bent and feet wedged under her.

Last night had affected her more than she cared to admit. The weirdness of the club and her dance with a stranger had knocked her off kilter, reminding her of those inappropriate fantasies of Adam, which explained but did not excuse her craving for loss of control and her overindulgence in champagne. Everything spiraled so far out of whack after that. She had to tell Adam about her celibacy decision, to make it clear to him nothing more could happen between them.

It wasn't only the club or Adam. She'd stayed with Devon for two years, and though he frequently pestered her about moving in with him, she'd shied away from it. Her reluctance should've clued her in that something was wrong in their relationship. Why had she stayed with Devon for so long? How could she have missed the clues to his true nature? He cheated on her, numerous times, and she remained oblivious. She may not have loved him with a grand passion, but she had trusted him and he shattered that trust with his disgusting behavior.

Her attraction to Adam had been exposed. She couldn't deny it anymore, but neither could she indulge it. Until she understood her own behavior, her own sinful desires, she had to stick to her moratorium. No more kissing or flirting with Adam. No more daydreaming about him. It would ruin their friendship, for sure, because he was more than her best friend, he was her...*Ugh*. Why couldn't she define his role in her life? He meant too much to her to risk their entire relationship for a night of hot sex. Possibly hot sex. Oh hell, definitely hot sex.

She would never, never, ever go there.

Taking off the hoodie, tossing it aside, she jumped off the sofa to snag her purse off the table. The cake captured her attention and she stared at it for a moment. A crumb-dusted plate sat beside it. She'd eaten two slices after Adam left.

The jewelry box caught her eye. A lump lodged in her throat. She averted her gaze to the cake. Red velvet. Adam knew her so well, but his behavior this morning made her wonder if she knew him at all. Staying friends, with no complications, was the smart course.

Mel dug her phone out of her purse and called Adam's cell. It rang six times before his voicemail picked up, the sound of his deep voice awakening her most carnal urges. She hung up without leaving a message.

Good thing she'd sworn off sex. She supposed celibacy was like swearing off chocolate. Suddenly all you could think about was chocolate and everything started to look like chocolate, even your best friend, who'd always been health food. Yes, that explained it. She didn't actually want Adam. She craved a yummy indulgence that was no good for her.

These fantasies about him felt weird and wrong for reasons she couldn't quite elucidate. Yet still, underneath the crusty exterior of wrongness, hid a warm and silky center of rightness. When his lips had caressed hers, when his tongue had coiled around hers, the notion of stripping naked for him had seemed natural and even appropriate. When he announced he'd show her why people liked fucking...

She hit the speed dial for Kaya's number. Her friend answered on the first ring, her voice far too cheery for the morning after their tipsy night out. "Mel, sweetie, how are you today?"

"Good. You?"

"Right as rain. Is Adam there?"

Mel hesitated at the odd question. "No, he's not."

"What have you done with him?"

"I—Nothing." Mel glanced at the sofa, where she and Adam had almost kissed again. "He had to go help his dad with a flat tire."

"Hmm..." Kaya paused. "Like father, like son, eh?"

Mel rubbed her temple. "What are you talking about?"

"Adam had a flat tire last night and today his father gets one." Kaya's voice dropped to a mutter. "You'd think the Arsonist would be more creative."

"I heard that, but I have no clue what you mean."

Her friend harrumphed. "Never mind. I'm sure I imagined it."

Now both her best friends were keeping things from her. Two friends to grill. Which reminded her of why she called Kaya. "How about lunch together at the Frontera Grill?"

"Sure thing. But aren't you working? It is Saturday, after all."

"Adam was here until a couple hours ago. Stayed the night, actually. I'll go to work after lunch."

"Oooh, Adam stayed the night?"

Mel rolled her eyes heavenward, shaking her head. "Don't get any ideas, Kaya. He slept on the sofa to keep an eye on his tipsy best friend."

"He sure is dedicated."

Something in Kaya's tone made Mel suspicious the girl knew more than she was saying.

They agreed to meet at their favorite restaurant at one o'clock, a scant hour away, and said goodbye. Mel put the cake in the fridge, changed clothes lickety-split, and headed for the front door, just as a knock rattled it.

She yelped and reached for the knob. *Adam.* He'd come back at last. She cracked the door open a few inches, with the security chain barring the gap.

Devon McCallister gave her a lopsided smile. His black hair, slicked back, glistened in the yellowish lights in the hallway. The top three buttons of his long-sleeve maroon shirt hung open, exposing a smattering of hairs on his chest. When he leaned against the jamb, his loose-hanging shirt rode up just enough to reveal a glimpse of his abs above his low-slung, dark-blue jeans.

She frowned at him. "What are you doing here?"

His flint-gray eyes explored the length of her before settling on her face. His sharp gaze made her fidget. "Came by last night, but you weren't home. I'm here to wish you a belated happy birthday."

"Bullshit."

He canted toward her and she drew back. Devon's lips flattened. "Come on, Mel, we had a good thing once. Don't throw it away on a whim."

She snorted. "A whim? You'd been cheating on me for how long? The whole time, apparently."

And he'd recorded many of his encounters, storing the videos on her cell phone, which he'd often borrowed because he kept forgetting to charge up his phone. She stumbled onto the videos three weeks ago—fifteen recordings of him with various women, sometimes two or three at a time. Why would he document his conquests, and why would he keep those videos on *her* phone? It was as if he wanted her to find them. To see. To know.

She'd promptly walked out on him, for good.

Her gorge rose in her throat. All those women. The positions, the screaming, the unbridled hedonism of it all. He'd never behaved that way with her. In fact, he'd said once or twice a month was often enough to have sex. He just wasn't that sexual, he'd told her.

"I repeat," she said, "what are you doing here?"

"Told you, I'm here to say happy birthday." He poked his face into the gap between door and jamb. "And give my girl a birthday kiss."

"I'm not your girl anymore."

He snaked a hand through the gap, holding it palm up. "I miss you, baby. Give me a second chance."

"Give it up, Devon." She pushed the door, but his body wedged it open. "Move, or I'll get my stun gun."

Bob Caras had given it to her for self-defense. She glanced at the table beside the door, at the drawer where she kept the stun gun. It was too bulky to carry in her purse.

"Chill, girl." Devon backed away from the door. "But think about it. We belong together."

She slammed the door. The sound reverberated off the windows and walls. Only when she heard his footsteps recede down the hallway did she let out the breath she'd held. Devon seemed to think she owed him another chance. Though her celibacy decision was no business of his, she must prove to him she would not take him back, not ever.

No dating, no men, no sex.

Memories of Adam surfaced in her mind. She'd make an exception to the no-men part for him. But absolutely, without exception, there would be no sex for her. Not with anyone. Especially not with Adam.

To salvage their friendship, she'd have to sublimate the hell out of last night and this morning, and her naughty thoughts about Adam. Direct the energy from her sexual frustration toward work. Forget about Adam's muscles and his lips and the way he stoked her fires with so little effort.

Yes, forget all of *that*.

She straightened her shirt and smoothed her hair. Her new life plan must include celibacy. It was the prudent choice. Adam went on duty again tomorrow, for his usual twenty-four-hour shift, giving her the rest of today and tomorrow to exorcise her illicit lust for him once and for all. *No sex.*

She could do this, because Mel Thompson always stuck to her plans.

Adam slouched in an overstuffed armchair in his father's house, trying to understand the crazy turns life had taken this week. He couldn't concentrate on any one thought and his jaw ached from the tension infecting his whole body. He and his father hadn't spoken a word to each other for the entire ride to Dad's house. Adam tried to relax, to look calm for Dad's sake. Christ, it was hard.

What if my father dies?

Adam rubbed his chest, to chase away the sharp pain behind his ribs. His palms had gone clammy. He longed for Mel to be here with him, holding his hand and soothing him with her empathetic smiles and soft words. How could he keep spouting lies to her, pushing her further away when all he wanted was to throw his arms around her and never let go?

Returning his attention to his dad, he scrubbed his face with one hand. "How long have you known?"

"Six months." Dad slouched into the sofa cushions. "I went to the doctor for a bad cough. He ordered x-rays and blood tests, which all came out fine. Except…"

Adam's pulse thundered in his ears. He didn't want to know the rest, but he had to hear it.

His father let out a long, groaning sigh. "Turns out, for any guy my age, they automatically order a PSA test whenever they do blood work. My PSA was twenty-six."

"What does that mean?"

"It means I got cancer. Had a biopsy to prove it. And with a PSA that outta whack, and a Gleason whatsit of eight, I'm at high risk."

"Risk?" Adam bolted upright, his fingers digging into the overstuffed arms of the chair. "Risk for what?"

Dad shrugged. "Complications."

"What kind of complications?"

"I dunno." Frustration tightened his voice. "It's all so damn confusing. The urologist said I need to have my prostate ripped out, but the oncologist says radiation is the only way to go. Everybody says it's my decision, though, and I ain't got a flipping clue." Dad leaned forward, elbows on his knees, and sank his head into his hands. "I started looking up stuff online, like Jack says everybody should do for medical shit. But there's too much of it. I dunno what to believe, but if I do nothing…"

The despair in his father's voice clawed at Adam's heart. "You could get sick."

"Yeah."

"Are you having symptoms?"

"Just needing to pee all the time. They got me on Flomax for that." Dad lifted his head, but his eyes stared straight ahead at nothing. "And I'm on something called Lupron, but I don't understand what it does. Other than muddle my brain and give me hot flashes, like a goddamn little old lady."

"Holy hell, Dad, this is huge." Adam scooted forward to the armchair's edge, his gaze glued to his father. "You should've told us when you found out."

Dad's head whipped toward him, his eyes went wide. "You can't tell nobody, Adam. You promised."

"Yeah, I know. But you've got to—"

"No. Please, do what I say."

Adam scowled at his father, not because he was angry, but because he couldn't understand this at all. "I don't get it. Why won't you tell anybody? Cancer's nothing to be ashamed of."

His father turned his head away, hiding his face. "I get hot flashes, I can't think straight, sometimes I cry at sappy TV commercials. I'm turning into a girl. How can I tell my kids about that?"

"Aw, Dad, that's a dumb-ass excuse and you know it. You don't have to talk about the personal stuff." Adam braced his palms on his knees. "But you have to tell Jack, Rick, and Toby you've got cancer."

Bob Caras swung his head to stare at his oldest son. "Nobody else knows. Nobody. Got it?"

Adam's shoulders fell. Once his father shifted into stubborn mode, there was no arguing with him. For the time being.

"Okay," Adam said, in the most conciliatory tone he could muster. "I won't tell anybody. I swear."

"Not even Mel."

"Yeah, not even Mel." His gut twisted at the memory of abandoning her this morning. He remembered her flushed cheeks, her shortened breaths, the glossy look of desire in her eyes, and the way her tongue kept flicking over her bottom lip. Instead of making love to her right then and there, he'd lied and run off.

His father's gaze narrowed on him. "What's the matter? Is it all this cancer crap? I knew I shouldn't've called you, but you're the level-headed one."

Level-headed. Adam almost laughed at that. His ridiculous scheme with the mask had been reckless and selfish, and he'd shown his weak will when Mel nearly shattered his resolve with her pleas for him to kiss her last night. Now he'd set his sights on seducing her, as a prelude to making her realize she loved him as more than a friend.

He didn't feel level-headed at the moment. He felt like he was riding an asteroid on a collision course with the sun.

"Sure," Adam said, "the cancer stuff is a lot to take in. But I did something really stupid last night. I—" He could not tell his father. No way. "Forget it."

"Spill the beans, kid." Dad managed a shaky smile. "I told you about the hot flashes. The least you can do is tell me what lame-ass thing you did."

Adam felt the corner of his mouth twitch up. "Good point."

"So spill."

"I was at a club with Kaya and Mel." Adam fixed his attention on the loops of thread poking up out of the carpeting. "I wore a mask so Mel wouldn't recognize me and I got her to dance with me." He scratched the back of his neck, grimacing. "It was, well, a hot dance. Really hot."

His father said nothing, his expression unreadable.

Adam coughed. "After that, I ran away, changed my shirt, took off the mask, and walked back into the club like I'd just gotten there. Mel has no idea it was me she danced with." He dropped his chin to his chest and words tumbled out of him. "I was planning to tell her the truth. About the dance, about how I feel. But last night she and Kaya drank too much champagne before I came back into the club and…Mel tried to kiss me."

"Did you kiss her?"

"No, of course not. She wasn't herself." Adam let his head fall back against the puffy chair. "Mel says she knew exactly what she was doing, but it was a mistake and a fluke. She feels something, I know it. We did kiss this morning and it was amazing. Trouble is, she's got this fear of getting involved with me, romantically. Says it'll ruin our friendship. I've got to find a way to show her we can be good together as more than friends, but still be best friends too. Made some progress on that front, but then you called and she pulled back into her shell again."

Adam risked a glance at his father. Dad was smiling—a full-on, kids-are-so-dumb smile.

"Sorry I ruined your plans, kid. You'll work it out, though." The smile turned into a knowing smirk. "Sure took you long enough to figure out you're crazy for her."

Adam's shoulders sagged even more. "I love her, Dad. I've never loved anyone else. But she still thinks of me as the boy next door, not a man. I did that stupid mask stunt to prove to myself she could have other kinds of feelings for me." He shook his head. "She felt the connection, I know she did, but I don't have a clue how to make her see me. All I know how to do is…uh…"

"Get a woman in bed?"

His father said it without any judgment in his tone. Everyone, even his family, knew how he lived. How he had lived. No one else mattered anymore, no one but Mel.

"Tell ya what." Dad straightened, as if a weight had lifted from his shoulders. "You help me figure out what to do for my cancer and I'll help you figure out what to do about Mel."

"Seriously? I've never needed your help with women."

"Mel's not women. She's the one."

"Yeah." Adam gulped down a lump in his throat. "She is."

Dad spit on his palm and held out his hand to Adam. "We got a deal?"

Adam spit on his own palm and took his father's hand. Giving it one strong shake, he said, "Deal."

Maybe he did need his Dad's help to woo Mel. Seducing her, he could do that on his own. But convincing her how much she meant to him and how much he meant to her…

Adam would take any help he could get.

"First," Dad said, "you gotta stop being afraid of her."

"I'm not afraid of Mel."

Dad shook his head. "Shut your pie hole and listen to your dad for once. I'm about to give you the key to a woman's heart."

Sure he was. Adam nodded, though, and feigned deep interest in every word his father spoke. More deceit. When, and how, would he ever find a way out of this sinkhole?

"Now the ladies," Bob Caras began, his tone solemn, "are like cats. You can't control 'em, so you gotta learn how to finesse 'em."

Adam tried to listen, but thoughts of Mel distracted him. When she'd seen him in the towel, the raw lust on her face had stripped him of all reason and he dived headlong into an all-consuming kiss that cemented his plans. Operation Seduce Mel had commenced. Stage one, fuck her sense-less. Stage two, fuck her senseless some more. Stage three? That was the hardest part of all. Somehow, he had to seduce her heart and mind. Unless she admitted she loved him, none of it mattered. For the moment, he had to focus on one step at a time.

Soon he would kiss her again. Very soon.

Mel hunched in front of the open refrigerator door, eying the food inside with a cross between hunger and disgust. She wanted to eat, needed to eat, but the idea of lunch left her less than enthused at the prospect. Her mind kept noting the time, whether she wanted to know it or not, and measured the passing hours with a single starting point—the moment her best friend had walked out the door yesterday.

Sunday. One o'clock. No Adam for twenty-seven hours.

He'd called last night, to apologize again for taking off and to assure her they'd talk on Monday. She couldn't decide whether to look forward to see-ing him again or dread what he intended to say to her. Adam wanted more than friendship, but was that "more" sex? A romantic relationship? She still couldn't fathom the changes between them, how fast they'd come, how drastic they were, what they meant.

Of course, if she could pull off brutal honesty with herself, something had changed between them a long time ago. Neither of them had acknowledged it. Maybe they had known each other too long to accept…whatever it was. Somehow, though, Adam had adjusted to it in a split second.

While she floundered, terrified of the implications.

She shut the refrigerator door, her stomach growling.

Brutal honesty? Bad idea. She did not want to consider her illicit thoughts of Adam, or how long she'd entertained them, or what they'd driven her to do even before Adam kissed her. Maybe if she'd been more self-aware, she could've talked to him about her desires and they—

What? They could've been having sex for the past two years instead of him screwing random women and her enmeshed in an unwanted relationship?

The doorbell rang.

Mel spun around and froze. What if it was Adam? *Need to see him, don't want to talk, need to kiss him.* She groaned at her own idiocy. Adam was on duty today, so her visitor couldn't be him. If it was Devon, again, she'd slam the door in his face—again.

Hustling across the living room, she reached the door and peeked through the peephole. The sight of her mother eased her tension a bit, and she swung the door open, ushering her mom inside.

Jillian Thompson raised an insulated bag, her smile crinkling her eyes and twinkling in the blue-gray irises. "Kaya called and I got the feeling you might need these."

"Need what?" Mel glanced at the bag, feeling her brows scrunch up.

"Banana pancakes. Maple syrup. Bacon, crispy the way you like it."

Mel's stomach grumbled at the scent of gooey goodness wafting out of the bag. "Yes, please. I haven't eaten lunch yet." She led her mom into the open kitchen and the bar that delineated it from the living room. "But pancakes for lunch? I remember having them for dinner once in a while, but never lunch."

"First time for everything." Her mother extracted a plate from the bag, a plate laden with a stack of pancakes, each one separated with a small piece of wax paper and the whole thing covered with plastic wrap. "Sit. I'll warm this up for you."

Obeying the order, Mel climbed onto a stool and rested her elbows on the bar. As she watched her mom unwrapping the plate, removing the sheets of wax paper, Mel couldn't help smiling. "Aren't we a pair? I'm a control freak and you're a neat freak."

"Neither one of us is a freak, Melly." Her mom popped the plate in the microwave to heat it up. "Who calls you a control freak?"

"Me."

"Well, stop it. There is nothing the matter with you."

"Yes, there is." Mel slumped against the stool's back. And for some reason, she blurted out, "Adam kissed me."

Her mother's eyes flared wide for a second, then she gave her daughter a knowing look. "When did this happen?"

"Yesterday. He said he was going to kiss me, gave me a chance to say no, but I wanted him to do it." Mel shook her head. "It was crazy and it will never happen again."

"Adam kissed you out of the blue?"

"Uh…not exactly." Mel fidgeted, avoiding eye contact. "Friday night, we—me, Adam, and Kaya—went to a club for my birthday. I drank a little too much champagne and kind of…made a pass at Adam." Pass. Striptease. Same diff, right? "He wouldn't touch me, thank God, but he slept on the sofa to keep an eye on me. In the morning, that's when the kissing thing happened. He was half-naked and wet, and I lost my mind for a minute."

Her mother's lips twitched, as if she were struggling not to smile. "Wanting to kiss a wet, half-naked Adam Caras is not insanity. Can't believe it took this long for you two to get it on."

"Mom!" Snapping ramrod straight, Mel gaped at her mother. "We did not get it on. And I can't believe you're using that term. We kissed, that's all. It was a mistake we will never repeat."

She couldn't believe she'd told her mom about it. What in hell had possessed her to say Adam had been half-naked and wet? But her mom, for heaven's sake, she talked like Mel had dragged Adam to the floor and had her way with him.

Of course, she had thought about it. Many times since Friday night. Most recently, about twenty minutes ago.

Cut that out, woman. No chocolate for you, remember?

"It's okay," her mom said, coming around the bar to pat Mel's arm. "You and Adam have been infatuated with each other for years. We parents can see it, even if our children are blind."

Ridiculous. She was not infatuated with Adam. Fantasizing about him, that was…

She couldn't finish the thought. Had no idea how to. *Damn.*

Infatuated. Yesterday at lunch, Kaya had made a similar claim, saying, "You two are totally into each other."

Mel had scoffed at the idea, even after admitting to Kaya Adam had kissed her.

Wait a minute. *We parents*, her mom had said. Mel pursed her lips. "Have you been talking to Adam's mom about him and me?"

"Maggie and I have been discussing you and Adam for years. We thought about meddling but decided it would be a mistake. You two have to get together on your own." Her mother winked. "Glad it finally happened."

"One kiss is not a happening. It was a fluke."

Jillian Thompson curved her lips into a secret smile. "You shouldn't be ashamed of kissing Adam, or of having feelings for him."

"I don't have fee—Oh, never mind."

"Maybe you should sleep with him and see how it feels."

"What?" Mel all but screeched the word, flying off the stool. "You're my mother, you're not supposed to encourage me to have casual sex."

"It's Adam, not a stranger." Her mom shrugged one shoulder. "If it's good, you'll know there's more than friendship between you two."

"And bad sex means we're just friends? Gimme a break."

Jillian Thompson patted her daughter's arm. "A simple suggestion, Melly. Live in denial as long as you like."

The microwave beeped. Her mother went to retrieve the pancakes.

Grateful for the reprieve, Mel mulled over the conversation. Suggesting Mel should sleep with Adam had shocked her. But it was the last thing her mom said that had Mel's world wobbling on its axis.

Live in denial as long as you like.

Was she in denial about Adam? About the nature of their relationship? It would explain why she couldn't make it work with Devon, aside from the fact he was a cheating ball of slime. Maybe she was infatuated with Adam or totally into him or whatever else other people claimed.

Mel squelched a growl of frustration. She was sick and tired of everybody telling her what she wanted, what she felt, what she should do. Devon told her she belonged with him. Adam told her she wanted him. Her mother told her to sleep with Adam. Once the captain of her own ship, Mel had allowed others to hijack her life. She, the control freak, had let it happen.

No more.

Time to take back control. If everybody told her to turn left, she'd keep her ship pointed straight ahead. This was her life, after all. She'd had all the surprises and changes she could handle lately and a nice cruise along a boring, straight-ahead river sounded like just the thing. As for Adam...

No matter how much he tempted her, no matter how badly she craved his lips and his hands on her, she would never give in.

No chocolate for you, missy.

Chapter Seven

Adam fidgeted in the metal chair in Mel's office, his jeans scritching on the cushioned seat. Someone much smaller than he was must've designed this frigging chair, because no full-size man could fit in it. The metal arms dug into his thighs and hips. For the past two days, since finding out about his dad's cancer, the one thing that kept him from freaking out was thinking about Mel.

His gaze shifted to the tall windows on one wall, which provided a crystal-clear view of Chicago from a fifth-floor vantage point. Mel had slaved eighty hours a week or more, he knew, to make her web design company successful enough she could afford a nice office space like this one, which included a reception area, a conference room, and two smaller offices. Mel occupied the biggest office, of course, as the big boss.

His heart swelled with pride at the thought. The shy girl he grew up with matured into a strong, independent, and brilliant woman.

Adam surveyed her office, as he'd done so many times. Her desk, glass-topped with shiny metal legs, always struck him as incongruous with the woman he knew. Mel was strong and capable, for sure, but she had a softness and subtle sensuality that didn't call to mind sterile metal and glass.

He bent forward and craned his neck to peek at the clock on her desk. It had actual minute and second hands, not glowing digital numbers.

With a sigh, he leaned back in his chair. He'd been sitting here for fifteen minutes. Kaya told him Mel was in a meeting and it might be "a few minutes" before she could see him. Fifteen seemed like more than a few to him. But then, the dictionary defined a few as more than a couple but less than many. He'd looked it up. In the dictionary Mel kept on her desk, propped upright by book-ends and carefully placed between the phone book and a huge paperback about something techie.

Mel was smart. He loved that about her. Hell, he loved everything about her. If he screwed up again, if he pushed too hard, he might lose her forever. After two days away from Mel, he itched to see her and advance his plan, slow and easy.

He drummed his fingers on the chair's arms. *A few minutes, my ass.* Adrenaline coursed through his veins, fueling a painful anticipation. Where the hell was she?

The wooden door swung inward inches from Adam's right arm.

Mel breezed into the office, humming softly, a faint smile on her lips. As the door clicked shut, she circled behind her desk and plopped the stack of file folders she carried onto the desktop. Her humming ceased as she straightened the jacket of her tailored suit. The skirt part of it featured a hem below the knee. Disappointment fluttered through him. No sneak peek of her thighs today. Still, the sight of her creamy calves lit an ember inside him.

Her smile broadened when she met his gaze. The lavender suit brought out matching highlights in her gorgeous eyes, which glittered in the sunlight streaming through the windows. He sat up and cleared his throat, aware of a sudden constriction. "You look nice today."

She was stunning, but his mouth refused to form those words. His dad was right. He was afraid of her—well, afraid of how she affected his emotions. Of what she'd say when, at last, he confessed his true feelings. If he lost her…

He couldn't let that happen. *Slow and easy.*

"Thank you, Adam." She lowered her perfect, round ass into the leather executive chair. "What can I do for you?"

It was more a question of what she'd let him do *to* her. To those tempting lips, the ones he'd savored and ravished. And that body, heaven almighty, the things he could do—

Adam ran a hand over his mouth. *Focus, idiot.*

Mel tilted her head and her dainty eyebrows converged over her nose. "You don't normally stop by my office unless we're meeting for lunch. Did I space out on our plans?"

"We agreed to talk on Monday." He waved a hand, trying to look casual, not like he was about to pop if he didn't kiss her soon. "It's Monday. Let's talk."

Her eyebrows rose. "Talk about what?"

Adam grinned. "About when and how we're going to fuck."

Her cheeks turned a lovely shade of rosy pink. "Really, Adam. That's no way to start a conversation."

Slow and easy, out the window. *Damn, damn, damn.* Mel fried every caution circuit in his brain. Besides, whenever he talked dirty to her, she got aroused, with plenty of visible evidence of it. She never looked more beautiful.

He leaned forward, holding her gaze. "You want me."

"I'm over it."

He couldn't help laughing. If he was the Arsonist, she was the Woman of Steel, with her impenetrable self-control. Ah, but he'd set his sights on penetration.

The intercom buzzed.

Mel held up one finger and punched a button on her large and complicated phone. "Yes, Kaya, what is it?"

"Mr. Stupin is calling about his social media icons again. You wanna talk to him?"

"Ugh." Mel rolled her eyes. "Tell him one more time that if we make those icons any bigger, nobody will see anything else on his website. They'll overwhelm the other content."

"I did, but he insists on talking to you."

"Take a message. And tell him if he demands any more changes to his website, we'll have to start charging a hundred dollars an hour."

"That oughta shut him up." Kaya laughed. "Is Adam still in there?"

"Yes. Why?"

"No reason." Kaya's tone suggested otherwise. Friday night, he'd thought she figured out his semi-pornographic, anonymous-dance plan. Since she'd said nothing to him about it, though, he decided she was just screwy.

"Go back to work," Mel said, and shut off the intercom. She fixed her un-wavering gaze on him, her lips compressed. "What were we talking about?"

"Sex." He roved his gaze over her breasts and back up to her face. "You. Me. Naked. It's going to happen."

"Does this bossy act work with other women? I have to say, I expected more from the Arsonist."

Her dismissive tone rankled, but he knew she was only trying to distract him from his goal. "Tell me why you think sex is nothing special."

"Because..." She worked her lips, her eyes diverting to the wall at his left. "It's pleasant."

"Pleasant?" He scooted forward in the chair, knees loose, and her eyes flicked down to his crotch. When she blinked and resorted to fiddling with papers on her desk, he knew he'd gotten her back on track. "Sex is an adventure, Mel. Two people come together to explore their desires and, when it's done right, find intense pleasure."

She made a derisive noise, still intent on reorganizing her desk.

Time for a new tactic. He sat back in the chair, propping one ankle over the other knee. "Do you masturbate?"

Mel's hand twitched, knocking over a stack of papers. She pushed away from her desk and locked her gaze on him. "None of your damn business."

Adam braced one elbow on his chair's arm and rested his chin on his coiled fingers. "That means yes."

She sputtered. He'd never known anybody actually sputtered, but she proved him wrong. Mel moved her arms this way and that, as if trying to remember what she'd intended to do with them.

"You're cute when you're flustered," he said.

"For heaven's sake, Adam." She grabbed the edge of her desk, yanking her chair forward, and clasped her hands on the desk. Rolled her shoulders back. Elevated her chin. "I am not discussing sex with you."

"Hmm." He uncurled one finger, stroking it up and down his cheek, absorbing the evidence of her arousal—cheeks flushed again, chest heaving, pupils blown. Just mentioning masturbation had gotten her so hot he imagined she was clenching her thighs tight. "Tell me something, Mel. When you touch yourself, do you ever think about me?"

Her eyes flared wide. She opened her mouth but clapped it shut again.

"When I do it," he said, "I think about you."

"Adam—" Her lips had turned dusky pink, ripe for a heated kiss. Her gaze flitted around the room, but then she seemed to reach a decision, confronting him eye to eye. "We are not discussing this."

"If your lovers can't satisfy you," he said, "I'm thinking you take care of satisfying yourself in private. I've seen your passion. Felt it too, when we kissed."

She snatched up a pen to tap it on the stack of papers under her arms. "Maybe I'm just not a sexual person."

Laughter burst out of him. A full-on, head-thrown-back guffaw. He couldn't help it. She had to be the most stubborn woman on the face of the earth, saying anything for the sake of contradicting him, in hopes of quashing his hunger for her. No chance of that.

He rolled his tongue over his bottom lip, reliving the taste of her mouth. His dick twitched at the sight of her breasts flouncing upward with her every labored breath. "You're a bad liar, Mel. You are sexual, we both know it. I'll prove it to you."

"How?"

From the horrified look on her face, he knew she wished she hadn't asked, but the question had sprung from her lips before she considered it. Ah, her control was slipping. And what a beautiful thing it was, watching her shell crumble away before his eyes.

"I'll prove it," he said, rumbling the words, "when I'm inside you, fucking you while you beg me to never stop. I'll make you come so hard you scream."

Her grip on the pen faltered mid tap and it flew across the room to smack into the wall, tumbling to the floor.

Then the shell dropped over her again. She sat up straight, hands on her lap, her face a placid mask.

"Oh, I forgot to tell you," she said, her attempt at being blasé derailed by the slight quaver in her voice. "Devon came by my place on Saturday."

Every thought evacuated his brain. He sprang upright, perched on the seat's edge. "What did he want?"

"Me." She scowled, her focus on her fingers. "He thinks we belong together."

"What do you think?" If she said Devon was right, Adam would vomit and then...die inside.

She sank back in her chair, weariness draining her face of vitality. "We were a couple for two years. That's a lot of history."

He watched her face, his heart hammering, but couldn't puzzle out her thoughts.

She sat up again, the old Mel shining through the bad memories. "But no. I slammed the door in his lying, cheating face."

That was his girl. Mel took no guff from anyone.

Adam jerked his head, as he abruptly realized what she'd said. "Devon cheated on you?"

"Yep," she said, drawing out the word. "Over and over and over."

"Why didn't you tell me? You said things just didn't work out with Devon."

Mel's shoulders caved in, her voice grew hushed. "It was too humiliating to talk about. Didn't mean to tell you now, but it kind of slipped out."

"I'm sorry, Mel. You deserve better than that creep."

"Which reminds me. I have some news." She clasped her hands on her lap and looked straight into his eyes. "I've come to a decision. No more men, in the romantic sense. I'm done with all that nonsense."

Shock slammed into him, a tsunami of ice. "What?"

"I'm done with dating." She gave a sharp nod. "And with sex. I'm going celibate."

The world tilted and he nearly fell off the chair, clinging to the arms for purchase. "Mel, you can't be serious."

"I am." She studied him for a couple seconds, her brows scrunching together. Her expression ironed out into an inscrutable serenity.

He sat forward, intent on unraveling the mystery of her expression but failing. "Is this about Devon?"

"Not really. I have a number of reasons for reaching this decision."

"One guy cheats on you and this is your response?" He rested his forearms on his thighs. "Come on, Mel, you're too smart to turn a knee-jerk reaction into a lifestyle choice. Devon's a prick. Move on." He watched her bristle, with a barely perceptible tensing of her shoulders and a lift of her chin. The rational part of him warned against pushing, but his male reaction proved too strong. "You can't give up on sex."

Her lips twisted. "Of course, you latch onto the sex-free part of my decision. Men."

"I only meant you're a beautiful, sexy woman. You should be touched, and often."

An endearing, pale blush rose in her cheeks. "Let me guess. You think I should sleep with you, so you can prove to me how wrong my decision is. You're certain you can blow my mind with orgasms only you can provide."

Well…yeah. He couldn't admit it, though, not after her announcement of her no-sex plan. He'd work on that problem later. Right now, for reasons he couldn't understand—since he did not want to hear the answer, no way—he asked, "Why did you stay with Devon so long?"

She pressed her lips into a pucker. With a popping sound, she separated them. In a serious tone, she said, "He was charming, attractive, and great in bed. Ruined me for other men, actually, so I'm abandoning my worldly possessions to go live in a Tibetan convent."

Adam's mouth fell open.

Her lips kicked up at the corners.

"Nice deadpan," he said. "You had me for a minute."

She smiled and his heart swelled. "You are so easy. In many ways."

Was she flirting with him again? He had the feeling she didn't realize she was doing it. "So you were joking about the celibacy thing."

"No." She swiveled her chair side to side. "I was joking about the convent."

"And the stuff about Devon." *Please, God.* "The other day, you said sex was nothing special."

She crossed her arms on the transparent surface of the desk. "Remember the pact, Adam."

"That was in high school. We're adults now. We can talk about sex." When Adam was nineteen and Mel was sixteen, he'd started playing the field and she hadn't liked it. They'd agreed never to discuss their romantic lives with each other. He still remembered Mel's explanation of their pact: *Ignorance preserves our friendship.*

But they weren't kids anymore, and besides, his goddamn mouth would not shut up. Hear about her sex life with Devon? It would be the worst torture imaginable. Still, he suffered from a perverse fascination with this topic.

"You really want to know?" Her gaze zeroed in on his and he stopped breathing. "Devon was not fantastic in bed, at least not with me. He saved his best moves for other women." She stared down at her hands. "I found videos he'd made on my phone, videos of his...encounters. They were far more passionate than anything he shared with me."

"Jesus. You said he cheated, but I had no idea." Adam clenched his jaw. "The bastard has some nerve wanting you back."

She shrugged. Her lustrous blue eyes focused on him again, with a mischievous glint in them. "Shall we discuss your sex life?"

Hell no. A double standard, he knew, but one he intended to enforce.

Maybe he needed to adjust his tactics, try something a little more personal in his quest to get her naked underneath him, take a step back to his original idea. He straightened and looked directly at her. "Go out with me, Mel. On a date."

Her laugh wasn't sarcastic, but a little sad. "Celibate. It's in the dictionary. C-E-L—"

"I know how to spell it."

"But you're clearly confused about its meaning."

He tried to rein in his annoyance, with little effect. "You had crappy sex with Devon, okay. You can't give up on—"

She eased her chair back and stood. "I'm sure you rock women's worlds and all that nonsense, but for me sex is not a big deal. I won't miss it."

He jumped up, his hands fisting. "You're also giving up on love. That's unacceptable."

"This is my life and it's a temporary moratorium. Why are you so upset about it?"

Because I love you and I want to make love to you every night for the rest of my life.

But the woman he adored had just stomped all over his dream.

Mel bent forward, her hands on the desk. Adam had gone pale and looked like he might throw up any second. "Are you sick?"

He dragged in three long breaths and color seeped back into his face.

She plunked down in her chair, but kept her gaze trained on him. Ever since their kiss, Adam continually perplexed her. And she'd let him get to her with his sex talk and the way he watched her like he was plotting out every way he might drive her to a screaming orgasm.

Don't let him hijack you again. She let him stew for a moment while she got her mental shields back up, her willpower strengthened by her resolve to stick to her plans for her life, instead of permitting others to rewrite them. Not even Adam. No matter how mouthwateringly good he looked today, in form-fitting jeans and a tight black shirt with a V-neck that revealed a glimpse of his rock-hard chest.

Adam coughed and muttered something about his dad being right about cats. Whatever that meant. He braced his elbows on his knees, his caramel-brown eyes fixated on her with that unnerving intensity he'd displayed of late. A warm little shiver sidled up her spine.

When he'd asked if she thought of him while touching herself, she'd had no choice but to deflect the question. She had a dirty little secret, one she could never share with him, especially not when he seemed hell-bent on seducing her. The answer to his question was yes. For years, on occasion, she had daydreamed about Adam's hot body—but for the past two years, she'd fantasized about him more often and with vivid detail while pleasuring herself in the secrecy of her bedroom, when Devon was "away on business." She'd eventually learned that meant "out screwing anything with breasts."

Adam was right about the other thing too. Her lovers hadn't satisfied her but getting off to fantasies of him did the trick every time. That fact had disturbed her at first, but after a while, she convinced herself it meant nothing. Still, she kept on doing it. Apparently, she couldn't resist Adam even in her imagination.

She could resist him. She *would*.

But was she any better than Devon? Hiding out in her room, indulging in wet dreams of Adam. Wasn't that a kind of cheating? Devon had betrayed her trust, yes. But her own behavior fractured her faith in herself, in her judgment, and in the woman she'd thought she was. Another ironclad reason she must stick to her new life plan. She needed a break from all the craziness that came with romance. She was sending herself to emotional rehab, for an indeterminate length of treatment, until she figured out what she'd become. And how to fix it.

"You can't be serious," Adam said, pulling her out of her ruminations. "I love you, Mel, but this is the worst idea you've ever come up with."

He got that sick-to-his-stomach look again when he spoke the words *I love you*. He said them all the time without vomiting, so why should the words bother him today?

"I am serious," she said, flipping through folders on her desk. "One hundred percent. No more men. Celibacy is the best choice for me."

"For how long?"

Even when she avoided his gaze, it seared into her skin, enlivening her body. Remote detonation? She flung her body back against the chair. No way could she be succumbing to the Arsonist's charms.

"How long, Mel?"

Elbows on the chair's arms, she steepled her fingers under her chin. "As long as it takes."

"Long as what takes?"

"I need time to sort out my feelings." She raised a finger to stay his complaint, since he'd already opened his mouth to offer one. "Not about you, not in particular. I made this decision before we kissed."

"Explain it to me. I'm trying to understand why you'd do this."

"I'll explain it to you when I figure things out. Right now, please accept that we are friends only."

"You say that, but you haven't told me to leave you alone."

Why couldn't she speak the words? *Stop trying to seduce me, Adam.*

"Don't need to say it," she told him calmly, "I have willpower."

"Willpower, hm?" He smirked. "Like you did on Saturday, when I said leave or else I'd kiss you."

His know-it-all tone chafed her nerves. She assumed businesswoman pose—shoulders square, hands clasped on the desktop, chin raised a touch. "That was a—"

"Fluke?" His voice was reasonable, but it still irritated her.

"Yes, precisely," she said, flattening her palms on the pile of folders and papers on her desk. Her thoughts gravitated back to Devon and his cheating, and her own unfaithful daydreams. Those videos, the ones Devon recorded on her phone. The things he'd done with other women. If he'd made love to her that way, maybe she wouldn't have needed her fantasies of Adam. Maybe she wouldn't be so confused these days.

"Earth to Mel." Adam's voice snapped her out of the past. "About this celibacy plan of yours—"

"Why do you care, anyway?"

She swore his nostrils flared, like an angry bull. "I care about *you.* And this is the most cockamamie, dumb-shit idea I've ever heard. You're way too smart to believe it's a good plan. Give it some time and you'll feel differently, trust me."

For her entire life, she'd trusted Adam more than anyone else in the world. She ought to share her angst over her sexual fantasies with him, to talk it out like they talked out everything, but how could she? He was obsessed with getting her in bed.

Worst of all, she wasn't entirely sure she didn't want him to succeed.

You've got willpower, dammit. Use it.

Adam tilted his head, eying her with a strange expression. "What's really behind all this? Talk to me, please."

"Maybe some other time."

He gave her an affectionately exasperated look.

She rolled her chair back. The wheels rumbled across the wood floor. Getting to her feet, she said, "I have work to do."

"Mel—"

"Please, Adam." She let her head fall back, frustrated in too many ways to count, some of them more salacious than others. "I'm running a business here."

Rising from the chair, he unfurled his body to full height. Muscles rippled under his snug-fitting jeans and shirt. He strode toward her, tall and strong and impressive in his confidence and easy sensuality. Halting right in front of her, their bodies inches apart, he slanted forward enough she had to tilt her head back to meet his gaze. She couldn't move or breathe, her body thrumming with crackling energy, transfixed by the luster of his caramel eyes.

"I'm sorry," he said. "Maybe I came on too strong. But I can't agree with your decision. Not ever."

"It's my life."

"Yeah, I know." He shook his head. "You should be loved and made love to, Mel, not shut up in your office or apartment, all alone."

"I'm not alone. I have friends."

He regarded her for several seconds, and then took her face in his big, callused hands. He lowered his face so near to hers she thought, for a dizzying moment, he might kiss her.

When he spoke, his voice rushed through her like champagne—alluring, intoxicating, unchaining her inhibitions. "Let me prove to you how half-baked your plan is."

"I've made up my mind."

"But you don't have all the facts." He sealed his hands over her buttocks, his grip gentle yet unyielding. Tugging her closer, their bodies a hair's breadth apart but not touching, he moved his mouth close enough his lips almost grazed hers. "I can give you the information you need."

Oh God. How did he make the word information sound filthy?

His hands massaged her ass. "What if I back you up to the wall and kiss you so deep and hard you come for me?"

She couldn't orgasm from a kiss. It was ridiculous.

If anyone could make her come that way, Adam was the man to do it.

No, no, no. Willpower. Where was it? She'd lost her grip on it somewhere between his hands settling on her ass and his husky suggestion of an orgasmic lip-lock. Though she struggled to regain her composure, the racing of her pulse and the fire consuming her sex thwarted her attempts.

In the most collected tone she could muster, Mel said, "Your stubborn determination to prove me wrong is not a valid reason to have sex."

"Sure it is." He slid his hands up to her hips, and higher still to rest on the small of her back. "But I didn't mention sex. I suggested a kiss. Guess you want me so bad your mind goes straight to the hot-and-sweaty stuff."

"I—"

Adam swept his hands up her back, pulling her tight against his body, crushing his erection into her belly. Before she could object, if she'd been capable of speech, he darted his tongue out to trace the seam of her lips. She stiffened, battling against the impulse to thrust her tongue between his lips and savor the drugging feel of his slick, hot mouth.

He coasted his lips across her cheek, down to her throat. One of his hands came around her side to slip beneath her suit jacket and palm her breast, his skin warming hers even through the layers of her blouse and bra. He nuzzled the juncture of her throat and jaw.

"I missed you," he murmured against her skin, "over the past couple days."

"Less than two days," she said, her voice barely a whisper, but hoarse and infused with need.

"Yeah." He licked his way up to her chin, as he scraped his thumb over her aching nipple. "But I missed you all the same."

His other hand skated down her thigh to the hem of her skirt. Fingers sneaked under the fabric, questing ever upward on the inside of her thigh. When he found her panties, he cupped her sex in his large palm. She was throbbing for him, her mind blank, her body dissolving at his touch even as she fought to control her response. Like she could. His fingers stroked her lightly through her panties.

"Ah, God," he groaned, his mouth so close to hers she felt the quivering of his lips when he groaned again. "You're wet, so wet."

A single, long finger dived inside her panties to rub down her cleft, from her clitoris straight down to her opening. She swallowed a cry, her body so primed for him she couldn't prevent her hips from rocking into his palm. He shoved his whole hand inside her panties, forcing the fabric aside to accommodate his palm and his fingers, as they covered and explored her inflamed flesh.

Her knees went weak. She clutched at his shoulders, head thrown back, lost to the sheer ecstasy of his touch. His other hand kept kneading her breast, his mouth was pressed to her face near the corner of her mouth. The hand stroking her shifted lower, until one finger pushed inside her.

A cry burst out of her.

He silenced it with his lips, sealing his greedy mouth over hers. They devoured each other with wild lashes of their tongues, both panting and desperate for each other. With her willpower annihilated, she had no qualms about shoving her hand down between their bodies to clasp his erection through his jeans. He withdrew his finger from her sex, then plunged two inside her, as his thumb rubbed at her clit.

So close, so close. Her body tensed. She stopped breathing, her heart pounding. *So close, oh God, so close.*

The intercom buzzed.

Adam froze, his hand still on her slick flesh. He turned his head, seemingly in slow motion, to scowl at the intercom.

Mel tried to wriggle free of him.

"Ignore it," he growled, even as the intercom buzzed again.

"Can't." She stumbled toward the desk, her skirt hiked up around her hips, and reached for the intercom button. Her finger missed it. She took a shaky breath and tried again. Her finger punched the button. "Kaya?"

"Sorry to interrupt," Kaya said, sounding hesitant. "But your mom's on line one."

Rough hands grasped her hips from behind. Mel glanced back at Adam and mouthed *cut that out.* Instead of cutting it out, he moved his hands around to her belly and slid them lower, between her thighs. She almost moaned.

"Uh, Mel?" Kaya said. "Should I tell your mom you're with Adam and she should call back later?"

"No." Nothing wrecked a mood faster than hearing the words *your mom* while being petted by a sex god. "Adam's leaving now. I'll take that call in a sec."

She pushed Adam away and straightened her clothes. "Time to go. I have—"

"Work to do." He hit her with that sexy, smoldering smile. The one that made her shiver. "You've got a funny definition of celibacy."

All she could manage was a frustrated grunt.

"We'll finish this later," he said.

"No, we won't." She smoothed her hair, squaring her shoulders. "This will never be repeated."

His smile turned amused and he seemed on the verge of laughing. "Bet you'll keep saying that even after I've had you naked and writhing under me, while I'm burying my cock inside your sweet little body."

She locked her arms over her chest. "Not going to happen."

Adam wiped his mouth with one hand, erasing from his lips the glistening dampness from their fevered kiss. "Have a good day, Mel."

He ambled toward the door, and out of her office, without glancing back.

As the door clicked shut behind him, she resisted the impulse to run over there and poke her head outside, to watch him until he disappeared into the elevator. Why had she let him touch her? Why did her willpower disintegrate every time she saw him? He wanted more from her—and she wanted more from him. More passionate kissing, more dirty talk, more of his hands between her thighs, more of everything leading into hot, sweaty, incredible sex.

Oh, it would be incredible. Her body assured her of that.

Mel collapsed onto her chair, as Adam's words echoed in her mind. *You should be loved and made love to.* Her chest ached, for no reason she understood.

You should be loved and made love to.

Part of her yearned for exactly that, but no. She'd made a plan and she would enact it. To the letter. So what if she remembered the feel of his strong, sure fingers plying her flesh. So what if her body recalled the delicious tension of craving his touch. She'd let him take control of the situation again. A mistake she would not repeat. No, really, she wouldn't.

Reaching for the phone, she wondered how far she would've gone with him, here in her office, if her mother hadn't called.

And how far she'd go next time.

Chapter Eight

el struggled to concentrate on work, but her thoughts kept drifting back to her argument with Adam and his statement would replay in her mind. *You should be loved and made love to.* He'd made it clear, with no room for reinterpretation, that he aimed to get her in his bed. Jeez, he had not only decreed they'd do it, he'd predicted how much she would enjoy it.

I'll make you come so hard you scream.

Oh dear lord. As Adam's voice echoed in her mind, her body warmed and softened—except between her thighs, where her clit pulsed and her sex grew damp. She never screamed during orgasm, either with a man or on her own. Could Adam really drive her that wild? If they had sex…

She couldn't finish the thought. Wouldn't finish it. Adam was Adam, her best friend, the boy she grew up with, the one who—though three years older than she was—had been her protector, her hero. All through high school, when a boy got too fresh with her, Adam would set him straight with a stern talking-to and she didn't have to ask him to intervene. He simply did it.

Adam. Her rock.

Since Friday night, though, she'd become obsessed with his rock-hard body, forgetting all about his rock-steady loyalty. Those shoulders, broad and strong. His arms, corded with muscles. The T-shirt he'd worn this morning stretched tight over his pecs and abs, all sculpted into sinfully hard lines. In her dreams for the past two nights, she'd licked her way up his six-pack abs, mapping the curves of his chest with her tongue, straight up his throat to those sensuous lips.

What was wrong with her? Secret fantasies were one thing, but panting for him in real life was an entirely different kind of wrong. Letting him stroke her to near climax, that was just insane.

A knock sounded at the door. She bid the visitor to enter and the door eased inward a foot or so. Kaya poked her head through the opening. "You've got a meeting downtown in forty-five minutes."

Dammit. She'd completely spaced out, hadn't even glanced over the proposal she was supposed to deliver to a potential client.

"Are you okay?" Kaya crinkled her nose. "You forgot, didn't you? Mel, sweetie, you are so out of it today."

"I know." Mel gave an exaggerated whimper. "I can't focus anymore."

"That's not like you at all. You're OCD about business."

"I am not OCD. Today has been weird, that's all."

"You were fine before Adam stopped by. Did you guys have a fight or something?"

Given her emphasis on *or something*, Mel suffered a fleeting worry Kaya had overheard her encounter with Adam. No, she couldn't have. Mel had cried out once, but not loud enough for anyone outside the office to hear. *I hope.*

She flapped a dismissive hand at Kaya, with a touch of sarcasm. "Scoot. Maybe you need more work to do, since you have time to pry into my personal life."

"Friends do that, you know." Kaya's eyebrows bounced up and down. "But I know how you feel about Adam and the way he feels about you."

Mel's fingers curled, the nails scraping the glass desktop. "I am not into him, either totally or partially."

Kaya bobbed her head side to side. "Come on. He's your go-to person. You guys have a *special* relationship." Again, her eyebrows bobbed.

"I—" Mel tugged down the hem of her skirt. "Back to work. Please."

"Whatever you say, boss." Kaya left and the door shut, sealing out the rest of the world.

Mel pulled up her proposal on her computer and tried to concentrate on it. A big website. Lots of details to hammer out. *Focus.*

Adam's face flashed in her mind. His horror when she announced her celibacy plan. The way he covered up his shock swiftly, though a hint of it lingered on his masculine face and in his deep voice.

She blamed her distracted mind on the stranger who'd lured her into a steamy dance at the club. His moves had ignited a fire deep inside her, exposing a longing she'd suppressed for so damn long. A need for Adam. God, how she had yearned to strip naked for him and let him touch her any way he wanted. She'd almost done it earlier, mere inches from her desk.

With Devon, sex had been wham, bam, back to watching CNN and yelling at the pundits onscreen. She'd rarely felt satisfied afterward, but then she never had with any of her boyfriends. She assumed it was normal. How Adam had figured out the truth, she had no idea. He just seemed to know, to see it on her face or hear it in her voice, even before she told him sex was no big deal to her.

Footsteps clapped outside her office.

The walls muted Kaya's words, but Mel still recognized the frantic strain in her voice. Mel jumped up and raced around her desk, tripping over a power cable. Her hip crashed into the desk's corner and pain lanced through her body. With a muttered curse, she rushed out the door.

And smacked into Devon.

Gasping, she stumbled backward into the threshold of her office. All six feet of Devon McCallister loomed far too close to her. Despite her low heels, she had to look up to meet his gaze. He smiled in that way of his, with a slight tightening of one corner of his mouth that injected a shot of arrogance into the expression. Once upon a time, she'd found it sexy. Anymore, it ticked her off.

Devon thrust up one hand, shoving a bundle of red roses in her face. "These are for you. Roses for my rose, the flower of my heart, who is as delicate and beautiful as these blossoms."

What bullshit. Flower of his heart? That didn't even make sense.

She blinked several times, gulped, opened her mouth, but nothing emerged. She wanted to tell him off, but she could do nothing except gape at him and his stupid flowers.

Devon waggled the flowers. The plastic sheet surrounding them rustled.

"Come on," he said, his tone wheedling, "you can't turn down roses. They're your favorite."

"No, they're not." She shifted her arms so they were folded over her chest in a defiant pose. "You decided roses should be my favorite. I've never cared for them. What do you want?"

His lips compressed into a slash. "Okay. I'll skip right to the point."

"Please do."

Peripherally, she noticed Kaya and her other employees gathering in a semicircle a discreet distance away. If she had to talk to Devon, which it seemed she did, she'd do it her way—without an audience.

She half turned toward her office door, tipping her head in a follow-me gesture. "Let's talk in my office."

Devon shook his head. "I want the world to know how much you mean to me."

He dropped to one knee.

Mel's eyes flew wide. He wasn't—he wouldn't—not after everything he'd done to her.

He set the roses on the floor, dipped a hand into the inside pocket of his suit jacket, and brought out a small velvet box. Her mind reeled back in time to Saturday morning and the moment in her apartment when Adam offered up her birthday present. Her heart had pounded then. It hammered again now, but for a different reason. Dread and panic fused inside her into a roiling mishmash of anxiety.

With an exaggerated flourish, Devon flipped open the box and raised it to her. His expression morphed into equally exaggerated sincerity. "Melody Thompson, love of my life, will you marry me?"

A round of gasps whispered through the reception area. Devon plucked the ring from the box and reached for her left hand.

Hot air blustered out of her nostrils. She backed up a step, but Devon clutched her hand and tugged. The sunlight glaring through the picture windows in the reception area glanced off the ring.

"Marry you?" She jerked her hand free. "Is this some kind of practical joke?"

He had the gall to look confused. "I love you, Mel. Losing you is more than I can take."

"Maybe you should've thought about that," she hissed loud enough for him to hear but too soft for anyone else to make out her words, "before you screwed every woman in the greater Chicago area."

"That's over and done with, baby, I swear." His voice dripped saccharine, his expression too. "When you left me, I realized how bad I'd messed up." His fingers hovered near her left hand. "Please, Mel, I miss you. I'll never hurt you that way again."

She kept her expression calm, but inside she seethed. Take him back? He must've lost his mind to believe she would.

Devon rested his head on her belly and gazed up at her with teary eyes. "You're my one. Please marry me, Mel."

"No."

He stared at her, his face blank.

Mel took a step back and pointed at the main doors. "I think you'd better leave."

His lips ticked downward. "You can't do this to me. We belong—"

"It's over, Devon. For good."

For a moment, he stared at her as if utterly mystified. Then he stuffed the ring back into the box and clapped the lid shut. He scrambled to his feet, hustling for the double doors. She didn't move until he'd left the offices and gone out of sight.

She wanted to hit something, anything. Instead, she relied on what she did best. She rounded up her wild emotions and penned them deep inside herself.

Her employees watched her. Kaya's mouth fell open, as if she wanted to speak but couldn't find the right words.

"Show's over," Mel said. "Get back to work."

Ten heads nodded. Everyone except Kaya wandered back to their desks. Kaya took a step toward Mel.

With a sharp shake of her head, Mel halted her. "Not now."

Her friend nodded and returned to her desk.

Mel shut her office door, relieved to be locked inside her bubble. She sank into the chair Adam had occupied not so long ago.

How dare Devon ambush her at work. How dare he force her into a public confrontation. She supposed this was what happened when two control freaks collided. He needed to regain control of the situation, and she needed to keep an iron hold on herself.

What must her staff think after Devon's display? Hell with it, let them gossip. Kaya would be discreet, but Mel didn't know about the others. Oh well. At least everyone would know she'd never take Devon back and maybe that would convince him.

Scuffling behind her desk, she dropped into the executive chair. Reached for her phone. Called up the keypad. Hovered her thumb over the button to speed dial Adam.

He always helped her through moments like this. His grounding presence and calming words kept her from losing it. But things had changed between them.

She checked the clock on her computer. Thirty minutes until her presentation.

No time to talk to Adam, or anyone. Since he was off duty today, she could find him at home after work.

Mel grabbed her purse, the six copies of her proposal, and the flash drive with her presentation on it. Time to suck it up and keep going.

Through it all, Adam stayed in her thoughts, in the background, ever present.

Adam fanned his cards, closed them, fanned them out again. The colorful pictures on the cards blurred, as his mind drifted. *Dad has cancer. I should be researching right now.* But shit, he needed a break from mind-numbing technical articles about radiation therapy and hormone therapy and God knew what else.

At least the research had helped him understand his dad's reaction. Most men were ashamed of the diagnosis. Prostate cancer and its treatments could affect their sexual health, and that was one thing men didn't like to talk about. Even doctors were uncomfortable discussing it.

His brother, Jack, prodded his arm. "Wake up. It's your turn."

What were they doing? Playing poker, yeah, that was right. But when Adam managed to not think about his dad, his thoughts circled back around to Mel. All day he fantasized about her. About touching her in that office. About not stopping next time, showing her the kind of pleasure she deserved. He drove himself to the brink of disaster, so distracted by daydreams of her that he almost ran a red light on his way home—at rush hour.

His brother nudged him again. "Man, what is your deal? You're a demon at poker. But tonight, you're either frowning or you've got this dreamy look on your face."

Brett Avadon, Adam's fellow firefighter, made a grossed-out face. "The Arsonist has gone soft. Thought I'd never see the day."

Adam slapped his cards on the table. Five bottles of beer wobbled. "I fold."

The other men at the table—Trevor Gannon and Adam's brother, Rick, both firefighters—grumbled their agreement that Adam had gone "squishy like jelly," most likely over a "smoking-hot babe."

Adam snatched his beer up and downed the remaining half in two long gulps, then thunked it onto the table. He shoved his chair back. "Gotta hit the head."

Hiding in the bathroom was dumb, but he had to get away from the guys. He usually loved poker night. It gave him a chance to hang out with his buddies from the fire station and his brother Rick, who was assigned to a different company, away from the stress of work. Jack had glommed onto their group a few months ago, determined to spend more time with his oldest brother. Adam appreciated the effort, since he and Jack had never been close, but tonight he couldn't marshal the energy for male bonding.

Mel distracted him, sure. His dad's illness, though, had him cinched up in knots. He'd spent hour after hour today researching prostate cancer treatments and hunting for specialists who might help him and his dad figure this stuff out. Dad was high risk. He had to take some kind of action soon, and from what Adam had read so far, the Lupron wasn't enough. It'd lower Dad's PSA by tanking his testosterone level, but he needed an aggressive treatment to get rid of the cancer. External beam radiation, cryotherapy, brachytherapy, blah blah blah. It all ran together in Adam's mind, too much information too fast.

What if I pick wrong and he dies because of me?

The burden of finding the right course of action had landed on Adam's shoulders. His father was no burden, but medical stuff was not Adam's forte. He'd promised Dad he'd take over the research task and he would not break his vow. He'd man up and take care of it, even at the risk of choosing the wrong treatment. He had no choice.

God, how he yearned to feel Mel's arms around him, to hear her sweet voice and take comfort in her. She'd always been his home. He wished it hadn't taken him so long to figure that out.

After ten minutes in the bathroom, Adam gave himself a mental kick in the ass and emerged to stride into the living room.

The guys beckoned him to the card table. Brett said, "Get your butt back in the game. I need to win back the money you swiped from me already."

"Not my fault you suck at poker."

Brett pretended to be wounded, mouth agape and one hand on his chest. "I'm an ace."

"In your dreams." Adam headed for the table.

The doorbell rang.

Adam held up a hand. "Gimme a minute."

"Oooh," Trevor said. "Which girl is it tonight? Lara, the one with the legs that go on forever and the tits—"

"Shut your trap. I'm not seeing anybody."

"But are you doing anybody?" The question came from Jack, his own damn brother.

Adam scowled at him, then swerved toward the door. His apartment was small, which meant the door was maybe a dozen feet from the living room. He swung the door open.

Mel huddled there, hands in the pockets of her slim-fit jeans. Her short-sleeve pink sweater, soft acrylic, fit her form to perfection, accentuating her lush breasts and full hips. He recognized the sweater. He'd bought it for her last Christmas. Strands of her hair spilled out of the clip she'd used to pull it away from her face. The wavy locks hung artfully around her face, framing it.

His chest tightened, his throat too.

She gave him a sheepish smile. "I was hoping we could talk."

"Ah…" He glanced back at the guys. *Screw them.* "Yeah, come on in."

Her head shook, bouncing the curlicue locks of hair. One brushed her mouth. His lips burned to taste hers—until he noticed the way she was biting the inside of her cheek, her hunched shoulders, the uncertain look in her eyes.

"Mel, are you okay?" he asked.

Her shoulders hiked up a bit more. "Devon came by the office, kind of ambushed me. He proposed."

Adam's heart sank into his stomach. "How did you answer?"

"Told him no way." She straightened, her chin up. "What did you think I'd say?"

"Dunno. You were with him for two years."

Jack popped up beside him. "Hey, Mel. You joining our game?"

"Game?" Her brow wrinkled, then her eyes widened. "It's poker night. I'm sorry, I should've called first."

She turned to leave.

Adam pushed his brother away, marched out the door, yanked it shut, and grasped Mel's arm. She looked back at him, brows arched. He let his hand slide down her arm to her wrist, his fingers teasing her soft, warm palm. "Don't go. I want to talk to you."

"But the guys—"

"I'll get rid of them." He glanced back at the door. "Wasn't into poker tonight, anyway."

He threaded his fingers with hers and led her into the apartment, past his brothers, who each greeted Mel with a quick hug and the usual pleasantries. She knew the other guys too, since she'd often stopped by the station to bring Adam snacks. Though Brett and Trevor smirked, Adam thought he was out of danger—until Brett piped up.

"We were just saying how the Arsonist has gone mushy on us."

Mel wriggled her hand free of Adam's, her brows lifting the tiniest bit. "Is that so."

Adam glowered at his friend, but Brett's grin only widened. "Sure. Adam's given up his harem and everything."

"Harem?" Mel recoiled from him, inching toward the door.

"Yeah, you know how some firefighters have those spotted dogs? Well, Adam's got chicks instead. They slobber all over him." Brett winked at her. "But not anymore."

Adam slapped a hand on Brett's chest to push him away. "Mel doesn't want to hear your asinine fireman jokes."

"Sure I do," Mel said with a slight smile.

Adam let his shoulders sag. He couldn't decide whether to be relieved she wasn't disgusted with the mention of his sex life or pissed at his friends for razzing him about it in front of her.

Brett scuttled up to her, leaning close. "Adam's kind of a player, but I'm sure you know that. The Arsonist makes women spontaneously combust and they don't mind one bit."

"Combust?" Mel cast a sidelong look in Adam's direction, her cheeks dimpled by a half-repressed grin.

"Aw, come on." Jack pushed Brett away from Mel. "Leave the poor girl alone. She doesn't get your fire comedy."

"Nope," Rick chimed in as he gathered up the cards. "Mel's a refined lady, not a firehouse groupie. She wouldn't get our jokes."

Given the humor in her eyes and the way she kept eying him sideways, and those dimples in her cheeks, Adam figured she understood. Either she thought all the talk about his sexual past was laughably sad or it...aroused her.

She turned her face toward him, her eyes seeming a deeper shade of blue, and drew the tip of her tongue across her lower lip.

Definitely aroused.

Adam shooed his visitors out with no excuse or explanation, not giving a crap if he seemed rude. Saturday morning, he'd missed a chance to be with her. This evening would be different. For one, his dad was more relaxed, thanks to Adam's promise to help him coupled with a new prescription for Xanax. He wouldn't be winding up in the ER again from a panic attack.

In five minutes flat, Adam had gotten rid of his friends and brothers. Jack had to pause on his way out to poke Adam in the gut and, with a suggestive glance at Mel, say, "I'd go jelly for her too."

A few minutes after that, Adam had settled onto the sofa with Mel. She sat stiff beside him, staring straight ahead, arms locked over her full breasts. Adam had positioned himself next to her, one arm on the sofa's back, behind her head. They were so close, if he'd bent over a smidgen, he could've kissed her.

"Forget what the guys told you," he said, aiming for a neutral tone. "They're morons."

She swiveled her head toward him. "Have you ever had a one-night stand?"

"What?" He tensed, unsure where this conversation was going. Unsure what she was trying to figure out by asking. "Yeah, a few times. Not in years, though. I like spending time with women, talking to them, getting to know them a little."

"Getting to know them? But you rarely spend more than a couple weeks with any one woman."

"You make it sound like I use them." He rubbed his jaw, wondering again where this line of questions was going, not sure he'd like it when he found out. "I don't. They all know what they're getting into with me and they come willingly."

"Do they now." Her lips relaxed into a faint smile. "You've made a lot of women come willingly, haven't you?"

Adam stared at her, dumbfounded. Was she making an off-color joke? Now? Considering her questions, he'd worried she might berate him for his lifestyle—not that she ever had before. She'd never asked him about his sexual past either. Her response was…unexpected. He'd go along with it, though, and take advantage of her playful mood for as long as it lasted.

He leaned in just a touch. "I could demonstrate for you."

She settled her hands on her thighs, absently rubbing them up and down. "Show and tell?"

"I'm not feeling talkative." He covered her hands with his and stroked lazy circles with his thumb. "I'm more interested in showing."

Mel's gaze searched his, though for what he couldn't say. Her pupils were large, her lips parted. She slanted toward him.

"I thought you'd be disgusted," he said, "when the guys started talking about my sex life."

"Don't care about the past. The present and future worry me." Her hands stilled on her thighs and her mouth tightened. "That's why I decided on celibacy."

"I am not Devon."

"Yes, Adam, I can tell the difference." Her eyes shut for a second, then she peeked at him through her lashes. "I've never been able to reconcile the man I know with the legend of the Arsonist. I know you sleep around, but it makes no sense to me. You're a good person."

Legend of the Arsonist? He put that aside for the moment, more concerned with the rest of what she'd said. "I enjoy sex, Mel. I enjoy women. It's that simple."

"I won't be another notch on your bedpost?" She got that teasing gleam in her eye again.

He chuckled. "You can relax. I don't have a bedpost. But you already know that, since you've been in my bedroom."

"It's different now." The humor sifted out of her, and she crossed her arms over her belly. "I'd rather be celibate for the rest of my life than wreck our friendship by having sex. It's not worth it."

"A few days ago, you said our friendship is already wrecked."

"We can save it, I think." She met his gaze, her expression serious. "But we can never have sex."

He let his hand float up to graze her cheek. "I don't cheat. I would never hurt you that way."

"This isn't about infidelity." She turned her head away from his touch. "At least, not the way you think. I'm not sure I can trust my own judgment anymore."

"Why?"

She looked at him again, pressing her lips together as if pondering whether to share her reasons with him. "Doesn't matter. I'm staying celibate. You and I will not have sex."

"Then why do you keep flirting with me?"

Mel stopped blinking for a couple seconds. "Do I?"

"Yeah, you do."

"Purely accidental."

"Uh-huh." He considered reaching for her hand but held back. Her mood was so mercurial tonight, he didn't know if she'd welcome his touch or shy away. "I suppose what we did earlier today, in your office, you probably decided it's another fluke."

She faced forward, the old impenetrable shield dropping down again. "I'm sorry if I've led you on, I didn't mean to. Please accept my decision. No sex, period."

Chapter Nine

She studied Adam, knowing he wouldn't like what she'd said, but uncertain how he'd respond. He'd gotten so upset when she announced her celibacy plan.

This time, he merely shook his head, appearing more bewildered than irritated. "I get that you're scared for some reason, about more than losing our friendship, and you don't want to tell me why yet. But you can't go on pretending there's no spark between us."

Spark? It was an inferno. "I told you. For me, sex is nothing special."

"You pick morons for boyfriends." His lips warped as he struggled not to smirk. "Guess they're limp dicks too."

"Honestly, Adam."

"Well, it's true." He flexed and relaxed his fingers, over and over, the tips dancing over her shoulders. "Let me show you how it should be. I know you want me."

She shrugged one shoulder, contemplating the coffee table. "Doesn't matter. I'm committed to celibacy and I intend to focus all my energies on my business."

"You're already obsessed with work. The no-sex rule is the only different part."

"Well, I'm reaffirming my commitment to my business, along with committing to the other thing."

But why couldn't she say the word all of a sudden? Celibacy. No sex. Confronted with the embodiment of male sensuality, in the form of Adam Caras, her resolve began to founder—again. She was fighting not to gaze into his eyes, which left her staring at his biceps. His T-shirt stretched tight over them, highlighting every line of muscle. She imagined those arms wrapped around her, cradling her to him while he drove into her.

Dammit. Where was her iron willpower? In a puddle on the floor, liquefied by the inferno he set off inside her.

Adam leaned in close, not touching her, though his breaths rustled her hair, tickling it over her skin. His voice lowered into a deep, sultry register that shivered through her every nerve. "Don't you like orgasms?"

Her throat went thick. She rubbed her hands on her thighs. "Don't really have them, not with a man."

"Not with a man?" He pulled away the slightest bit. "Women?"

She threw him an annoyed glance. "I've only been with men."

"Then wh—" His smirk, the one she couldn't see because she was *not* looking at him anymore, colored his voice. "Ahhh, I get it. You only come when you touch yourself."

Her shoulders bunched, she picked at the hem of her shirt. "Uh, yeah."

"But not with men."

"Nope."

"You mean, like, *never?*" He sounded so shocked she couldn't resist glancing at him. Brows furrowed, mouth open, he stared at her. "Never at all?"

"Maybe once or twice." She tried to look away, but his jewel gaze captured her focus and her breaths grew shallower. "Wasn't any big deal. I assumed that's how sex always is. Good for the man, disappointing for the woman."

"Disa—" One corner of his decadent mouth angled downward. "I repeat, you pick morons for boyfriends." He laid a hand on her arm, sweeping it up and down her skin. "A real man makes sure his lover comes first."

His tone had gone lava-hot again, unleashing molten currents of electrified energy. Sexual energy. God, she knew the sensation so well by now she couldn't ignore it. The dampness between her thighs surged into a liquid fire that soaked her panties. She squirmed, but couldn't make herself move away from him, even when he leaned in again, so close the heat of him washed over her skin and awakened every hair, every nerve, until she struggled to catch her breath.

"You keep flirting with me," he said, sliding his hand down to her wrist, massaging the pulse point there. "You want me to fuck you. And I want the same thing. I want to bury my cock inside you and drive us both to the edge of insanity, when we come so hard we're mindless from the pleasure of it."

She was already mindless. Her thoughts spun away from her, cast out on the tatters of her self-control. Tatters? She had nothing left. If he kissed her right now, she'd let him do anything to her. Anything.

And all of a sudden, her celibacy plan seemed like the worst idea ever.

No. She must stick to it.

Could she? Adam's proximity endangered her willpower, her commitment to her work-focused life, her determination to have a moratorium on sex.

Adam glided the back of one long finger down her cheek, the faintest caress, but it reverberated through her with erotic power. She bit the inside of her lip, desperate for his kiss yet terrified to take what she hungered for with an earth-shattering need. If she truly intended to stick to her plan, she ought to shut this down.

His fingers on her wrist moved to her palm, circling, teasing. "You never answered my question. Do you think about me when you're making yourself come?"

She opened her mouth to deny it, but she'd never convince him of her commitment to celibacy if she lied about this. She'd evaded the question before. Now, she had to tell him the truth, if she had any hope of salvaging their friendship. Besides, she was a bad liar. "Yes. I have, uh, thought about you on occasion when I...you know."

"Oh yeah, I know," he murmured, angling his head nearer hers, his lips brushing her ear, "I can show you how sex should feel. How it can feel."

"Adam..." Breathless, she floundered for a rational response. No chance in hell of that. "We can't."

That finger, it brushed her cheek with such tenderness yet evoked such a firestorm in her. He shifted position, his hip suddenly pressed to hers, his thigh plastered against her. She swore she felt his skin through their clothes. Crazy, and yet—

He dragged his lips down her jawline. "Let me give you pleasure, Mel. I won't take you, not tonight. But I want to be the one who shows you sex can be good for you."

"Mm." The little gasp-moan was all she could manage. The scent of him—spicy, earthy, tinged with sweat and the dark, musky cologne he preferred—it propelled her past the limits of reason. Without thinking, she turned her face to his. Their lips grazed each other. A bolt of lust ripped through her and her answer tumbled from her lips. "Okay, yes."

That smile, the one so slow and intimate it dripped sexual promise, spread across his lips. He tipped her away from him, slipped a hand under her ass to rotate her hips, and laid her down on her back on the plush cushions. On all fours, his hands at either side of her head, he admired her, his brandy eyes darkened by desire.

"Relax," he said, running his fingertips down her jaw, her neck, across her collarbone and down her bare arm. "I'd never hurt you."

"I—know." And she did, with every fiber of her being.

"After this, you can still say we haven't had sex. Because, technically, it's not sex—not intercourse, anyway."

The back of her throat hurt with a strange tightness. He was giving her an out, accommodating her screwy logic, so she could cling to her celibacy plan while allowing him to pleasure her. That he cared enough to provide an excuse for her, that he understood her so thoroughly he knew she needed one, signified more than she wanted to acknowledge.

He settled his body atop hers, his weight a welcome pressure, the heat of him stimulating. His erection was caught between them, but he didn't seem to care. He skimmed his lips across hers in slow sweeps, over and over, until at last, he crushed his mouth to hers. His silken tongue slipped inside, consuming her with swirling motions, provoking her to coil her tongue around his. She opened her mouth wider, inviting him in for a deeper, searing kiss, their tongues mating as their teeth scraped each other's lips. She moved her hands, intent on plowing them into his hair, but he snared her wrists and held them down.

When Adam finally pulled back, he gazed down at her with raw lust. "I love kissing you."

"Me too." Love didn't seem a strong enough word. She was addicted to his kiss.

He crawled backward, inching down her body until his head hovered above her groin. He moved one hand to rest alongside her right hip and curled his fingers around the bone, kneading the sensitive hollow with gentle, insistent strokes of his thumb. His other hand dipped inside the waistband of her sweats. Inside the band of her panties. Oh God, the sensation of his skin on hers, dangerously close to her sex, shot a wicked thrill through her. Every thudding beat of her heart throbbed in her ears. And oh yes, she throbbed down there, just south of where he was fondling her.

With purposeful slowness, as if relishing every second of it, he tugged down on her clothes enough to expose a patch of skin. He pulled in a deep breath, smiling with blissful satisfaction. "The scent of your desire is like honey and cream. I can't wait to taste you."

Taste. With that one word, he shut down her brain. Her head grew light, her entire body felt weightless, tethered by only his hands.

Adam pressed his warm, damp lips to her belly, making her sex clench in anticipation. With both hands, he rolled her sweats and panties off her hips, down her thighs, to let them bunch around her ankles. Bound by her clothing, she was at his mercy.

His tongue sneaked out, sweeping over his lower lip. "You will come for me. Only me."

A choked noise caught in her throat. Her breasts had grown so tight, her nipples straining against her bra, she longed to rip it off and free them. An image of his mouth on her aching nipples had her squirming again, panting, wriggling her hips.

He lowered his head between her thighs, his breaths a whisper across her drenched flesh. He grasped her hips, pinning her in place. An instinct, a deep-seated need, urged her to spread her thighs as wide as possible, knees bent, offering her body up to him.

A long groan resonated in his chest. Never breaking eye contact, he nuzzled the hairs on her mound. His lips skated over her skin, firing jolts of hunger straight down to her core, deep inside where she burned to feel him. He hovered his mouth above her clit. She tried to thrash, but his hands restrained her. He puckered his lips and blew a gentle stream of air across her taut nub, the tickling sensation almost more than she could bear.

"Oh God," she moaned. "Oh, Adam. Please. I need—I—unh."

"I'll take care of you, don't worry." He dipped his tongue to her flesh, skimming it along the inside of her folds, first up, then down, then up again to glide it around to the other side. His tongue flicked across the edges of her clit as he laved her folds, tormenting her with what she needed most yet not quite giving it to her. She clutched at his hands, ablaze from head to toe, her blood sizzling, her skin so sensitive the lightest whisk of his shirt on her thighs had her thrashing her head. He shifted his head lower still and his tongue lapped at her opening. Incoherent sounds burst from her lips. He plunged his tongue inside and swiped it left and right, gradually, deliberately.

Her hips bucked.

Adam lifted his head, licking his lips clean of her glistening wetness. "You taste so good, like honey and sweet cream with a hint of dark chocolate. I could spend all night devouring you."

Holy shit. The things he said. No man had ever spoken such things—dirty, intensely erotic things—to her, not ever, not in her entire life. She'd never imagined words could amp up her need, but his inflamed her without fail.

Staring into her eyes, he let go of one of her hips, reaching down to part her folds with his thumb and forefinger. His mouth sealed over her clitoris.

White. Hot. Scorching. Need.

He suckled her hard, his tongue swirling round and round the head of her clit. His hand drifted down, sneaked between her thighs to find her opening. One finger dived inside.

She gasped.

His lids eased half shut as he sucked, nibbled, licked her nub. The pleasure coursed through her like swells on the ocean, building toward something more powerful than she could fathom. His finger thrust into her again and again, in time with the lashes of his tongue.

She shoved her hands into his hair, desperate to hold him against her.

Another finger plunged inside her. He lunged his fingers as deep as they'd go, curled them, and petted a spot inside her she'd never known could be touched. His other hand burrowed under her ass, hoisting her up to grant him better access. He raked his tongue down her cleft and back up, nipping at her clitoris before he devoured it once more, while his fingers pumped in and out, in and out, with a maddening rhythm. Her back arched up off the sofa, her fingers clenched in his hair, the nails dug into his scalp.

His fingers rubbed across the flesh inside her. Fast, powerful strokes.

"Adam!" Her body went rigid. She couldn't breathe, couldn't move except to thrust her hips up into his kiss. Her climax struck with such force her entire body convulsed, bucking up off the sofa, as the ecstasy of her orgasm thundered through her and thudded her heart painfully against her ribs. Her knees pulled up on their own, her head and shoulders caved in toward her belly.

She screamed.

When the last spasm faded away, she collapsed in a heap. Between panting gasps, she said, "Oh, Adam. That was…incredible."

Between her legs, Adam raised his head. "Told you."

She grabbed the pillow from behind her head and lobbed it at him.

His grin warmed her in a completely different way, a deeper and more intimate way, and yet no less profound in its effect. Though her body still simmered from the passion he'd shown her, his smile made her heart ache.

Adam settled on top of her, his hard shaft pressed against her belly, and rolled to the side, taking her with him so they lay face to face. His back was against the sofa's back, his arms were around her. The embrace seemed even more intimate than what he'd just done to her, for her, and when his hands splayed over her back to draw her even closer, a lump formed in her throat. His tenderness, it scared her more than the lust he evoked in her. His need to introduce her to real pleasure, it was part of his seduction, but she had the strangest feeling he was seducing her into more than hot sex, so much more.

He nuzzled her cheek, placed a sweet kiss on her cheek, caressed her back.

A hardness pushed against her belly and she glanced down at the erection straining his jeans. "Aren't you uncomfortable?"

"I'm fine, it'll go away after a while." He buried his face against her neck and she felt his smile on her skin. "Probably."

She pulled her head back to meet his gaze. "Thank you."

"For what?"

The way he was looking at her, so adorably befuddled, she stifled a wince at the pang in her heart. He was beautiful, sensual, masculine, and so...wonderful. She took a shaky breath. "Thank you for giving me the best orgasm of my life."

"We haven't even gotten to the best part yet."

She laid her cheek against his chest and closed her eyes. Wrapped her arms around his waist. Listened to the thump-thumping of his heart. Everything had changed, despite her desperate attempts to stop it. They'd blasted past a line and they couldn't go back. If this—whatever it was, whatever it could be—didn't work out, she stood to lose everything that mattered most to her in the world. Tears pricked at the backs of her eyes. It wasn't what he'd done to her body that affected her this way. It was what he'd done to her heart and mind, the undeniable change between them. Nothing could ever undo it.

And that scared the hell out of her.

But in this moment, she needed the closeness. Needed him. She snuggled closer, grateful for his warmth and strength and the way his hands cradled her to him. Tomorrow, she'd worry about the rest. Tomorrow.

She nestled deeper into his firm body.

His erection jerked.

Mel pushed up into a sitting position, regarding him, her bottom lip trapped between her teeth. She pointed at his cock. "You sure you're not suffering?"

"I'll live." His voice was strained, though, as if his condition was uncomfortable.

Technically, they hadn't had sex—intercourse. As long as she was swimming in the River Technical Denial, she might as well revel in its steamy waters. The thought of taking his erection in her hand and pumping, of watching his reactions as she manipulated his rigid cock with her fingers and her tongue, made her mouth water.

"What are you thinking?" he asked, his voice throaty and deeper than ever.

"I can't let you suffer." She couldn't help moistening her lips, her gaze glued to the hard line of his erection under his clothes. She was getting wet just imagining what she might do to him. "Sit up."

He stared at her, unblinking. His lips parted, his pink tongue traced the edges of his front teeth. "Mel, if you're thinking about doing what I think you're thinking about doing—"

"I want to make you scream."

He choked. Coughed into his fist. "How, exactly?"

She coasted her finger up the ridge of his cock, with nothing between her skin and his except the fabric of his jeans. "Mmm…I'm thinking a combination of my mouth and my hands."

He sucked in a breath that inflated his chest, held it for a moment, and released it in one big huff. "Christ, Mel."

She leaned in and kissed him, exploring his mouth with her tongue, relishing the taste and the textures of him, and the way he groaned into her mouth as he gave in to her demands, responding with equal ardor. When she pulled away, he was breathing hard, his eyes hooded.

"I've never done this before," she said, "but I'm a quick study."

He opened his mouth but no sound came out.

"Sit up," she said, gesturing with her hand for him to do so.

Adam hesitated for a second, but then rose to sit beside her, his feet planted on the carpet and his arms at his sides. She sidled up to him, tucking her legs beneath her, and fanned her fingers over his chest.

"I have a feeling," he said, "you're going to kill me tonight."

"A person can't die from pleasure."

He seized her head in one hand, dragging her in for a quick, hard kiss. "The French call orgasm *le petit mort*. The little death."

"Since when do you speak French?"

"I looked it up this morning, online." He hissed as she trailed her fingers down to his waist, bumping the head of his erection. "Thought I'd learn a few French sex words to impress you."

"No need to impress me." She lifted his shirt and unhooked the rivet of his jeans. "Not after that orgasm."

She pulled his zipper down, the rough sound of it more sensual than she would've ever imagined it could be, freeing his cock inch by inch. He wore no underwear, like a true hedonist.

He let his head fall back against the sofa.

Overwhelmed by the sight of his erection, she closed her fingers around it and eased them down his thick length, admiring the veins threaded through his velvety flesh. When she guided her hand back up, his body stiffened. A bead of moisture poised atop the head of his cock. She leaned down to roll her tongue over the rosy-red tip, lapping up the liquid, loving the salty flavor of him.

A scratching sound drew her attention to his hands, and his fingers punching into the cushions, crooked so tight they seemed about to snap.

Mel rested her chin on his shoulder, drinking in the exquisite need on his face. "Shall I alleviate your suffering?"

"Fuck, yes."

She began a measured pumping, the pace languid, her grip on him firm. "Is this okay?"

He writhed in place, his eyes squeezed shut, letting out a sharp grunt with each stroke of her hand.

Emboldened by his response, she pumped harder, faster, until he was thrusting into her movements, gasping, his mouth wide open. Her clitorus throbbed, she was so aroused by what she could do to him. He went rigid, his back frozen in an arched position.

Then, as she milked him with her hand, his hips bucked and creamy liquid shot out of his cock.

He screamed—in a hoarse, manly way.

A sensation rippled through her clitoris, like a tiny orgasm.

Beside her, Adam slumped, breathing hard, his face ruddy. "Shit, Mel. You are, absolutely and positively, the hottest woman on the face of the earth."

She laughed. Giggled, actually.

He pulled her close, gathering her under his arm, and pressed a kiss to her forehead. "You're amazing."

"You don't have to shower me with compliments."

"I absolutely do. Not only are you sweet and smart and strong, but you did the impossible." He tipped her chin up with his finger. "You made me scream."

"You've never…"

"No. Never."

She wanted to say something, but she had no clue what. How did a woman respond to being told she gave a man so much pleasure he screamed? Even worse, she had no idea what to do now. Were they friends? Uh, not really. Were they lovers? Well, not quite. Besides, she'd sworn off romance and sex. Yet here she was, enjoying a steamy session of mutual getting-off with him.

Adam's phone rang, startling them both.

He sighed, digging the phone out of his pocket. When he glanced at the screen, a frown etched lines on his face. "It's Dad. I better take this."

She clasped her hands on her lap as he extricated his arm from around her and answered the call. "Dad? What's up?"

He grimaced, pinching the bridge of his nose between his thumb and forefinger.

With nothing to do, she let her gaze wander the apartment. The shelves on the far wall grabbed her focus, especially the middle shelf—the Mel Shelf. It featured a crowd of framed photos of her, from childhood to the present day. Adam had photos of his family too, but none of them rated as many frames as she did.

Unease quivered through her, chilling her skin.

She was being silly. The Mel Shelf had been there for as long as Adam had lived in this apartment, and another version of it had occupied a prominent place in his old apartment. Still, she swore he'd acquired more photos of her lately. Why did it bother her? Why did her heart speed up when she looked at it tonight?

"Aw, Dad," Adam said, turning his gaze to the ceiling, shaking his head. "Calm down. Take a zan—do that thing we talked about. It'll relax you."

That thing? What on earth were they discussing? Come to think of it, why had his father been calling him so much lately? Bob, though retired, liked his independence and rarely asked his sons for any kind of help. Now the stoic ex-cop was dialing up Adam to talk about secret things that put Adam on edge.

"Okay, okay," Adam said, sounding defeated. "I'll come over right away."

He hung up and jammed the phone in his pocket.

Mel's shoulders flagged. He had that apologetic/pathetic look on his face that she knew meant he was about to ditch her again.

"I'm sorry," he said. "I have to go. Dad needs help with his car again. Damn thing's breaking down constantly these days."

He winced.

"Better hurry," she said. "Your dad must be in dire straits if he called you for help. Again."

"Well, I…" He stared down at his hands on his lap, silent for several seconds. At last, he turned to her and said, "Come with me."

She drew her head back. "What? I thought these were secret missions."

"My dad doesn't want me telling anybody what's going on, but you could come with me to his house." Adam sighed, shutting his eyes for a moment. "At least then you'll know I'm not lying about where I'm going."

"I know you're not lying."

"You do?" He seemed genuinely surprised by her assertion. "But—I mean, you've been so skittish about the changes in our relationship, I figured…"

"This has nothing to do with Devon. It's not you I can't trust, it's me."

His whole face tensed, and lines etched across his forehead. "I don't get it. Wish we had time to talk about this, but I really have to go."

"Give your dad a hug for me."

"Thanks for not asking me to give him a kiss for you." Adam pushed up off the sofa and stretched. "And thanks for understanding. You can let yourself out?"

She rolled her eyes. "Yes, Adam, I can manage to open the door and close it again all by my lonesome."

He bent to peck a kiss on her lips. "I'm off tomorrow. Maybe you could take a personal day, for once."

"Can't. Too busy."

He bumped her nose with his. "Meet me for lunch. Please. You do still eat, don't you?"

"Uh-huh."

"Lunch, then. A date."

She shook her head, trying not to smile at his tenacity. "Not a date."

"Sure," he said, patting the top of her head. "Whatever you need to tell yourself."

While she made an irritated noise, he hurried out of the apartment. The door thunked shut.

Mel heaved her body off the sofa, heading for the door. One again, she'd succumbed to her lust instead of standing firm in her commitment to celibacy. She would've loved to claim she'd do better from here on, but given his single-minded determination to seduce her, she couldn't convince even herself she might succeed in resisting him. Still, she had to try.

How could she examine her illicit desires, and what they meant, if she kept going further and further with Adam?

As the apartment door shut behind her, she leaned against the jamb.

This would not happen again. Positively never again.

Next time she saw Adam…

Resist, resist, resist.

Chapter Ten

Mel hunched over the table in the coffee shop, absently stirring her mocha latte while studying the swirly patterns made by her spoon. She'd been waiting for Adam to show for their "date," which was not a date, but he was fifteen minutes late. Not like him at all.

Not like the man she'd thought she knew. But last night she'd met the Arsonist and experienced the heart-stopping sensuality he was renowned for, the side of him she'd longed to know. Adam the confident, sensual lover who valued her pleasure above his own. How could she go back to seeing him as a friend only? As sweet, dependable Adam?

The better question was, why had she gone to his apartment last night? To talk. To explain her celibacy choice. At least, those were the reasons she told herself. Throughout today, her thoughts had kept returning to him. More than thoughts. Vivid memories of his mouth on her clitoris, suckling and licking until she screamed from the profound bliss of her orgasm. Fantasies about what he might do to her next time.

Not that there would be a next time. She'd resolved—or rather, re-resolved—to be celibate.

Coffee splashed out of her cup. Her stirring had turned a tad manic, so she set the spoon on her napkin. Two powdered donuts had not quelled her real hunger, the one buried under layer upon layer of self-doubt and guilt. Was she as bad as Devon? She'd masturbated to thoughts of another man. He cheated on her, but in a way, she'd been unfaithful to him as well. Hadn't she?

Even if she'd wanted a real relationship with Adam, she couldn't go there. He wouldn't betray her, she knew that, but she no longer felt sure of her own trustworthiness. Adam trusted her, called her amazing and strong and held her with genuine tenderness, let her keep saying she was celibate when they both knew she wasn't. He wouldn't give up, but maybe he should. He should be with a woman who could promise never to stray, even in her mind.

A pang stabbed into her heart. She wasn't that woman.

Things had been so much easier before he demonstrated his sexual talents for her. Back when she could stick to their old rule of not talking about their love lives. No more. Ignorance hadn't preserved their friendship. It had set them up for failure.

She gazed out the floor-to-ceiling glass window beside her. Outside, people meandered past on the concrete sidewalk. A couple, smiling and holding hands, traipsed by and, right in front of Mel's vantage, they gave each other a sweet kiss.

Mel's heart clenched. Memories unreeled in her mind, this time a flashback to their first kiss. Adam's lips grazing hers, over and over. That moment when everything froze, the anticipation a palpable energy between them. And then his mouth claimed hers. She surrendered to the passion, and oh, the kiss had been life-altering.

She slouched in her chair, nabbed the spoon, and twirled it in the brown liquid.

Her phone rang. She ditched the spoon in her mug to dig her phone out of her purse. The untouched coffee whorled for another few seconds. Her eyes focused on the caller ID: Adam. She stared down at the screen, immobilized by the sight of his name, until the third ring. Then she picked up.

"Hey," he said, guilt tainting his voice, "I'm so sorry, Mel. Stuff came up and I completely forgot about lunch."

"Your dad again?"

His heavy sigh gusted through the speaker. "Yeah, actually, it is Dad."

"Is he okay?"

"Dad's fine. Stressed, but fine." He hesitated. "Something's bothering you, I can tell."

"Let's not talk about this on the phone, okay?" She should explain her fears to him, but not like this.

"How about dinner? We could hash things out." A pause, and then: "You have my word I won't leave until we're done."

Done doing what? she almost asked, flashing back to their last encounter in his apartment. Ohhh, not a good idea to be in the vicinity of that sofa. "We should meet at a public place this time."

"Afraid if we're alone you'll seduce me?"

Despite herself, she felt a smile tightening her lips. "I think I can keep my hands off you. How about we meet at the Downtown Diner?"

A client of hers, the first client she'd ever signed, owned the diner and gave her a discount whenever she visited. She loved the place and so did Adam. Great fries and chocolate malts.

"Sure," he said. "Sounds good. How about seven tonight?"

"Okay. But it's not a date." She switched to her businesswoman tone, anxious to convince him. "And for the record, I am off the market. Celibate. I told you this already, so please respect my wishes."

"Yeah, you told me. Right before you let me suck you to orgasm."

With an annoyed grunt, she said, "That was a fluke."

"Another one, huh?"

She could hear the humor in his voice, and suddenly, it seemed like they'd traveled back in time to before *that* night at the club. They were talking like they used to, like best friends. "I'll meet you there at seven."

"Great." He sounded so relieved she could picture him slouching in his chair, a slight smile on his lips. "I'll be there at six forty-five, to show you can count on me."

"I know I can." And the weird thing was, in spite of her misgivings of late and his flaking out on her for lunch, she did know she could rely on him. "Goodbye, Adam."

He muttered a goodbye and disconnected.

The waitress stopped by her table, started to ask if she needed a top-up, but then spotted her full mug and excused herself.

Adam had introduced her to this coffee shop. They had the best bagels in the city, but today, she'd needed donuts instead. In the past three days, Devon had filled up her answering machine and voicemail with thirty-eight messages. His emails glared at her every time she checked her account, a dozen a day. And the texts. He kept begging her to forgive him, to take him back, to allow him one more shot.

One more shot at humiliating her? Even if she'd loved him, she wouldn't take him back. Since she'd realized she hadn't really loved him, no way would she let him back into her life. Maybe she was partly to blame for the implosion of their relationship, but it hardly mattered. They were over and done.

She slid her coffee mug across the table, the smell of it suddenly nauseating. She rummaged in her purse for her wallet.

"Baby, it's kismet."

Devon's voice scraped her nerves. She fumbled with her wallet. It slipped away and plopped onto the floor. Devon nabbed it, offering it to her with his palm up. She ripped it from his hand.

He brushed a finger across her cheek. "I get why you're ignoring my messages, I do. But it's pretty childish, don't you think? We're grown-ups and grown-ups work on their problems."

"I dumped you." She slapped a couple bills on the table and stuffed her wallet back in her purse. "And I rejected your proposal."

"You didn't mean it."

"I said no. N-O. How much more definitive do I have to be?"

He smiled, lips sealed.

She thrust her chair backward. It tumbled over, clattering on the floor.

Devon righted the chair and cupped her elbow in his palm. "Let's have a real, adult conversation."

Mel suppressed a groan of disgust. "You are not an adult, unless you mean in the porno movie sense. You could start your own production company."

He gave her a long-suffering look. "Mel, baby, come on. We hit a stumbling block, that's all."

She snorted. "You stumble into the vagina of every hot babe you meet."

The waitress took a few halting steps toward them, her eyes on Mel, a question in her expression. Mel gave her a grateful, if tight, smile and shook her head. Clearly relieved, the waitress headed back to the counter.

Mel pushed past Devon to stalk out the door. He trailed after her, his pathetic entreaties echoing behind her. She yanked her car door open, dropped into the seat, and slammed the door just as Devon bent to speak to her.

Devon rapped his fist on the window. "Please, let's talk. I want to explain."

She rolled the window down partway and said, "Not interested in excuses. It's over, move on with your life."

"But I love you."

"I don't love you." She hated being so brutally blunt, but he'd left her no choice.

His eyes widened, his face went pale. "You don't mean that."

"Sorry, but I do." Rolling up the window, she waved her hands to shoo him away from the car. When he simply stared at her, she mouthed, "Move."

At last, he stumbled backward across the sidewalk.

The tires squealed as her car rocketed out of the parking space onto the street. Celibacy was her plan. She hoped Devon would accept it was over, accept she didn't love him, and find someone else to snag in his charming little trap. Though Devon had bruised her, Adam seemed intent on destroying their friendship and stealing from her the one good thing she had left.

Adam. In spite of herself, she softened a little thinking of Adam. The man who'd consoled her during her darkest hours. The lady-killer who detonated women. He set her off, for sure.

During the drive home, a different question haunted her. After last night, could she ever go back to being just friends with him? Her mother's words replayed in her mind, echoing until she couldn't ignore them anymore.

Maybe you should sleep with him and see how it feels.

The scent of burgers and fries wafted over Mel, inciting her growling stomach. She'd skipped lunch, too enmeshed in an anxiety attack to eat. Every time she looked at food, her stomach churned. Until she'd walked into The Downtown Diner. She loved their bacon cheeseburgers and chili fries.

From her position at the rear of the restaurant, seated in a booth, she had a clear view of the front doors. She drummed her nails on the Formica table, in a panicked rhythm in time with the tapping of her right foot. Dread wormed its way through her. She knew what Adam wanted to talk about this evening, but she had no clue what to say to him. How could she meet his eyes without blushing crimson? Or getting wildly turned on again?

Which seemed to happen every time she saw him these days. Every time she heard his voice. Every time she thought of him. So, pretty much every second of every day. Perpetual arousal could not be healthy.

If she tried to explain her guilt over her fantasies of him…Maybe she had to tell him, but she wasn't at all sure she could make the words come out of her mouth.

The doors swung open and Adam strode into the diner.

Her heartbeat sped up, her palms grew moist, her fingers and foot stilled. Dressed in dark blue jeans and a hunter-green shirt, Adam took her breath away. His long sleeves concealed the muscles of his powerful arms, but the jeans were snug. Everywhere. He'd done something to his hair, to make it glisten in the golden light within the restaurant. He stood tall, shoulders back, relaxed yet alert, every bit the firefighter tonight.

Adam scanned the restaurant and their gazes converged. He smiled—a closed-mouth expression that managed to be reserved and suggestive at the same time. She squirmed in her seat. As he sauntered toward her, those hips swaying with each step, masculine and casual in his demeanor, she couldn't help wetting her lips.

Ugh. After years of paying little attention to his body, except in the privacy of her daydreams, all of a sudden she couldn't stop gawking at him. It might have something to do with the memory of his tongue on her most intimate flesh, demanding she yield to him. And holy heaven, she had yielded. Completely. It had felt amazing. Relinquishing control, giving in to her passion.

Her skin prickled with unease. The reason for it was striding toward her right now, breathtakingly hot and delectable. She was dangerously close to feeling things she did not want to feel. Irrevocable things.

Adam lowered his lean body onto the bench across from her. Thank heavens he hadn't tried to sit beside her. She needed a barrier between them, because her stupid hands itched to touch him. When she'd assured him she could keep her hands off him, she hadn't counted on him arriving in this state, looking too good for her good.

He rested his hands on the table, fingers interlocked. "Thanks for coming."

She shrugged. Her stomach fluttered at the way he watched her with intense interest, his gaze never leaving hers. Her grip on pretty much everything was faltering.

He skimmed his gaze over her, as much of her as he could see with the table between them. His appraisal stalled over her breasts. When he focused on her eyes again, heat smoldered there. "You are gorgeous."

"Thanks." Was that a slight squeak at the end? No, she did not squeak.

Adam leaned forward. He waved one finger at her powder-blue silk blouse. "You're wearing one of my birthday presents from a few years ago."

Oh, fudge. She'd forgotten he gave her this. Sitting as straight as possible, hands on her lap, she lifted one shoulder. "I picked a top at random."

"Since I bought you half the tops you own, the chances were fifty-fifty you'd pick one of mine."

"Yours? They were gifts, which makes them mine." She sounded prissy, not like herself at all. Trying too hard to seem like she didn't care.

Adam gave her a long-suffering look. "I didn't mean it that way."

Her shoulders sagged, but she buttressed them with a long breath. "I know. I'm sorry."

For a moment, he studied the tabletop, head bowed. Just when she thought he'd fallen asleep, he raised his head. "Devon really did a number on you, didn't he?"

She folded her arms over her belly, not quite ready to delve into that subject. "We need to talk about last night."

Why had she mentioned it? She'd intended to steer way clear of the topic, but here she was veering straight into oncoming traffic. Okay, so what had she meant to discuss with him? Not a goddamn clue.

"I'm thirsty," she blurted out. She took a menu from the napkin stand and pretended to be obsessed with it. "Starving too. Let's order first, okay?"

His irritated sigh raked across her nerves. "Whatever you want."

There was the problem. She had no idea what she wanted. Celibacy, she'd thought. Adam made her question that plan. So, what did she really want?

Maybe you should sleep with him and see how it feels.

Flipping through the menu with harsh movements, she tried to shove the thought out of her brain.

After ordering, they waited in silence. Adam regarded her with a shadow of a frown, and she painted invisible lines on the tabletop with one finger, watching it slide over the surface. The waitress brought their drinks—root beer for her, coffee for Adam—and sashayed off to the kitchen. Mel dared to glance up then, at her best friend, and struggled to catch the thoughts swirling in her brain but couldn't latch onto a single one. From the kitchen behind them, she recognized the sizzle-snap of a burger flipped on a griddle.

Her hands, wrapped around the chilled glass of her drink, absorbed the cold of the ice cubes that bobbed inside it. She jammed her hands under her thighs.

Adam observed, his barely visible frown ticking up at the corners. He sipped his coffee and his lips puckered to draw in the hot liquid. Oh those lips, how they snared her gaze. The lips that had claimed hers the morning after her birthday and again last night, the ones that drove her wild in the naughtiest way on his sofa, the ones she couldn't stop fantasizing about at inappropriate moments, like in the middle of a business meeting. She latched her gaze onto the drop of coffee that lingered on his bottom lip.

His tongue darted out to lick it away.

An odd sensation fluttered in her belly. She ripped her gaze away from his mouth and counted the ice cubes in her glass. Ten. No, eleven. Wait, there was another one, sneaking out from behind a bigger chunk. Twelve, then.

"Mel?"

Her gaze jerked up to meet Adam's. He reclined against the booth seat, his arm stretched across the back. The pose pulled his shirt taut, widening the gap created by the two undone buttons at the top. She spied firm, toned flesh, glazed a golden brown by the sun. He spent a lot of time outdoors, playing touch football or working at odd jobs on his two days off in between every twenty-four-hour shift at the firehouse.

Visions of sweaty, shirtless Adam flashed in her mind.

She cleared her throat. "What we did last night cannot happen again."

His eyes pored over her, from her breasts, up her throat, to her mouth. His gaze affected her like a caress, arousing every nerve. "Sure, next time we'll try a different way. Maybe I'll slide my hand inside your panties and make you come for me while I kiss you mindless."

"You know full well what I meant. I am celibate. No more hands on any part of me that isn't suitable for public viewing."

A tingle rippled through her when his eyes focused on hers. "No hands, hmm? This time I'll take your nipple in my mouth and swirl my tongue around it until you come like a flower blossoming beneath me."

"Honestly, Adam."

He settled a palm on the tabletop, fingers spread. "I won't apologize for wanting you."

"It can't happen again."

"Tell yourself that all you want. I'm not sorry I fucked you with my mouth." His fingers curled on the tabletop. "My only regret is we didn't go all the way."

"We never will. This goes no further, ever."

"Don't try to make me believe you didn't feel anything other than turned on."

In spite of her doubts, she couldn't lie to him. "I felt something, don't know what it was."

"Stop running away and maybe we can find out together."

Mel contemplated the scene outside the window, needing a respite from his piercing gaze. "You're the one who keeps dashing off at inopportune moments."

He jerked his hand, knocking over a pepper shaker, the gray particles scattering over the Formica. "I am helping Dad."

She picked up her napkin, using it to sweep the pepper particles into a neat little pile. "I'm not accusing you of lying. I believe you, but it's another complication we don't need. This is one more reason why we should stay friends—and only friends. The universe is trying to tell us that."

"Bullshit. You're using fate as an excuse to push me away."

Mel sipped her root beer, anything to gain a few seconds to think. The fizzing of the carbonation unleashed a sense memory of the champagne she drank at the club, which led to visions of the mysterious dancer, and finally her clumsy attempt at seducing Adam. Everything after the club had unfolded because she'd gotten so discombobulated by her dance with a stranger. An oddly familiar stranger.

Oh please. No one she knew would've slapped on a mask just to dance with her in secret.

In her apartment the next morning, she'd noticed his black pants and suffered a momentary and insane thought. The dancer had worn identical pants. Of course, she'd realized after a couple seconds that lots of guys wore black pants. Besides, Adam wouldn't have tricked her that way.

"The stuff we did last night," she said, "it was too much. I need to concentrate exclusively on my business, with no distractions."

"You keep saying that, but you keep letting me touch you."

"Never again. I mean it, business only and friendship only."

"Baloney." He wound his fingers around the coffee mug and massaged it, with a motion reminiscent of when he'd kneaded her hip while his mouth plundered her body. Warmth shivered down to settle between her thighs. He smirked, clearly certain he'd guessed what she was thinking. "You say it can't happen again, you're celibate, but then you flirt with me and let me shove my head between your legs. What you don't say is 'Adam, cut it out and leave me alone'. You've never had a problem telling me to shut the hell up. Why can't you do it now?"

"I don't want you to go away. I want you as my friend."

"Face it, Mel. You want me, period."

She laughed, but instead of sounding sarcastic, it came out panicked. *Damn.* What was wrong with her?

"Look me in the eye," he said, "and tell me you don't feel it. A shift in our relationship."

"We're friends. That's all I can handle."

His voice was soft, husky, his gaze irresistible. "You're scared. We both felt a connection last night, something deeper than friendship. Our relationship is changing, but it doesn't have to be a bad thing. It can be incredible." He dipped a finger into his coffee, plunged the finger into his mouth, and withdrew it slowly. His lips puckered around his finger, relaxing as the tip slid out of his mouth. "Our first kiss was incredible. The best first kiss I've ever had. But every kiss after that has blown me away, and I know it's affected you the same. I feel it in the way you kiss me back."

"We can't do this. I won't do it." She grabbed her glass and guzzled a third of it. The onslaught of carbonation sent her into a coughing fit. Once it subsided, she told him, "I want to stay friends. *Only* friends."

He tilted his head to the side, one eyebrow raised. "If you say that one more time, it'll stop sounding like words."

"Celibate," she said. "You still haven't picked up a dictionary, have you?"

"Don't need to." He grinned. "I looked it up on Wikipedia."

"There's no point in talking about that…thing we did together." Her vocal cords refused to form the words to describe it. Her gut roiled, yet an odd excitement had her head floating. "I am done with romance."

"Your body told me the exact opposite." He held up two fingers. "Twice."

"Twice?"

"Once in your office, when we got interrupted. The second time when we came."

She just had to ask, didn't she? "Strictly friends. I don't want more."

Adam's mouth quirked into a knowing smile. "You're blushing, which means you're lying."

Her throat went dry, her mouth cottony. For the first time ever, she wished he didn't know her so well. "What do you want me to say? I've known you my whole life."

"That's the problem. We've been too close for too long and you can't see the broader picture. How everything has changed. How we've changed. Pretending you don't want me won't solve anything."

She swigged a mouthful of root beer, then slapped the glass down a little too forcefully. Cold, sticky liquid sloshed onto her fingers.

Adam snatched a napkin out of the dispenser, offering it to her. She did not move. Couldn't move. Her heart raced. The way he was holding the napkin, she'd have to touch his hand to take it. A muscle in his jaw ticked. He tossed the napkin onto the table. "Christ, Mel. It's not like I'm gonna throw you down on this table and take you right here."

The image of it blasted through her mind. Adam on top of her, his mouth on hers, his hand diving under her blouse to unhook her bra, their bodies entangled.

He froze, his jaw going slack. "Would you like me to?"

Yes. No. Her heart thudded. *No, no, no.*

"You would." Wonder filled his voice. He slid his hand across the table to grasp hers before she could yank it away. If she'd wanted to yank it away. Did she? Yes, of course. But his big, warm hand closed around hers, trapping it. "Relax. We can take this real slow."

"Take…what?" A breathless question.

He gave her a gentle smile imbued with more fondness than she'd ever received from anyone. It tugged at something deep inside, loosening a thread, unraveling a tapestry of longing and fear and desire. Her body ached for his touch, but as his fingers caressed her palm, she knew this was not enough. She thirsted for more. For those lips teasing hers. For those strong hands on her naked flesh, rending passion from her with every stroke.

Oh no, no, no. This was Adam. Sweet, thoughtful, best friend Adam. She couldn't. They couldn't. Black dots appeared in her vision and she realized she'd stopped breathing. She pulled in a draft of burger-scented air. "How do I know this is the real you, not your alter ego? The Arsonist?"

"I'm not two people. It's just me." His fingers rubbed harder. Her body slackened. Her gaze flitted, only to latch onto his. He covered their joined hands with his other palm. "I won't burn you."

"How many women have you slept with?" She didn't want to know, the mere idea of it made her throat hurt, but she had to ask.

His smile faded. "More than you'd like, but less than you think."

More than she'd like? She had no idea how to process the statement. Why had she asked? To steer the conversation away from sex. To end the argument about their status—friends, or more. To delay the moment when she had to confess her worst fear.

Adam was gazing at her with concern clouding his beautiful eyes. "Tell me what's really going on inside that brain of yours."

"What if—" She choked on the words, unable to finish the thought. Closing her eyes, she focused on the feel of his hands around hers. The warmth. The safety. He wasn't dangerous, he was the only person who'd never hurt her. She opened her eyes, cleared her throat, and said, "After the way Devon fooled me, how many times he cheated and I had no idea, I don't trust my judgment anymore. Not about men, not about you. About me. I think I might be as bad as Devon."

He jerked his head back, his chin tucked. "What? No way."

"You have no idea what I've done. I realize you have this idealized view of me, like I'm a perfect angel." She wrestled her hand free of his and clasped both her hands on her lap. "I cheated on Devon, more times than I can count."

Adam's expression blanked. "You had sex with other guys?"

"Well, not exactly." She rubbed her palms on her cheeks, then dropped them to her lap again. "I fantasized about someone else. A lot. I had orgasms while thinking about—" Her cheeks flamed, but the rest of her had gone cold. *Might as well go all the way.* "While thinking about you."

"You told me that already." Eyes wide, he gaped at her for several seconds in silence. Then, a sly smile stole across his face, crinkling his eyes. "Do you have orgasms only when you think about me?"

"No, of course not." Though it seemed impossible, her cheeks grew hotter. Soon her hair would burst into flames. She fought the urge to fan herself and instead swigged the rest of her root beer. Clapping the glass down on the table, she started to speak—but a belch cut her off.

Adam grinned and laughed, his eyes twinkling. "You burp and I still want you."

She squashed her lips together. "You're missing the point. Getting off to thoughts of someone else is infidelity. I'm a dirtbag cheater like Devon."

"You're not. No way."

"Adam." She flattened her palms on the table. "You're just being contrary."

"The word is stubborn." He laid his hands over hers, his fingers stroking her wrists. "Did you think about me when you were having sex with him?"

"No. But—"

"Then you absolutely are not anything like him." His fingers kept gliding over her skin. "Dreaming about me isn't cheating. It's a sign you were never happy with Devon because he couldn't get the job done."

"Not everything is about sex."

Adam snorted. "No, but it means something when you're masturbating to thoughts of me while your boyfriend's out fucking other women."

"I know." Her mouth had gone dry, but her palms were clammy. "It means I'm as bad as—"

"No." He closed his fingers around her wrists, restraining her with gentle pressure. "You are a sweet, loyal, smart, incredible woman. You have lousy taste in guys, but I think I finally understand why."

No one else would call her sweet. Driven, sure. Contained, probably. A lot of men clearly found her intimidating.

Adam's words sank in gradually, until at last she realized what he'd said. "What do you mean you understand why I have bad taste in men?"

"Because I do." As he withdrew his hands, he let them slide over hers. "You pick these guys you can't fall for, not all the way, because you're already in love with somebody else."

She stared at him, unblinking, awareness rippling through her with a hot tingle chased by a faint chill.

He leaned forward, his arms folded on the tabletop. "You're in love with me, Mel."

Chapter Eleven

Aw, shit. Adam knew the second he lost her. The way her fingers twitched and her eyes got squinty, those things told him he'd pushed way too far this time. Seducing her, that had forced her out of her comfort zone. But announcing she loved him…

He'd blown it. Big time.

Why couldn't he keep his damn mouth shut? He kept screwing up with her because getting it right had never mattered this much before. He'd never needed to win over a woman. Never loved a woman. No one but her.

The waitress stopped by to refill Adam's coffee and replace Mel's empty glass of root beer with a fresh one. Adam noticed her peripherally, but he refused to take his eyes off Mel. She was staring right back at him, her expression defiant and her hands clasped on the table. The waitress asked, in a hesitant voice, if they needed anything else. Adam glanced at her and muttered, "No, thank you."

Once the waitress had gone, he reached out to lay a hand over Mel's. "Please talk to me."

"Talk?" She arched her eyebrows. "You seem to prefer dictating to me. First, you tell me I want you. Then, you tell me I can't keep my hands off you. And now, you have the gall to tell me I'm in love with you."

"I'm sorry, I shouldn't have said it." He curled his hand around hers, heartened by a slight softening of her expression. "The fact is, I've been in love with you for a long time."

"In love with me? I don't understand, you never acted like you…felt that way."

How the hell could he explain it? Probably couldn't, but he'd waded too far in to scramble back out. No choice but to dive into the depths. "I didn't realize how I felt until it was too late. You were already with Devon, and I wouldn't get in the way of that. I may be a player, but I don't steal other guys' girlfriends."

"You said you've felt this way for a long time."

"Two years seemed like forever. Two years of wanting you and not knowing if you felt the same way, wondering if Devon wasn't in the picture…" He shrugged. "Maybe you'd pick me."

She sighed, bowing her head briefly. "What am I supposed to say? You didn't tell me any of this until tonight—and you were sleeping around while you claim to have been in love with me."

He straightened, and despite the nausea rising in his stomach, he told her the truth. "You're wrong. One of us went celibate, but it isn't you. It's me."

She went stock-still, not blinking, then glanced away. When she looked him in the eye again, her expression had turned incredulous. "How long?"

Adam didn't ask what she meant, because he knew. "I've only had sex three times in the past two years, and not at all in the past year. I tried to, uh, get back in the game but it didn't work. I kept thinking about you, so I gave up on sex."

Mel's eyes flared wide, though she regained her composure a second later. "*You* are celibate?"

"Yeah."

He sat back, shoulders slumped, arms slack and his hands resting on the cold vinyl of the booth's seat. With his secret out, he had no idea what to say next. Mel didn't move or speak for an eternity. Probably a minute, but damn, it dragged on like a decade. He scratched the nape of his neck, though it didn't itch.

She slouched against the back of her seat. "Adam, I honestly don't know what to say. Don't know how I feel about what you've said, or about anything or anyone. All I know is I don't trust myself. I can't make any serious decisions until I sort myself out." She rubbed her eyes, suddenly looking exhausted. "That probably sounds selfish, but I can't help it. This is why I planned on being celibate, because I need a break from all the demands."

"Demands?" He shook his head. "I don't understand. If Devon's harassing you—"

"It's not just him. It's you too."

A pain lanced through his chest and suddenly the aroma of coffee wafting up from his untouched cup turned his stomach. *I've lost her, for real.* What could he say? She was right. He'd been pestering her when he knew she wanted to be left alone. Trouble was, he knew her too well to believe she really wanted that. She believed she'd been unfaithful to Devon and nothing Adam could say would convince her otherwise. No wonder she was so tangled up inside.

Maybe he should leave her be.

His gut twisted at the thought. He missed her when he couldn't see her for one whole day. Or half a day. Or one hour.

"Okay," he said, "I understand I pushed you too far too fast. If you need some time…"

God, he couldn't finish the sentence. *For how long?* he ached to ask. But he couldn't. She needed him to back off and he would do anything for her. Even rip his own heart out.

"Thank you," she said, her voice barely more than a whisper.

"I pushed you," he said. "Should've given you more than three weeks."

"Adam, it's not the timing. Three weeks or thirty weeks, it wouldn't make a difference because the problem is what I realized about myself. I need a break. I'm sorry, I can't do this with you. I just can't."

Tears shimmered in her eyes, about to spill down her cheeks. She sucked in a breath through her nostrils, swiped at her eyes with the back of her hand, and stumbled out of the booth. Her hip bumped the table, shaking it. Her glass of root beer rocked and splashed brown liquid onto the tabletop and the booth seat she'd vacated a second earlier.

She fled the diner.

Adam started to rise, to run after her, but stopped himself. He flopped back onto the seat, a breath blustering out of him. He'd messed up so bad, he didn't see a way out.

The waitress approached the booth carrying a tray full of food. Their food. Mel had run away without eating her dinner.

"Your girl go to the restroom?" the waitress asked.

"No."

The waitress waved at the tray. "You still want this?"

Adam studied the food, the steaming scent of burgers making his mouth water. Would he really let Mel go hide in her apartment, to cry alone? She wouldn't bother to eat, he'd bet. The hell with it. He could at least make sure she had a good meal before she kicked him to the curb.

"Yeah," he said, "but can I get it to go?"

Adam hesitated outside Mel's apartment, one hand raised to punch the doorbell button. In his other hand, a takeout box from the Downtown Diner balanced on his palm. He shouldn't have come. Mel was too upset. But dammit, she was supposed to talk to him about her problems, not shut him out.

The door to her apartment loomed like the fortified walls of a medieval castle, impenetrable and full of hidden dangers. He hit the doorbell button. The chime sounded, muted by the door. Seconds ticked by, heavy as a ram striking the castle gates.

The door crept open six inches. The security chain stretched taut. Mel peered at him through the gap, her eyes red, her expression unreadable. Although she'd changed into sweats and a baggy T-shirt, the sight of her still made his heart thump. One bare foot was visible. She avoided direct eye contact.

He held up the takeout box. "You didn't eat, so I brought your burger and chili fries."

She sniffed, her delicate nostrils wrinkling. One hand dropped to her stomach. "I am starving."

"Take the food." He proffered it again and kept his voice neutral. "I won't ask to come in. Just wanted to make sure you'd eat something."

She clapped the door shut. His heart sank.

A scraping ensued, then the door swung wide. She backed up to the entryway wall, one hand clamped around the door knob. He sidled past her into the living room.

Mel lifted the takeout box from his palm and carried it to the bar that separated the living room from the small kitchen. She plopped the box on the counter, hopping onto a stool. Her little bottom shimmied as she found a comfortable seating.

"Let me warm that up for you." He commandeered the box and took it into the kitchen. He sensed her gaze on him as he got out a plate, slid the food onto it, and popped the whole thing into the microwave. Buttons beeped under his fingers. With a quick sideways glance, he caught her watchful gaze on him. The microwave hummed to life and still she watched him. While he waited for the food to reheat, he turned toward her, one hip braced on the kitchen counter. The second their gazes connected, she averted hers to her hands, linking her fingers atop the bar.

"What was special about Cynthia?" she asked.

The hairs on the back of his neck stiffened. He cleared his throat. "Why do you ask?"

"You were with her for six weeks, twice as long as your next-longest liaison."

She didn't call them relationships. He couldn't blame her, because he'd never had a real relationship with any woman. Except Mel. Friendship counted.

He scratched his head, but the odd prickling sensation lingered. "Cynthia was a nurse, so she understood the screwy hours I work. She was smart, like you. She didn't take any guff but she was kind and compassionate, like you. Actually, the two of you would've gotten along really well, I'm sure, because you're a lot alike."

"You're saying I'm the type of girl who has six-week flings without commitment."

"Of course not." His skin itched, his throat went dry. *Screwing up again.* "I told you what I mean. You're both smart, independent women."

Mel fiddled with the buttons on her shirt, refusing to look at him. "Is that why you picked her? She's a duplicate of me?"

"No." He pressed both hands into the countertop and bored his gaze into her, willing her to glance up, even for a second. She didn't. He let his chin fall to his chest. "Nobody could replace you."

Her stool creaked. He raised his head to find her wriggling on her seat, face pinched. They had to get off this subject right this instant. He said the first thing that popped into his brain. "I pushed. About the sex thing. I thought three weeks was plenty of time for you to get over Devon's cheating and be ready for something new." He rubbed his neck, frowning at himself. *Go slow and easy, even if it kills you.* "All I thought about was what I wanted. I'm a jackass."

"Told you before it isn't the timing." Her eyes rolled up to look at him, though her head stayed bowed. Through her thick lashes, he spied her deep blue irises. She lowered her hands to her lap. "And you are not a jackass."

"You had to bolt to get away from me."

"It's not you." She winced. "Sorry. I know that sounds like a brush-off, but it isn't. The problem honestly is with me."

"Devon's a cheating bastard. That's his problem, not yours." He couldn't help the hint of anger in his voice. If he could've strangled Devon McCallister without risking life in prison, he would've done it a long time ago. "And you are nothing like him. Fantasies about another guy don't make you an unfaithful girlfriend. Everybody thinks about stuff like that once in a while. It's normal."

"You still don't get it." Mel shut her eyes and sighed. "I have never fantasized about anyone but you."

Adam froze, his eyes locked on her face. "Never?"

Her shoulders jerked upward in a nervous shrug. "Maybe a fictitious character or a famous actor once in a while. You know, the unattainable types. You are the only real, here-in-my-life man I've ever imagined having sex with."

Though he knew he shouldn't ask, because it was none of his business, he couldn't shut down his raging curiosity. He tried, really, he did. But he failed. "Uh, how—how often did you have those thoughts about me?"

She remained perfectly still and silent for so long he worried he'd gone too far again. But then, she lifted her face to look at him. Her expression was neutral, her voice even. "Far more often than I should have, considering I was in a relationship with someone else. I tried to convince myself it didn't mean anything."

"How often, Mel?"

"Over the past year or so," she said, "maybe once every month or two. After I found out about Devon's trysts, I realized my daydreams about you were a symptom of a huge problem between me and Devon. Between me and any man."

"Every month or two? Come on, that's nothing. You're being way too hard on yourself." He shook his head. "Devon's a sleaze, that's not your fault."

"No, but—" She groaned, slumping into the counter. "It's complicated."

The microwave beeped, its hum ceasing.

Screw the food. Adam stared at her, unable to move one inch until he understood. "Explain it to me."

Mel bit her lip. Her teeth scraped across it as she released her flesh. Her mouth opened.

The blasted microwave beeped again.

She raised her hands, joined as if in prayer, and rested her forehead on them with her elbows propped on the counter.

Adam ripped open the microwave door, grabbed the plate, and slung it across the bar counter toward her. She didn't budge. He snagged a can of Coke from the refrigerator, popped the cap, and thunked the can down beside her plate.

Mel peeked at him over her hands.

With more restraint than he'd tried for in years, he planted both hands on the counter, leaned into them, and waited for her to speak.

She lowered her hands, her lips twisted into a half frown. "I finally figured out why I pick men I can't love. Guys who don't…excite me."

"Why the hell would you stay with a guy you don't love and who's crap in bed?"

"I told you, sex wasn't a big deal for me."

Adam couldn't bite his tongue any longer without risking serious blood loss. He crossed his arms over his chest. "Let me get this straight. Devon sucked in bed. He sucked at fidelity. What did the creep have that made you stick with him? He hit the jackpot with a woman like you, but what did you get out of it?"

"I didn't find out he was cheating until recently. We had nice conversations and he could be a lot of fun to be with, charming and attentive. He didn't mind

I worked long hours and he accepted my business came first. I realize you hated him from the start, but you didn't know him the way I did."

"Obviously, you didn't know him that well either."

She flinched and he instantly regretted the words.

But she said, "You're right. I didn't know the real Devon. That's what scares me about whatever's going on between you and me lately."

A wave of ice-cold dread crashed over Adam. He gripped the edge of the counter hard enough to shoot pains through his knuckles. "You think you don't know me? That's crazy. We've been best friends our whole lives, Mel. Nobody, and I mean nobody, knows or understands me the way you do."

She clasped her hands before her face and let her forehead drop onto them. "I'm saying this all wrong. I trust you. That's never been the issue."

"This is all Devon's fault. That guy—"

"Not all his fault." She raised her head, her chin propped on her hands. "I never thought I'd be the kind of person who'd have erotic fantasies about her best friend while being involved with someone else. Never imagined I could be so...craven. I need to figure out why I'm this way."

What could he say to that? Craven? Mel? No way.

He stared down at the countertop until he felt able to speak calmly again. "You didn't do anything wrong. I did this. I was hell-bent on seducing you, no matter what you wanted." He squeezed his eyes shut, shaking his head. "God, Mel, I'm so sorry."

"Don't apologize. I could've said no, but I didn't. I liked it too much, getting naughty with you."

He couldn't stop the smile from kinking his lips. "I liked it too. A lot."

"But it has to stop." She rubbed her temples, squinting as if her head hurt. "Do you see now? Why I need a break from all this?"

"I get why you think you do."

She made an irritated noise, dropping her hands to her thighs. "Sex isn't the most important thing ever, you know."

"Never said it was." He probably had acted like it was, though. *Damn.* What an ass he'd been. "You can talk to me about this. We can figure it out together. But avoiding your feelings is not the answer, Mel."

She leaned against her stool's back, giving him that *you're impossible* look he knew so well. "Talking to you about my fantasies of you will not help clear my head. It'll probably lead to more things we shouldn't be doing together."

"If you're that hot for me, why fight it? You are in love with me, after all."

"Gah!" She threw her hands up in a melodramatic and slightly sarcastic gesture, letting them slap back down on her thighs. "You are impossible, Adam, and outrageously presumptuous. I'll decide how I feel, thank you."

"Then hurry up and decide." He grinned and winked, rewarded by her poorly suppressed smile. "See? I can make you smile. It's more than sex with us. It's real."

Mel glanced down at her plate. "Could you warm up my food for thirty seconds? I'm starved and it's cooled off a bit."

"Sure thing." He grabbed the plate, practically flung it into the microwave, hit the thirty-second button, and watched the digits counting down as the contraption whirred. She was probably using food as an excuse to stop talking, but he had come here to make sure she ate. For now, he'd let her stall.

The microwave beeped, finished with its reheating. He retrieved the plate and knocked the microwave door shut with his elbow as he spun around to slide the plate across the bar to her.

Mel dived into the meal with all the gusto of a contestant in a pie-eating competition. Mouthfuls of food puffed out her cheeks while her jaw worked hard. Once she'd finished, she took a swig of pop and sighed with contentment.

Adam smirked and waved a finger at her face. "Even with ketchup all over your face and on your fingers, you're still the hottest woman on the face of the earth."

She snagged a napkin from a dispenser on the bar and scrubbed her face and hands with it.

"Relax," he said, "I've seen you messy before. I'm glad you still feel comfortable enough with me to pig out in front of me. Did you get messy when Devon was around? Or any of your boyfriends?"

"No, of course not." She crumpled the napkin, tossing it on the counter. "Why would I want them to see me like this?"

"Because it's part of who you are. Anybody who loved you would accept it."

She made a noncommittal noise, her face pinched. "What if we get involved, romantically, and I start fantasizing about someone else?"

"Nice conversational U-turn. Real subtle."

"I'm serious."

"Yeah, I know."

She gulped down another mouthful of pop. "There's something fundamentally wrong with me. I'm defective, incapable of being satisfied with what I have."

Hurrying around the counter, he stopped in front of her. Not touching her. Just being there, close to her.

"Listen to me," he said, "you are not defective. Did you ever think maybe you weren't satisfied with any of your relationships because you just weren't in love with them? They clearly couldn't get the job done in bed either. No wonder you weren't happy."

"What if I can't be satisfied with you either?"

Adam slanted toward her until their eyes were level. "We both know I satisfy you."

Her beautiful eyes went soft, but she said, "I might cheat on you in my fantasies. I might think about some other man—"

Laying two fingers on her lips, he sealed them shut. "I'm the only one you've ever fantasized about. That's what you told me. Which means you've always wanted me, not those schmucks you dated. Me." He peeled his fingers from her lips. "Stop fighting it, Mel."

She stared at him for several seconds, her breaths shallow and fast, while his heart pounded and the blood thundered through his veins.

"Maybe you're right," she murmured. "But I still worry this could all blow up in our faces."

"That's life. You can't control it, no matter how hard you try."

For several seconds, she sat there staring into empty space, her eyes unfocused. When her gaze landed on him again, she nodded. "You're right. I keep trying to maintain a death grip on my life, to keep things from changing, but all I accomplish is making myself crazy."

"You are allergic to change."

A small smile tightened her lips. "I was just thinking that the other day. Amazing how often you seem to read my mind."

"With a time delay, huh? Must be jet lag or something."

"Or maybe," she said, her shoulders relaxing and her sweet smile warming him, "you just know me better than anybody else in the world."

"Definitely that."

"Makes me wonder if you might be right about other things."

Before he could ask what other things, Mel slipped her delicate hands into his and urged him closer. She eased her legs apart to welcome him between them, his hips snug between her thighs. She looped her arms around his neck, her supple body pressed to his, her lush breasts crushed into his chest. The heat of her enveloped him, intoxicating and irresistible.

Tipping her head up, she moved her lips toward his.

With her mouth a breath away from his, he bent his head back to evade the kiss. His heart hammered, his body sang with the need for her. He eyed her warily. "Have you had any alcohol tonight?"

"Not a single drop." She brushed her lips against his, and her tongue sneaked out to lick at the seam of his mouth. "I've decided you're right about me wanting you. Time to stop fighting, give in to my desires."

His cock shot hard. He fought to breathe, to stay rational. So damn hard with her lips teasing his and her warm arms around his neck and her soft body molded to him. Her fingers threaded through his hair, a sweet tickle on his scalp, sending electric currents down his skin that spread across his entire body. He slid his arms around her waist, glided them up to her shoulders, splayed his hands over her upper back. She moaned as her lips found his, her tongue thrusting inside his mouth, velvety and agile. Rocking her hips into his, she locked her ankles behind his ass and pulled him into the softness between her thighs. With deft fingers, she tugged his shirt free of his waistband. Her hands glided up his abs, around to his back, kneading his flesh as they traveled ever upward.

Groaning into her mouth, he shifted a hand to cup her breast and flick his thumb over her nipple, rigid and straining against her bra. She made a little gasping grunt. Her legs tightened around him. His cock was jammed into her crotch, with only a few layers of fabric between his hard length and her welcoming softness. Even through her clothes, he could scent her arousal. Musky. Heady. With a dash of sweetness. He groaned, half crazed with the need to plunder her mouth and her body, but one thought held him back.

She's still not sure about us.

Jesus, he couldn't do this. Not now. Not when she still had doubts.

He grasped her shoulders and pushed her away just enough to sever their kiss.

She gazed at him, her eyes hazy with desire, her lips a deep pink. When she spoke, her voice was hushed and dreamy. "Adam?"

"We can't do this." He did not miss the irony of it. After struggling to overcome her fears and get her to exactly this moment, he was the one cutting it short. "Not tonight. I have to work tomorrow and you said you need time to think, so I'm recommending you do that. I won't call you. I'll wait for you to call me. Okay?"

Her hand snaked down between their bodies. She cupped his erection through his pants, stroking up and down. "No, not okay."

"Mel—"

She unhooked the rivet of his jeans, her fingers taking hold of the zipper slider, dragging it down inch by mind-numbing inch. Her voice flowed through him, husky and wanton. "I want you inside me."

He choked on a gasp. How long had he waited to hear those words? And he couldn't let it happen. He caught her hand. "We can't do this tonight. I'm sorry. We've had a really intense, emotional conversation and it's got us both wired. I will wait to hear from you, when you've cooled down and thought this through. Okay?"

The emphasis he injected into the last word seemed to snap her out of her lustful haze. She blinked rapidly, her eyes clearing. "Okay."

Hands shaking, he zipped up his jeans and secured the rivet.

Mel canted her head. "I can't believe you just rejected me."

"Not a rejection. A rain check." He took her face in his hands. "You'll thank me for this later, I promise."

"If you say so." One corner of her mouth crimped. "Figures. The first time I throw myself at a guy, he tosses me back."

"Aw, Mel, it's not like that." He rubbed his thumbs over her still-swollen lips. "I want you more than I've ever wanted anyone. But I can't—I won't—mess this up by getting greedy. Waiting isn't my forte. But for you, I'll wait as long as it takes. Because this is more than sex."

She opened her mouth to speak, but he shushed her with a finger on her lips.

"Don't say anything." He kissed her forehead. "Get some sleep. Everything will look different in the morning."

Though it hurt with near-physical pain, he turned away and headed for the door, somehow appearing calm even as he battled his frenzied, conflicting needs to have her and to protect her. If he stayed in her apartment any longer, his libido would win out. So he did the only thing he could.

He walked out the door and didn't look back.

Chapter Twelve

Adam hunched on his sofa, exhausted as he collected the papers on the coffee table and began stuffing them back into file folders. Two days without Mel had strained his patience, but a long evening of medical mumbo-jumbo had sapped the remains of his energy. The phone consultation with the out-of-state oncologist had run almost two hours. Adam offered to pony up the extra fee to keep it going. The doc knew his stuff. Adam could tell his dad was relaxing just listening to the guy talk about the options, the pros and cons, and his advice.

Their other guest, Cynthia Harwood, lounged in the arm-chair across from the sofa. His dad had left already, insisting on taking a cab home. Adam had offered to drive him, since he didn't feel up to driving himself, but Bob Caras announced he'd had enough of being dependent.

"Cynthia, thanks." Adam had thought of contacting Cynthia after Mel asked him about her. It was weird and kind of creepy that the only woman he'd ever loved inspired him to get in touch with his former lover, the one he'd stayed with the longest. Cynthia had medical experience, though, and way more knowledge about this crap than he or his dad. "You knew questions to ask neither of us would've thought of."

"Happy to help," she said.

Cynthia moved over to the sofa, crossing the distance with her usual grace. She was nothing next to Mel, though, and the spark he and Cynthia once shared had fizzled out two years ago, at the same time Mel was hooking up with Devon. These days, Adam was grateful for Cynthia's friendship.

As if reading his mind, she settled a hand on his knee and said, "I will always be here for you, Adam."

"Your fiancé doesn't mind us being friends?"

"Paolo understands I have a past. He's not the jealous type."

Adam picked up a scattered stack of medical records, trying to straighten them. The papers slipped from his hands to spill across the floor. His thoughts kept straying to Mel, wrecking his concentration and his coordination. What if the past two days hadn't changed her mind? What if she was more determined than ever to be celibate? After trying to seduce him two nights ago, he didn't see how she could come to the conclusion. But her fears were irrational, and that kind of fear could make a person do stupid things.

He reached for the papers again, but his fingers slipped and the records scattered further across the floor. "Shit."

Cynthia's hand rose to his shoulder and squeezed lightly. "Take it easy. You've got a good treatment plan worked out. I know a radiologist at Northwestern who will take wonderful care of your father."

He laid a hand over hers. "Thank you. You're a great friend."

"Enough thanking me, Adam." She withdrew her hand, smiling. "Tell me about the woman you're in love with."

He startled, his gaze flying to Cynthia. "What makes you think I'm in love with anyone?"

She pinched his cheek. "A woman can tell. Besides, you kept checking your watch, like you have a hot date. And you're clearly distracted, by more than your father's illness." She rubbed her hands with exaggerated lust for the dirt on his love life. "Come on, at least tell me her name."

As uncomfortable as talking to Mel about Cynthia had been, the reverse would be even worse. Then again, Cynthia might have some sage advice for him about women. She was ten years older. Didn't age grant wisdom or some such bull? Worth a shot.

He rested his arms on his thighs, head drooping. "It's Mel."

"I had a feeling. Even when we were together."

"What?" He glanced at her sideways. "How could you know when I didn't?"

Cynthia patted his arm. "Adam, dear, it was painfully obvious. You'd run out on me to go be with her, anytime she called. Given our arrangement, I didn't mind. But it was hard to miss the signs of a smitten man."

Smitten. *No shit.* He'd waited two agonizing years for Mel to dump her smarmy boyfriend and now...

"Does she love you?"

"I think so. I dunno." Adam sank back into the sofa, overwhelmed by a sudden wave of exhaustion. On the table, his phone rang. Groaning, he threw his body forward to grab the phone and mutter a hello.

"Hi, it's me."

Mel's sweet voice made his heart stutter. Two days without her had eaten away at his heart. How painful would it be if she kicked him out of her life altogether?

He sat forward, the phone clutched to his ear. "Hey, Mel. What's up?"

Brilliant conversation. She'd leap into his arms for sure.

"I've done a lot of thinking," she said, her tone cautious. "Is it okay if I come over?"

"Now?" And of course, he all but shouted the word—sounding exactly like a lying creep who had another woman in his apartment. *Awesome job, Romeo.* He dropped his face into his palm. "Uh, yeah, come on over."

"Are you sure? You sound like you don't really want me to."

"I want to see you."

"Okay." She hesitated, probably biting her lip in her adorable way that made him want to ravish her mouth. "I'm already in the elevator. Be there in a minute."

She disconnected the call.

Adam sat frozen with the phone in his hand, suspended in front of his face. His brain couldn't form complete thoughts, everything got jumbled into disjointed words. Mel. Here. Cynthia. Trouble.

"Everything okay?" Cynthia asked.

He stuffed the phone in his pocket, numb and cold all over. "Not even close."

"Your father?" Concern tinged her voice.

Adam gave her a tight smile. "Dad's fine."

Deep down, he knew Mel wouldn't care about him hanging out with Cynthia, but she'd have to wonder why the other woman was here so late. He couldn't tell her, thanks to his father's gag order. Since Adam had apparently turned into a chicken shit this past week, he opted to avoid the discussion.

"It's Mel," he said. "She's in the elevator, be here any second, and—"

Cynthia arched her manicured brows. "You'd rather I weren't around when she gets here."

"I'm a moron, I know. But would you mind leaving through the stairwell?"

"No problem."

He kissed her cheek. "Thanks. You're a godsend, Cynthia."

"No, your godsend is on her way. Think of me as the fairy godmother."

Cynthia rushed out the door. It clapped shut behind her.

The papers on the floor and the table taunted him. He scrambled to scoop them up, no longer having the luxury of organizing them. Mel couldn't see these. He had to keep this damn secret, for his dad. He gathered the papers in a heap in his arms, kicked the lid off the storage ottoman, and dumped everything inside. He slammed the lid over the whole mess.

Rushing into the bedroom, he changed into a fresh T-shirt and replaced his sweats with jeans. As if it mattered what he wore. Mel was coming.

She'd done a lot of thinking, she said. She wanted to talk.

Anxiety like nothing he'd experienced before twisted his stomach in knots and sheened his forehead with a cold sweat. Mel was the only woman who'd ever mattered. The only one he couldn't bear to lose. Whatever her decision, at least the misery of waiting would end tonight.

He prayed she wasn't about to hurl him into a deeper, darker abyss.

Mel stuffed her hands in her pants pockets, tapping one foot on the floor. Was this the slowest elevator on earth? Sure seemed like it. Then again, maybe she was anxious about explaining her decision to Adam. Two days apart had given her more than enough time for self-reflection. Too much, maybe.

At last, the elevator halted with a little bump. The doors slid open—and Mel's heart dropped through the floor.

In the hallway, a woman froze mid step. She'd been heading down the hall, past the elevators, but now rotated her head to stare wide-eyed at Mel.

Cynthia's mouth fell open.

Mel stared, like a mute idiot. Adam was still friends with Cynthia, Mel understood that. But seeing the woman skulking away from Adam's apartment, that was…weird.

The other woman, Ms. Six Weeks, cleared her throat. The shock receded from her features and she smiled warmly as she moved toward the elevator doors. With one hand, she kept the doors from shutting, but she held out her other hand to Mel. "I'm Cynthia Harwood, a friend of Adam's. We met a few times."

"I remember." Mel blurted out a question before her brain had processed the implications of it. "Are you and Adam back together?"

They weren't. Mel knew it, because Adam would've told her if he'd gotten back with Cynthia and, more importantly, he would never two-time Mel. Not that they were a couple. Or dating. Holy hell, this entire situation confused her and it was her own damn fault. Tonight, she'd planned on sorting it all out with him.

Instead, she stood face to face with his ex-lover.

"Back together?" Cynthia waved a hand as if shooing away the possibility. "No-no. I'm engaged to a wonderful man I love more than anything in the world." The woman's gaze turned shrewd, focused on Mel. "I imagine there's someone you feel that way about."

Mel lost her voice again. A wonderful man she loved more than anything in the world. Adam's face flickered in her mind's eye. His sexy smirk. His tender smile. Those gorgeous eyes focused on her and her alone.

Cynthia strolled into the elevator. "Go on, dear, he's waiting for you. There's only one woman in Adam's heart."

The other woman urged her out the doors with one hand on her back, exerting gentle pressure. Mel stumbled out into the hallway. The elevator doors rolled shut behind her.

Mel stared at the elevator doors for a moment, struggling to sort out her encounter with Cynthia. Back when Cynthia and Adam had been involved, Mel had sort of met the woman a few times—though only in passing. They weren't friends or even really acquaintances. Why should the woman care about Mel's relationship with Adam? And what had he told Cynthia about Mel?

Well, Adam might've needed someone to talk to about things. Mel had Kaya, so she couldn't fault Adam for confiding in Cynthia.

Mel shook off her confusion and headed down the hall. She reached Adam's door, her stomach fluttering and her palms clammy. *Breathe, dummy.* What if Adam didn't like her decision? He hadn't understood the celibacy thing, but if he couldn't handle what she wanted now…She drew in breath after breath, exhaling for a count of ten each time, until at least she didn't feel about to pass out from lack of oxygen. Then she knocked four times. Seconds elapsed. She fiddled with her purse strap, scratched her arm, fiddled with her hair.

The door swung inward.

Adam studied her with an expression somewhere between anxiety and happiness.

She must've looked the same way, given her emotional state. Should she admit she saw his ex-lover in the hallway? The woman had seemed to be sneaking off—to avoid Mel, no doubt. But she was about to ask him for total honesty.

Well then, she better start things off.

Clearing her throat, she said, "I ran into Cynthia on my way in."

His face blanked. "You—what?"

"Looked like she was hightailing it out of here to avoid seeing me." Mel glanced down the hallway. "Or rather, to avoid me seeing her. It wasn't necessary."

"No?" He braced one shoulder against the door jamb, eying her with what she could only describe as admiring surprise. "Don't you want to know why she was here?"

"If you want to tell me." She shrugged one shoulder. "Otherwise, it's none of my business."

He stared at her, unblinking, his expression inscrutable. "You really trust me, don't you?"

"Of course. May I come in? I have something to say and I'd rather not explain out here."

Adam straightened with a jerk and waved her in, stepping aside.

Mel rushed into the living room and dumped her purse on the coffee table. She twiddled her thumbs. Seriously. She twiddled them, something she thought nobody actually did. Yet here she was, twiddling away. Rotating her thumbs around each other like hot dogs on spits. Adrenaline bolstered her body, but her mind ricocheted from thought to thought before getting stuck on what she needed to say next.

Adam sauntered into the living room to halt at the sofa. The six feet between them seemed both far too small and as distant as the moon.

She perched on the edge of the sofa, hands on her thighs, but could not make herself look at him yet. "I've reached a decision."

"Okay," he said slowly.

"This will take a bit of time to explain."

His eyes pinged back and forth, between the sofa beside her and the chair. "May I, uh, sit next to you?"

"Yes, Adam, you may." She cast him a sidelong look, trying not to smile. "Since when do you ask? You normally just plop yourself down beside me."

"Plop?" His lips twitched with a smirk that couldn't quite take hold.

"That's right." She patted the cushion beside her. "Sit."

"Yes, ma'am." He strode over and settled his big body onto the sofa, draping one arm behind her head.

She longed to lean back and rest her head on his arm. First, she had to confide the truth to him. "I realize it may have seemed like I don't trust you lately, but that's not the issue. I haven't trusted my judgment, even about my feelings for you."

"You told me this the other night. You think you're craven, which is total bull—"

"I agree."

He tilted his head, eying her with raised brows. "You agree with me?"

"Yes." She closed her fingers over her knees, but still felt oddly untethered. Drifting. In danger of floating away into outer space, weightless from excitement and nervousness. Though they'd talked about this before, she felt compelled to reiterate her fears, to make him understand how deeply they'd affected her. "I wondered if I'd turned into a perv. Maybe Devon cheated because I was saving all my passion for an imaginary lover, someone who was perfect because it wasn't real."

Adam leaned closer without touching her. "I'm real."

Oh yes, he was real all right. The scent of his cologne enveloped her, a tantalizing mix of spice and woodsy appeal, with a hint of pure Adam. His breaths fluttered her hair and his proximity ignited a spark inside her, one that could easily flare into an inferno. She closed her eyes briefly, hoping to tamp down her attraction to him for long enough to finish her explanation, but it didn't work.

She zeroed in on the armchair kitty-corner to her and let the corduroy lines in the armchair's tan fabric obsess her. "You were right, I've been beating myself up for having these thoughts about you and I have to stop. I didn't do anything wrong. It wasn't cheating."

"Damn straight it wasn't." He hooked a finger under her chin. "If you'd been a cheater, you would've run to my apartment late at night and ripped my clothes off."

His comment teased a laugh from her. "Never once occurred to me to do that. Until this week."

"Can we call the craven perv discussion closed?"

"Yes, please."

He inched even closer. The cushions wobbled under his weight. "Was this what you wanted to talk about?"

"No, not all of it." She sank back into the sofa—and straight into his waiting arm. She loved the warmth of his muscular arm cradling her head. "I think I've been in denial for a long, long time. Yesterday, I had an epiphany."

Angling sideways slightly, he relaxed against the sofa. "I had one of those once."

She swiveled her head toward him. "You did?"

"It happened not long after you got together with Devon. Hit me like a bolt of lightning."

"What was it about?"

"That's when I realized I love you." He nudged her with his arm. "Your turn."

She chewed the inside of her lip, needing a moment to gather her thoughts. "Yesterday, I tried to think about everything, to get some perspective and maybe some clarity. Instead, I kept thinking about you. No matter what else I tried to focus on, my mind kept gravitating back to you—to us. That's when I had my own bolt of lightning. Suddenly, I realized what I need to do. What I want."

"And?" He'd gone stiff beside her, his breaths no longer fluttering her hair.

She hesitated for a second, transfixed by the golden flecks in his caramel eyes. "I want you. Always have. I've known you my entire life and I think that's why it was so hard for me to accept the truth. Things changed between us before I met Devon. We are not friends anymore."

He sat motionless, his attention concentrated solely on her, as if nothing else existed in the universe. "What are we?"

"Not sure, but I want to find out."

"How, exactly?"

"Like this." She laid a hand on his cheek, sliding it into his hair to pull him closer, and pressed her mouth to his. With their lips barely touching, she said, "I want to explore our physical relationship."

"You mean sex," he rumbled against her lips, his words vibrating into her.

"Mm-hm." She captured his lower lip between hers, releasing it little by little. "But I need to start slow, if that's okay with you. The intensity of what you make me feel, it's overwhelming and not like anything I've felt before. I'm asking for a little time to acclimate."

Eyes hooded, he caught her hand and held it to his heart. "You've got it. Anything you need, I'm game. And I promise to be more patient about sex."

She laughed softly. "Adam, you've been so patient with me you deserve a medal."

"Guess my inner animal doesn't show through as much as I thought." He let go of her hand, brushing his fingertips down her cheek. "This is your play. Tell me what you need and I'll give it to you."

"I was worried you might react to my new plan like you did with my first one."

"Celibacy was a dumb plan." He shifted his weight, avoiding eye contact. "You're smart, determined, kind, beautiful, sexy, amazing...Are you sure you want to be with me? A guy who's spent over a decade perfecting the concept of meaningless sex."

She puckered her lips. "After pursuing me relentlessly, after I'm finally ready to do this, now you have doubts?"

"I'm just making sure you really want this. Want me. You had to be drunk before you could admit how you feel."

"Adam." She took his face in both hands, to make him look at her. "I'm not perfect, you know that. And all those things you said about me, they apply to you too." She kissed him, hard and quick. "You, Adam Caras, are an amazing man. Don't argue with me, because you left out the part where I'm as stubborn as you are. I want you and you're not getting rid of me, so suck it up and start acting like the confident, smart, brave, incredibly hot firefighter you are."

His lips twitched, as if he were fighting back a smile. He straightened, watching her with an odd expression, for long enough to make her sit up straight and open her mouth to voice a question. She never got the chance.

A grin spread across his beautiful face, lighting him up from the inside out, twinkling in his eyes. "Thanks, babe. I appreciate the vote of confidence."

His voice had dropped into that deep, sexy register that made her skin tingle and her sex grow wetter with each second his gaze scorched into hers. God, he was gorgeous. And irresistible. And completely irreplaceable. She didn't even mind he called her babe, a term she'd hated when other men used it. From Adam, the endearment set her pulse to racing, her mind to imagining all the ways they could explore their physical connection.

How could she have ever thought she wanted anyone else? No wonder her relationships invariably fizzled out. No other man could compete with Adam Caras.

"So tell me," he said, splaying a palm over her thigh, gliding it ever upward, inch by inch, "what's your plan for tonight?"

Mel smiled with her lips sealed.

He arched one eyebrow.

Tucking her legs under her, she rose into a kneeling position before him. Excitement rushed through her, heated and electric. He tilted his head back, his eyes drinking her in as she hovered over him. She dipped her head down to his, wrapped her arms around his neck, and devoured his mouth with her own. He opened wide for her, granting her deep access to his hot mouth, his hands coming up to her hips to anchor her. She wound her tongue around his again and again in a slow, decadent dance.

His groan resonated in his chest.

She pulled back a few inches, breathing hard. "It's true, you know. What I said on my birthday. I have always wanted to be naked for you."

His voice had gone smoky, his expression was tinged with confusion. "You said no sex tonight."

"Mm, yes." She pushed her hands up the back of his neck, into his hair, and dragged them down his cheeks. "But there's a lot we can do when we're naked. I want you to see me, touch me, kiss me. Can you handle that?"

"Oh, hell yeah."

"Do you think I'm crazy?"

He shook his head, grazing his lips over hers. "You're obsessed with controlling every aspect of your life. It's no surprise you need to hold the reins, to keep our libidos from stampeding away with us."

"In this metaphor, are you the wild stallion or the hot cowboy?"

"Whatever you want me to be, I'm game."

She slid off the sofa, rising to stand in front of it, in front of him.

Adam relaxed back into the sofa, his legs spread wide with his feet at either side of hers. His erection already bulged inside his jeans. She couldn't help licking her lips at the sight of it. Her thoughts flashed back to their previous encounter, on his sofa, when she'd held his swollen length in her hand. His cock was thick and sleek and beautiful. What would it taste like?

She startled at the thought.

He leaned forward to take her hands gently in his. "What's wrong?"

"Nothing. I'm not quite used to having these naughty thoughts about you while I'm in the same room with you."

A devilish smile curved his sensuous mouth, and he shifted his hands to her hips. "A naughty thought? You've got to tell me what it was."

Why not? She couldn't think of one good reason not to tell him. "I was remembering the time I took your cock in my hand and made you scream. Made me wonder what you'd taste like."

He hauled in a shaky breath. "Damn, you sure know how to get me fired up for you."

"I'm just getting started." She laid her hands on his shoulders and urged him backward. "Sit back and enjoy the show."

Slumping down a little, he reclined on the sofa with his hands on his spread thighs, his fingers lightly caressing the fabric of his jeans. She wondered if he was picturing his hands on her.

And all of a sudden, she couldn't wait any longer.

Taking hold of her shirt hem, she pulled it up slowly. Cool air kissed her stomach.

"Wait," he said, holding up one hand. "You sure you're not drunk?"

Chapter Thirteen

What the hell was he doing? Asking if she was drunk. *Way to wreck the mood, Romeo.*

"I'm positively, one-hundred-percent sober," she said, looking at him with amused exasperation. "Should I track down a Breathalyzer so you can test me?"

"No. Sorry. I guess I—" *Can't believe you really want this with me unless you're toasted.* "Guess I needed to make sure. Better safe than sorry."

"That's not it."

She bent over him and planted her hands on the sofa's back, at either side of his head. Her breasts hung in his face, cloaked in the thin fabric of her T-shirt and the bra underneath it. His heart sped up, pumping more blood into his rock-hard erection. He couldn't think with her this close, so he gave in and let his head fall back on the cushion.

"I think," she said, her voice soft and sweet, "you can't believe I'd take my clothes off for you unless I'm tipsy. Don't know why, after the things I've let you do to me. Guess you actually believe you're not good enough for me, don't you?"

Speechless. Paralyzed. Entranced by her angelic face. She'd read his mind, the way she told him he'd read hers. He couldn't respond, couldn't manage a coherent thought.

"The only one who's beneath me," she said, "is Devon. You belong on top."

An image of just that blasted through his mind. Mel writhing beneath him, while he drove into her wet heat again and again.

She rose before him, a stunning vision of beauty and sensuality.

If he'd thought she might kill him that night in his apartment, he'd been so wrong. Tonight, she wielded a weapon of such devastatingly erotic power he'd pray for death—for death from overpowering pleasure. *Le petit mort.* She could slay him with ecstasy and resurrect him with total satisfaction.

And he'd beg for more.

The Arsonist begging? Nobody would ever believe it.

For Mel, he'd fall down on his knees, a vassal pleading for mercy from a goddess.

She stripped off her T-shirt and flung it aside. The garment fluttered to the floor behind her. "You wanna see me naked or what?"

He nodded, incapable of intelligent speech. The best he might've managed was a grunt or a guttural groan. The smooth plane of her stomach seized his attention, pulling his gaze upward to her perfect little belly button, and higher to the delicate inner slopes of her breasts.

With the tips of her index fingers, she slipped the bra's straps off her shoulders. They tumbled down her upper arms, revealing a tantalizing glimpse of the upper curves of her breasts. She reached behind her back. The bra popped loose and she let it slip off.

Adam lost his breath at the sight of her breasts, bared to him for the first time ever. Rigid nipples jutted out from the dusky pink, puckered skin of the areolas. The plump mounds would fit perfectly in his palms. His mouth watered, his cock pulsed, and he battled the impulse to surge forward to suck one of those stiff little peaks into his mouth.

She ditched her jeans and panties in five seconds flat.

He ran his gaze down her body, following the contours of her slender waist to the swell of her hips. The thatch of dark hairs at the apex of her thighs tapered into the barely visible slit of her cleft. Drops of glistening moisture clung to the hairs there and his body burned at the knowledge of how wet she must be. For him.

"Am I getting you too excited?" she asked, a playful gleam in her eyes.

"What?"

She nodded toward his crotch.

He glanced down to discover he was stroking his cock through his jeans. No wonder his erection throbbed. She had turned him on more than any other woman he'd known—and he hadn't even laid a finger on her yet.

Mel went to her knees between his legs, skimming her hands up his inner thighs. "You look about to burst. Shall I render aid?"

Render aid. He flashed back to her hand on his cock and the way he'd lost every shred of control from just that simple act. He was so much hotter now, if she touched him…

"Think I should," she said, her fingers grazing his erection.

When he gasped, she smiled the most beguiling and wicked smile he'd ever seen on a woman. She sneaked her hands under his shirt and swept it up over his chest. He tore it off over his head, desperate to shed his clothes too. Licking her lips, she fanned her hands over his chest, moving them in circles, her skin like feathers brushing over his flesh. Each labored breath heaved his chest, as her fingers traveled lower and lower.

God, how he wanted to yank her close and ravage her mouth with a frantic kiss. But this was her show and he wouldn't get in the way. No matter how much it hurt.

He loved every second of the torment.

Mel unzipped his jeans. "Need a little help here."

Lifting his hips, he held himself off the cushions with both hands while she whisked his jeans off him in one swift motion. His dick sprang free, bobbing in the air between them.

She stared at it like she wanted to consume him whole, starting with his cock.

One of her soft hands closed around the base of his shaft. She ducked her mouth to within millimeters of the tip, then paused to peek up at him through her lashes. One corner of her mouth kicked up. "Ready?"

"Please," he rasped.

Her mouth descended on him. She lapped up a drop of moisture on the head of his penis, her eyes closing for a moment, and the feel of her velvety tongue on his flesh nearly drove him mad. With a little groan of pleasure, she took him deep into her mouth.

Both hands clenching the sofa cushion, he surrendered to her, his mind and his every nerve overpowered by the riot of sensations she ignited in him. It all blended into a kind of bliss he'd never experienced in his life. Her tongue raking over his skin. Her cheeks caving in every time she sucked. Her soft lips encompassing his hardness. And fuck, her fingers, the way they worked him...

Ecstasy.

Mindless, he thrust up each time she drew him into her mouth and hauled in a breath each time she withdrew. He tunneled his fingers into her hair to cradle her head, shut his eyes, and let the pleasure overtake him.

The orgasm hit him hard, without warning, like a bomb detonating inside him. Every muscle wrenched in a full-body spasm, his back bowed, and the breath exploded out of him. His hands fisted in her hair as he shouted a strangled cry, overcome by the most mind-blowing pleasure of his life.

When she released him, the air cooled the dampness her mouth left behind on his skin.

Prying his lids open, he gaped at the woman he adored. "Mel..."

"No need to thank me." She grinned, her cheeks pink and her lips glistening. "I enjoyed doing that."

"You did?"

"I love the way you react. Makes me feel like the sexiest woman in history."

"That's because you are." He sounded hoarse—probably from all but screaming, again, thanks to her sensual abandon—and he couldn't stop gaping at her. She kept grinning, her hands on his thighs, seeming to glow with joy and excitement. This woman, the only one he'd ever really wanted or needed, she made him lose control with so little effort.

She sat back on her heels and sighed with contentment. "I do love making you scream."

"It was a throaty yell." He smirked, because both of them he was full of it.

Mel laughed.

He loved her more than anything, had a desperate need to prove it to her, but right now he had other things on his mind. He leaned forward, cupping her chin. "How about that touching and kissing now?"

She lay on the bed, her head on a pillow, her body stretched out across the silky, powder-blue sheets. Adam knelt over her, his knees at either side of her legs. His penis, still semi-erect, dangled in front of his muscular body. His eyes were darkened with lust, but he beheld her with an expression of such tenderness her throat tightened with an undefined longing.

Undefined because she couldn't focus on it. Because part of her couldn't yet take a hard look at her own feelings. Soon, maybe. Her plan to avoid sex in hopes of getting some clarity had skidded off the rails in spectacular fashion. She couldn't resist Adam. And she no longer wanted to.

"You are so fucking beautiful," he said, his voice thick with emotion.

"So are you." Mel pushed up on her elbows until she was face to face with his penis. She sat up straighter and pressed her lips to his lower belly, exhaling against his sculpted abs, tracing her tongue over his skin. Then she laid back down on the bed, her hands clasped above her head. "Touch me, Adam."

He sat back on his heels, skating his hands up and down her thighs. She ignited wherever his skin touched hers, a deliciously hot tingle that swept through her from head to toe. Both his big hands danced over her hips, onto her stomach, where his agile fingers explored her with languid ease, as if he had days to memorize the swells and dips of her body. One hand closed over her left breast, the thumb flicking across her nipple, slowly, again and again. Lightning shot through her, straight down to her clitoris, with each rapid movement. The roughness of his thumb heightened the sensation. She arched her back, pushing her breast into his palm, mashing her flesh to his caress.

Bracing his free hand on the mattress beside her, he bent to seal his mouth over her other nipple, lashing his tongue over the rigid tip as he suckled it, his eyes half closed. His thumb kept flicking. His tongue kept lashing. The head of his erection, reddened and slick, rubbed across her belly. She reached down to take hold of its length, but he settled his body atop hers, pinning her to the bed with her hand trapped between their bodies. Releasing her breast, he tugged her hand free to raise it above her head again, his hands cuffing both of hers there.

Then he kissed her—and she forgot everything else.

His mouth claimed hers, stealing her breath. With delicate pressure, he urged her to open for him and she did, without hesitation. She plunged her tongue deep inside his mouth to savor the taste of him, the indescribable essence of Adam. He let her take charge, responding to her every demand, consuming her with a hunger matching her own, but never seizing control of the kiss. He truly did care more about her pleasure than his own and knowing that made her want him all the more, want to give him exactly as much as he gave her.

What he inspired in her, it was more than arousal. So much more. He made her feel…liberated.

He broke away, his eyes locked on hers. One of his legs had slipped between hers, with his thigh brushing against her sex.

"Christ," he groaned, "you're so hot and wet. You must be really wound up."

Oh, that hardly described her current state. Her clit throbbed, her sex ached, and the friction of his chest rubbing against her nipples kept sending wonderful shocks through her. She rocked her hips up, loving the pressure of his thigh scraping against her flesh.

"Yeah," she said, and couldn't believe the throaty voice was hers. "Forget what I said, let's fuck now."

He smirked, chuckling softly, and the vibration made her whole body thrum with need. "That's the first time I've heard you say fuck when you're talking about sex. I like it. But I'm not taking advantage of you when you're so turned on you can't think straight. I can help you relax, though." He dragged his lips up her throat to nibble the tender spot just under her jaw. "I can make you come quick and hard, without penetration. Do you want it?"

Excitement pulsated through her sex, already slick with need. Nipples aching, breasts aching, clitoris aching, she burned for a release only he could grant her.

"Yes," she whispered, "I want it."

Adam took her mouth in a leisurely kiss, every sweep of his velvety tongue rousing her to respond, to tangle her tongue with his over and over, even as he lowered onto one arm, his leg still between hers, and slipped a hand down to palm her mound. His fingers combed through the hairs as he dipped his head to her right breast. The sight of him, of his impassioned gaze, made her breath hitch and her fingers crook into the mattress. He opened his mouth, exhaling a torrid breath that shivered over her taut nipple.

"Ready?" he asked.

Unable to speak, she nodded once.

His mouth descended on her nipple, devouring the tip and areola, just as his tongue raked across it. His hand shifted downward, one finger dived inside her folds to circle her clit. His tongue flicked back and forth. His finger thrust up and down, up and down, over her pulsating nub. She arched her back, fingers clenching the sheets. He stroked her clit with quick, fierce motions of his finger. Up, down. Left, right. Up, down. All the while, his tongue tormented her nipple, the wetness of his mouth moistening her skin, the pleasure firing down from her breast straight into her clitoris, her entire body ablaze and alive. She writhed beneath him, whimpering and crying out.

"Oh God, Adam!"

Her climax ripped through her, stunning in its power and swiftness, wrenching a scream from her. He rubbed her clit and suckled her nipple until the electric shocks of pleasure faded away.

She took his face in her hands, raising it from her breast. "How did you do that?"

A grin overtook his features, so boyish and charming it set off a pang in her chest. "I was inspired. By you."

Still reeling from the ecstasy, she rolled her head side to side. "Wow. That was…unbelievable."

He rolled onto his back, bringing her with him, tucking her against his side with one arm looped around her. "Time to sleep."

"Are you frustrated we didn't go all the way?"

"Not even a little." He nuzzled her hair, rubbing her back with one hand. "After what you did for me earlier, there's no way I could feel cheated."

"I love the way you touch me."

"Ditto."

They lay in each other's arms, luxuriating in the closeness and the afterglow of their erotic adventure together. A lovely kind of drowsiness settled over her, a soft blanket of total relaxation and contentment. Little by little, she drifted down into a dreamless sleep.

She woke in the early morning, still snuggled against his body, shielded by his arms, her cheek on his bare chest. He'd given her more than sexual release. He'd given her the best night's sleep she'd had in ages.

Mel pushed up on one arm, gazing down at his face, overwhelmed by the flurry of emotions evoked by his sleeping expression. He looked so sweet, so content, so young. What on earth would she do about Adam? He called her stubborn, but he was just as obstinate. Adam Caras would not give up on winning her heart until he'd done it. She wanted him, she needed to explore the new dynamic between them, but beyond that…She had no idea what came next. Sex. Blistering pleasure. What then?

The pang in her chest, the one that got worse every time he showed her affection and tenderness, it unsettled her. He believed she was in love with him. Did she even know what love felt like? The real, soul-deep kind shared by two people? She'd never loved anyone like that. Like…this?

In sleep, Adam's lips curled into a faint smile.

The pain in her chest stabbed into her heart once more.

Adam's eyelids fluttered open and a lazy smile curved his mouth. "Morning."

"Good morning."

"Don't look so scared," he said, sweeping hair from her face with two fingers. "I'm not expecting anything, except to spend time with my best friend."

"Today? Ugh, I have a big meeting this morning." She flopped onto her back. "If it goes well, I'll be spending the afternoon devising a plan for a complex e-commerce website."

He rested an arm over her belly, his chin on her shoulder. "Can't you squeeze in a quick lunch?"

"Afraid not. I'll be finalizing the contract over lunch with the clients. Don't you have a carpentry job or something?"

"Nope. I'm completely free all day." He slid his hand down to her hip, while he skimmed his mouth over her cheek. "But my girlfriend's a workaholic, so I'm left out in the cold."

Girlfriend? Had he actually called her that? A chill iced through her, but a lovely warmth rushed in behind it. Even her body couldn't decide how to feel about their evolving…involvement. She knew only one thing for certain. She wanted him, every day, so often it had to be wrong—yet it felt right, very right.

Adam kissed her cheek. "What you did last night, nobody's ever done that to me before."

"Which part?"

He pinched her hip gently. "The part where you had my dick in your mouth."

"Ohhh, that." She eyed him sideways. "No one's ever done that? All the women you've been with and none of them would do it for you?"

"Not a one. It's my fault, though. I cared more about their pleasure and didn't give them a chance to think about mine, or to think about anything."

"I'm familiar with your mind-numbing skill."

"Didn't your boyfriends try at all? To make you feel good, I mean."

"Oh, they tried. But they'd give up rather quickly when I didn't fall into a fit of ecstasy in a minute or two." She picked at the hem of the sheet, tucked over her breasts. "Why do you care more about a woman's pleasure than your own?"

He pushed up on one elbow, looking down on her with a playful smile. "I like watching women come. Especially you."

"I've noticed." She spread a hand on his broad, muscled chest, fascinated by the smoothness of his skin and the softness of the fine hairs sprinkled over it. "Do you actually believe I'm better than you? That you don't deserve me?"

"Sometimes. But most of the time—like last night and right now—I don't think about it at all. You look at me like I'm…I don't know. Important, I guess."

"You are." Gliding her hand up to his neck, she curled her fingers around the nape. "You're the most important person in the world to me."

Though she hadn't intended to say it, the words came out anyway and she meant them. No stab of anxiety accompanied the statement or the associated emotion. In fact, a wonderful warmth spread through her, centered on her heart.

Adam hooked a finger under the sheet covering her breasts and tugged it down little by little, baring her to his admiring gaze. "Do you still worry you're a pervert?"

She considered the question for a moment, until a realization hit her. "No, I don't. Everything with you, no matter how dirty it is, feels right." With her hand still on his nape, she urged him to lower his head toward hers. "And so damn good."

"Love getting dirty with you, babe." His lips hovered a breath away from hers, his chest grazed her breasts. "Any chance I can convince you to meet me for a late lunch?"

"I could do dinner."

He winced. "Sorry, I promised Toby I'd do some odd jobs in their nursery, to get ready for the baby. Sonya's relaxed about the whole thing, but Toby's gone neurotic."

"Cut him some slack. He's hopelessly in love with his wife and it's adorable."

"The guys think I've gone soft over you. Does that make me adorable too?"

She combed her fingers through his hair and nibbled on his lower lip. "You've always been adorable and sweet. It's part of what makes you scorching hot and totally lickable."

"Mm, I love the way you lick."

She kissed him, soft and slow, only their lips touching.

He moved on top of her, the sheet covering them both. "I'm going to persuade you to get dirty with me again, before you go to work. You'll be relaxed and satisfied, not at all nervous about your meeting. I guarantee it."

"A guarantee?" She laughed—until he pushed her thighs apart with his knee and began rubbing his erection along her cleft. Her laughter turned into moaning, as she lifted her hips into each stroke, her body coming alive at the blissful friction of his rigid shaft on her flesh.

He proceeded to demonstrate the full meaning of getting dirty without going all the way. And he kept his word, leaving her so relaxed and soft she forgot about every one of her worries.

At least until she got to her office.

Chapter Fourteen

el sat straight in her chair at the head of the conference table, hands folded atop the shiny surface. Her clients—the five partners in a trendy, high-end bakery—were seated around the table, two on one side and three on the other. Afternoon sun streamed through the picture windows on the left side of the room, casting reflections on the large-screen TV mounted on the far wall. Via the laptop computer resting on the table in front of her, she'd displayed her entire presentation on the TV.

Her clients had asked more questions than she'd ever heard in a single meeting. They worked through lunch, hashing out details while they munched on sandwiches Kaya brought them. Mel resisted the impulse to yawn and rub her neck, though she was exhausted. Professionalism demanded she hide her true feelings—namely, that she wished these people would make up their minds and sign the damn contract.

She longed to retreat into her office and call Adam. Just to hear his voice.

"About the shopping cart," Peter West, the senior partner, said. "It has to be intuitive and human-centric."

Oh, for pity's sake. She'd already explained the details of the website's shopping cart feature in excruciating detail, twice. And she still had no clue what he meant by "human-centric." Maybe he wanted a little cartoon to pop up and offer to hold the customer's hand. Sometimes clients drove her batty.

Pasting on a professional smile, she said, "I've shown you examples on the websites of our other clients. We'll do something similar with your site and customize the cart to your needs."

"Yes, Ms. Thompson, we are impressed with your previous work. Of course, we do have reservations about working with a small company that has limited resources. Could you give us a moment to discuss?"

The third time he'd asked for that. She'd never met such indecisive people before. He'd mentioned "limited resources" several times as well, and every time she struggled to remain pleasant and unaffected by the insult. And no doubt about it, the statement was an insult. West had made passing comments about her "micro-staffing" and "need for outsourcing." Ten employees seemed like a lot to her, since she'd started with only herself, but clearly West found the number inadequate.

West and his partners operated the chicest boutique bakery in Chicago, called Feast of Sweets, which meant gaining their business might attract other big fish.

"Sure," she said, starting to rise from her chair.

West held up a hand. "No need. We'll confer in the corner."

Her five clients rose and ambled into the far corner of the room, gathering in a circle to speak in hushed voices.

With nothing else to do, Mel allowed her thoughts to drift back to this morning with Adam. His hands. His mouth. His wicked grin. The man was adept at setting her body on fire, then dousing the flames with an earth-shattering orgasm. Well, maybe not dousing it. He left her with a simmering hunger for him that never truly died away. The slightest thought of him, no matter how fleeting, whipped the smoldering into a blaze.

At last, she understood his nickname. He'd shown her the Arsonist, for sure, but he'd also revealed a part of himself she suspected he hadn't shown any woman before. The vulnerable part. The loving, tender man who wanted more than sex with her.

Her clients returned from their corner confab and took their seats at the table once more.

Peter West smiled at her. "We're ready to sign, Ms. Thompson."

"Since we're working together now," she said, sliding the contract across the shiny tabletop to him, "please call me Mel."

Horns blared in the outer office.

Mel jerked. Her clients went still, their eyes wide.

The horns—trumpets, she guessed—fizzled out and a feminine voice shouted words Mel couldn't make out. She recognized Kaya's voice, though, and knew something was wrong.

Jumping up, Mel straightened her suit jacket, smiled politely, and said, "Will you please excuse me for a moment?"

The five men seated around the table gazed at her with confusion but nodded their assent.

Mel hurried outside, easing the conference room door shut behind her.

A freaking circus greeted her. Four men in brightly colored sombreros and outfits that matched their hats stood grouped in the center of the outer office, in front of Kaya's desk. She was on her feet, hands on her hips, scowling as she spat her words at someone Mel couldn't see, since the sombrero-bedecked men blocked her view. Now, she noticed the instruments the men held—three trumpets and a guitar. A mariachi band? In her office?

Mel pushed past the musicians to get to Kaya and—

She halted so fast she nearly tripped on the heels of her own pumps.

Devon hunched beside Kaya's desk, gesticulating with slashing motions of his hands, eyes wild and a bouquet of—what, orchids?—clutched in one hand. The flowers lashed this way and that, as he continued to flap his hands.

"Go away," Kaya snapped at him. "This is a place of business. You can't bring mariachis—"

Kaya froze when she caught sight of Mel.

Devon swerved toward Mel, thrusting the flowers at her. "There you are, baby. No roses this time, see?"

Mel drew back. "What the hell are you doing here?"

"Wooing you." He scuffled closer, shoving the flowers in her face. "I've got so much to atone for and I'm pulling out all the stops to make things right. I know you love Mexican food, so I brought Mexican music."

"This is my office," she said carefully, summoning all her self-control to not shout at him. "Can't you see how inappropriate your behavior is here? You've made a scene in front of some very important clients."

"I needed a grand gesture." Devon dropped to one knee in front of her. "You are the Melody of my heart and I can't live another day without you. Please marry me."

Oh shit, not again.

She stared at him, utterly baffled. How could he think another proposal, even more outrageous than the first, would change her mind? Melody of his heart. What happened to flower of his heart?

Rolling her shoulders back, she lifted her chin and said, "No, Devon. No for today, no for tomorrow, no for the rest of eternity. There is zero chance we will ever get back together. Clear enough?"

His head drooped, his chin fell to his chest. The flowers tumbled from his hand as it fell to his side.

Someone cleared their throat behind her.

"Ms. Thompson," Peter West said, "we have changed our minds."

Her stomach plummeted through all five floors beneath her feet, straight into the basement. She shut her eyes, swallowing a curse.

Then she collected herself, reverting to full-on repression mode, and turned to offer her almost-client an apologetic smile. "Mr. West, please let me reassure you this…event is singular and will never happen again. Claddagh Web Design is committed to a professional atmosphere and—"

West waved a dismissive hand. "I'm sorry, Ms. Thompson. We require a certain level of savoir faire and sophistication, what you might call an uptown attitude. Clearly your downtown model of business doesn't suit our needs. Thank you for your time."

He handed her the unsigned contract.

As he and his partners exited through the double doors into the hallway, Mel dumped the contract into the trash can beside Kaya's desk.

Devon sat back on his heels and raised his face to gaze at her imploringly.

"I don't want to hear it," she said. "Get your circus act out of my office and stay away from me."

She marched into her office, snatched her purse from the floor by her desk, and marched back out to Kaya's desk.

Devon and the mariachi band had left.

Maybe she should've been relieved, but she kept getting flashbacks of the disaster Devon had instigated. Sure, he hadn't meant to ruin the biggest contract of her career. But he had. All because he couldn't accept she was in control of her own life, not him.

Right now, all she wanted was to lose control in the most magnificent way. To erase the stress, erase her anger, erase everything from her mind. To drown in pleasure.

She knew of one surefire way to accomplish the task.

"I'm going home early," she told Kaya, whose mouth fell open. Mel Thompson did not leave early or take days off or lounge around in her PJs on Saturday mornings. She slaved for her business. And she was damn sick of it. "If there's an emergency, don't call me. Handle it yourself. You are the most capable person on my team, Kaya, and I know you can run this place without me for one afternoon."

"Uh—I—" Kaya blinked rapidly, swallowed, and nodded. "Sure thing, boss."

Mel left the office at 1:43 PM.

Once inside her car, she dug out her phone and dialed Adam. She was about to tell him, without an iota of shame, exactly what she needed. Mind-blowing sex, for hours and hours, until they were both breathless and drenched with sweat. No halfway, no limitations, no rules. She needed to cut loose, get wild, shed every last vestige of her control—and only one man could give her what she wanted.

Adam slouched on his sofa, an open but full bottle of beer in his hand and the TV tuned to a home repair show. He wasn't paying attention to it. His mind had gotten stuck on one thought since he sat down here an hour ago.

Mel.

Not seeing her for a whole day, it made him antsy and edgy—and yeah, frustrated. Even before they got naked together, being away from her had bothered him. But now, he couldn't concentrate on anything except finagling a way to see her today.

Being in love with a workaholic sucked.

He could tempt her away from her job. He would tempt her. If he'd learned one thing over the past few days, it was how much Mel delighted in the carnal pleasures. At the thought, a vision of her naked unreeled in his mind. Her luscious body laid out beneath him. Creamy skin begging to be touched and tasted. The desire sizzling in her eyes and in her voice. The drugging scent of her arousal blooming. He burned to be inside her just once.

No, not once. Over and over, for the rest of their lives.

Adam glanced at the clock on the wall. It was five after two. Time to change into better clothes and head out to his dad's place, to pick him up for his doctor's appointment. Groaning, Adam pushed up off the sofa and stretched, trying to wake himself up after a long period of being a lazy-ass, then headed for the hallway. He'd hoped to see Mel tonight, but after driving his dad to the doctor, Adam had promised to spend the evening doing some odd jobs for Toby and Sonya. Tomorrow, he'd see Mel tomorrow.

Any longer than that and he'd go nuts.

His phone warbled. He glanced at the caller ID and warmth washed through him. While he walked down the hall, he picked up the call.

"Mel," he said, aiming for a low and sexy tone. It came naturally with her. "I was just thinking about you."

"I need you to strip me naked and fuck me until I'm incoherent."

Adam choked on a breath and tripped over his own toes, slapping his free hand on the wall to keep from landing smack on his ass. "Yeah, I'd love that, but—Is everything okay?"

He'd heard something in her voice, though he couldn't quite identify it.

"You know me too well," she said. "I had a shit day. Devon showed up at my office with mariachis and another moronic proposal. His ridiculous display wrecked a big deal for me."

Adam clenched his fist and imagined slugging Devon in the gut.

Mel's voice snapped him back to reality. "Adam?"

He took a deep breath, exhaling out the anger. Railing against her ex would ruin the beautifully sensual mood she was in. "I get it. You need a distraction."

"I need you." A breath blustered out of her. "Please, Adam, I don't want to think right now, I want you to shut down my brain and make me dissolve."

With his hand still on the wall, he curled his fingers. All the blood evacuated his brain, shooting straight into his cock.

"Are you free?" she asked, her voice as smooth and warm as buttered rum.

"Right now?" *Aw, hell.* His father. "I have to help my dad. I was about to head over to his place in a minute, and after that I'm at Toby and Sonya's."

"How late?"

"Toby wants me out by nine, so I won't bother Sonya when she goes to bed. Pregnant ladies need their sleep, he says. We could meet after, if you're not too tired."

Silence.

He counted the seconds. One, two, three—

Mel's contented sigh hissed into his ear, almost like she was beside him with her rosy lips pressed to his ear.

"What was that about?" he asked. "Sounded like the way you sigh when I've got my hands and mouth all over you."

"Exactly what I was picturing."

"More naughty fantasies, eh?"

"I need more than fantasies tonight." She hesitated, but only for a half second. "I need hot sex, all night. I need you inside me, making us both come again and again, until we're boneless."

He couldn't hold back the groan that escaped him as his cock throbbed with a powerful hunger for her and only her. "You can count on me."

"I know I can," she said. "Meet me at the club, ten o'clock. I'll be wearing the dress I wore on my birthday and I'll wait for you at our table."

"Why the club?" He leaned his whole body into the wall, eyes drifting shut, ensconced in the memory of that night. Now she wanted to shed her inhibitions again. "Are you going full-on wicked tonight?"

"You bet your ass I am, alcohol-free this time. Are you in?"

"Hell yeah." He paused, then added, "If you need to get off without me to tide you over until tonight, go right ahead. I know you'll be thinking of me."

"I think I can wait."

"Maybe I want to fantasize about you making yourself come while you imagine me doing dirty things to you."

"In that case, I wouldn't want to disappoint you."

He chuckled, in the way he knew made her tremble with excitement. "You couldn't if you tried."

"See you tonight."

"Guaranteed, this is one date I won't miss."

Not even a horde of demons straight out of Hell would stop him from getting to her tonight.

Mel perched on a stool chair, her body swaying to the heavy beat of the music. Lights the color of ripe plums and succulent strawberries coruscated around and over her. She eased her shoulders into the swaying, and finally, allowed her head to rock side to side with the rhythm. Her loose hair swished over her bare shoulders, a sensual tickle on her skin. She ran a finger down the strap of her halter dress, the same one she'd worn on her birthday. The dress accentuated her best assets, and tonight she'd need her entire arsenal on display.

Arsenal. The word led her brain to another one—arsonist. Her body heated at the memory of Adam's hands on her naked skin. Tonight, they'd consummate their physical bond completely, but she had no idea what that meant for the rest of their relationship. For this one night, she didn't care.

She might've had the luxury of pretending they weren't lovers as long as they stuck to erotic touching and oral sex. Before this night ended, she wouldn't be able to deny it any longer. They would become lovers, without qualifications or prevarications. Adam would be her lover.

Her stomach fluttered, her skin tightened. Lover. Adam. *Yes, please, now.*

Mel scanned the club and her gaze fell on a group of young men, probably younger than her, congregated near the partial wall that separated the club proper from the private rooms in back. A blond-haired man in leather pants and a silky white shirt caught her gaze with his own. His wide lips curved upward. He tipped his tumbler at her, the golden drink inside it sloshing.

Sorry, pal, no dice. She gave him a polite smile and nod but averted her attention. Only one man would capture her interest tonight—and he hadn't arrived yet.

Mel picked up her glass and sipped the sparkling water. This time, she needed no alcohol to get her buzzed. The mere thought of Adam, and the firsthand knowledge of what that body could do, triggered a natural high. Her head seemed to float in the clouds, while her body ached and sizzled with anticipation.

A large body stepped in front of her, blocking out her view of the dance floor.

She melted back against her stool chair, smiling with what must've resembled drunkenness. Gazing upon the glorious masculinity that was Adam Caras could make any woman tipsy, without a drop of booze.

When he leaned one hip on the high table, the black slacks and blue shirt he wore—the same outfit as on her birthday—pasted to every muscle in his torso, arms, and legs. His hair was wild, as if he'd just rolled out of bed. The top two buttons of his shirt, undone, exposed a wedge of tanned flesh dusted with fine, brown hairs. The strobe lights glinted off his rich, caramel eyes, enhancing the fire already smoldering within them.

He folded his arms over his chest, smirking at her.

The music segued into a slow, sensual number, the volume low enough to permit conversation without shouting.

Adam raked his gaze down the length of her body, dragging his focus back up to her face. "I'm here."

"Duh."

"What are we doing here, Mel?"

"I want to dance with you," she said, sliding off the stool, her high heels clacking onto the floor. "Show me your moves."

His eyebrows shot up but settled down as a devilish grin slid across his lips. He sauntered toward her, devouring the distance between them in one step. She bent her head back to stare into his hooded eyes. She was pinned there, between the chair and him, surrounded by his wall of muscles.

He snared her right wrist in his big hand, his fingers stretching down to her palm. "Are you ready?"

She nodded.

Hand in hand, they weaved their way out onto the dance floor, around couples writhing against each other and pumping their hips in blatant imitation of the sexual act. Mel bumped into a woman who had her head thrown back, eyes shut, mouth open as if in ecstasy. The woman seemed oblivious to Mel bumping her, oblivious to everything except her lover's hands on her waist and his hips thrusting into her.

Adam tugged her into him, snug against his hard chest.

They stood inside a vacant space on the dance floor, no more than five feet across.

His hands splayed over her bare back, exposed by the halter dress, the heat of his flesh and the roughness of his palms exciting every nerve. The fine hairs all over her body lifted as goose bumps flared up on her skin. She looped her arms around his neck, her heels bringing her face close to his, and when she tilted her head back a little, their gazes converged.

The naked lust in his eyes made her heart stutter.

He began to move, swiveling his hips, compelling her to move with him, their bodies bound in an erotic rhythm. Her breasts mounded against his chest, the fabric of her dress teased her sensitized skin. His hands roamed over her back while his swelling erection rubbed on her belly, the rigid line of it wedged against her. Not even a millimeter separated them, not a molecule of air could've squeezed between their bodies, and as they swayed around the floor in lazy circles, she melted into him a little more, and a little more, until her lips brushed against his cheek.

Both his arms clinched tight around her. He tipped his head down to catch her mouth with his own, even as their hips ground against each other. Her lips parted, commanded by the caress of his lips, the way they closed over hers only to pull away, then captured her lower lip to suckle and release it. She wrapped her arms around his neck, drawing closer, flattening her palms on the back of his head to urge him nearer. He crushed his mouth to her parted lips and forged his tongue inside, ravaging her with a deep, open kiss that stole her breath and set off a tidal wave of liquid heat that surged over her sex.

"No more dancing," he rumbled against her lips. "I can't wait one second more to have you."

She wound a lock of his hair around her finger as she moved the other hand down to cradle his face. "The wait is over."

A breath erupted out of him, ruffling her hair. Clasping her hand, he tried to lead her off the dance floor, but more couples had crowded into the space, creating an unmoving mass of sweaty, scantily clad flesh. The more they tried to push through, the more the pressure of the crowd held them in place.

Mel swung her head left and right, searching for a gap.

"There," she said, pointing to a narrow path. "Maybe we can squeeze through—"

Adam grasped her waist, hoisted her off the floor, and draped her over his shoulder with one arm barring her thighs to his chest. He strode down the narrow gap in the crowd, towering over most of the patrons and garnering surprised looks as everyone in their path scurried out of his way. With her head upside-down, dangling down his back, she couldn't help but stare at his ass, entranced by the sight of his taut buttocks, the way they flexed with each stride. His back muscles rippled against her stomach and breasts. Her groin rubbed on his pectorals, the sensation arousing her in the most delicious way.

They passed the bar and headed down the darkened entryway. Gasps whispered around them, from the people forced to step aside or get mowed down by the ruthlessly determined firefighter hauling her away.

In the parking lot, he halted and deposited her on her feet. "Where's your car?"

"Took a taxi. I assumed we'd leave in your car."

"I came in a taxi." His lips compressed, eyes darting, he closed his fingers into fists and popped them straight, then fisted them again, only to pop them out again. He kept up the repetitive motion as he scrunched his mouth and hissed a breath out his nostrils. "I see a taxi over there."

He seized her hand and they jogged to the yellow vehicle parked at the curb. Adam rapped on the taxi's window with his knuckle. When the driver rolled it down, Adam said, "We need a ride. You available?"

"Hop in," the driver said.

Adam rattled off the address of her apartment building, probably because it was closer than his place. They climbed inside the car, and as the taxi accelerated down the street, her pulse sped up along with the vehicle.

This was happening. Now.

Chapter Fifteen

The elevator doors spread wide before them. Butterflies flittered in her stomach.

Adam hustled out into the hallway, his hand clamped around hers, his expression one of pained resolve. The rock-hard erection stretching his pants taut might've had something to do with his expression—and his ruthless pace. They'd made out in the taxi, all the way to their destination, shamelessly oblivious of the driver. Her lips still tingled from his demanding, almost frenzied kisses. She'd responded in kind, as frantic as he was to get naked and get it on.

He halted them at the door to her apartment. His voice rough, he asked, "Key?"

Mel reached inside the neckline of her dress, to where she'd taped her apartment key under her breasts. Plucking it free, she handed the key to Adam.

Eyes locked on her cleavage, he took the key. "Strange place to keep it."

"Didn't want to take my purse and this dress doesn't have pockets. Besides, I knew you'd get me home safe, so all I needed was the door key."

"Uh-huh." He stared at her for a couple seconds, as if seeing her for the first time. Then he shook off his confusion—literally, with a flap of his head. He unlocked the door, ushering her inside with a hand on her back.

Her mind traveled back to the moment in the club when he scooped her up. No man had ever slung her over his shoulder. But she supposed a firefighter was trained to carry people out of burning buildings, so why wouldn't he resort to carrying her out of the packed club? It had gotten them through the crowd, for sure.

And damn, it had been the sexiest thing ever.

The door shut, the lock clicking into place. They were alone. Completely alone.

She took in the sight of him, his cock engorged and straining against his pants, his hair wilder than before thanks to the way she'd shoved her hands into it repeatedly during the taxi-ride make-out session. He was gorgeous. Melt-in-your-mouth, lap-up-every-crumb-of-him hot and delectable and irresistible. If he touched her again, even one fingertip on her skin, she might combust.

Gaze glued to her cleavage, he licked his lower lip. When his focus returned to her face, he said, "You're wearing my earrings."

"Of course." She fingered one of the ruby earrings. "What else would I wear tonight?"

Though he tried not to smile, the expression dimpled his cheeks and crinkled his eyes. "Guess you're not mad at me anymore for buying them."

"I wasn't mad, not really." She ran her fingertip over the earring once more, the metal smooth and slick under her skin. "I was nervous about our new dynamic, about how much I want you."

He skimmed a hand up her arm. "You don't seem nervous now."

"Because I'm not. I'm done fighting this. No man has ever made me feel the way you do."

The pad of his thumb stroked her skin. "How do I make you feel?"

"Free."

Adam stared at her, unblinking, his chest heaving with each breath. "I love you, Mel."

"But?"

"Nothing. I love you, that's all."

Mel opened her mouth to speak, but he rested two fingers on her mouth. "Don't. Not yet."

The longing on his face pricked at her heart. Gazing into his molten-caramel eyes—the eyes of the man who'd stood by her no matter what, who cared for her and understood her like no one else—for the first time in years she knew what she wanted. What she needed.

She stretched a hand up to caress his cheek. Cool. Rough with stubble. He leaned into her touch, eyes half shut, and exhaled with pure contentment.

"I want to be with you," she murmured, stroking his face, combing her fingers through his hair. "Since we kissed the first time, you've gotten me so fired up I can't see straight. When I'm at work, I think about you. When I'm at home, I think about you. I have the most erotic dreams about you every night and in the daytime too." Her hand traveled down his neck to rest on his shoulder. "I've been terrified of losing my best friend, but I finally realize I have to take the risk, because I want this more than I've ever wanted anything."

He took hold of her free hand and fluttered a delicate kiss over the palm. "You will never lose me. I don't care what happens, I'll always be here for you."

"I know. Can't believe it took me so long to get here."

He chuckled, low and sexy. "I believe it. You're stubborn as hell, but worth the wait."

"Stubborn?" She tapped a finger on his nose. "You'd know all about being pigheaded, wouldn't you?"

He took her hand, turned it over, and pressed a warm kiss to the tender underside of her wrist. "I heard you're looking for a night of wild sex."

"Oh yes, please."

"In that case..." He swirled his tongue across her palm and her breath hitched. "If you want a hot fuck, I can deliver."

An inferno. In her belly. Racing lower, eradicating reason.

"You are the Arsonist," she said, and skated her hands down his chest to the waistband of his pants. She hooked one finger inside it. "Detonate me."

He pulled her in snug against his firm, aroused body. "Yes, ma'am."

Adam's mouth sealed over hers in a possessive kiss, his tongue diving deep, swirling, tasting, taunting. She surrendered to him, burning for him to take her in every way. The flavor of him overwhelmed her senses, so masculine and exquisitely satisfying. His hands roved her back, fingers fanned out, until the tips latched onto her shoulders. Her breasts molded to his chest, her nipples tautened into rigid peaks, aching, sensitive to the slightest movement of his muscles. Wet, hot juices rushed over her sex and her whole body thrummed with need.

He groaned, the ravenous sound vibrating through her, and she sensed the second his control snapped. He devoured her mouth with abandon, grabbed her ass in both hands, and lifted her off the floor. She clung to him, lost to the sensations. He backed her up to the nearest wall, its surface cold and unyielding against her back. Pinned between the wall and one scorching-hot, rock-hard, very male body, she let go of the fears that had held her back and relinquished herself to him.

His voice rumbled in her ear, as his erection prodded her. "I'll take care of you."

She threw her arms around him. He would take care of her. In every way.

Adam pinned Mel's wrists above her head. He'd intended to make love to her, slowly, to show her how much he needed and cherished her. He shouldn't be taking her against her living room wall, but this ferocious hunger for her drove out reason. He rubbed against her warm, soft body. She yielded to his every touch, with little noises that amplified his need and made his cock throb. He slid his tongue around the shell of her ear, reveling in her sweetness. Her shudder broke his willpower.

"God, Mel," he rasped. "I can't—I need—"

She shoved her hand down between them to cup his erection through his pants. "Shut up and take me."

He yanked up the skirt of her dress, hooked his fingers in her panties, and ripped the delicate fabric. With one flick of his wrist, he sent the panties flying. The scent of her arousal, rich and musky, propelled him past the point of rational thought. He thrust his hand between her thighs, she parted them willingly, and he chafed his fingers over her slick flesh until he found her taut clitoris.

She shuddered again, with a little gasp.

He fumbled in his pocket, tore out one of the condoms he'd stashed there, ripped the foil, and rolled the condom on as quickly as he could without tearing the damn thing. His breaths were already quick and labored. Her chest heaved, her hands gripped his shoulders so tight it hurt. He didn't give a damn. He clutched her bare ass, his fingers digging into her pliant flesh, and rocked her hips up as he pushed her thighs further apart with one knee. She opened for him so easily, her cream rubbing off on his pants as his thigh ground against her sex.

"I need you," he rasped, positioning his cock between her legs, nestled against the slippery, hot flesh of her cleft. "Are you sure—"

"Yes, oh God, yes."

Her throaty, hoarse words broke him. He rolled his hips back and thrust his cock into her soft, slick heat, burying himself inside her to the hilt, going still as realization hit him. He was inside her, inside his Mel. His body shook with need, but for more than her body and the release it promised. He shook inside and out, with an intense longing for the love of his life, the woman clinging to him and begging for him to fuck her. He let his head fall onto her shoulder. He needed to show her how much she meant to him, to demonstrate his love and commitment to her so she'd have no doubts.

With his head still on her shoulder, he began to pump his cock into her sweet, luscious body. Slowly at first, wanting to get her there at the same time. But she moaned and whimpered, flung one leg around his hip, and tugged him into her body, the muscles inside her sex clenching around him. She couldn't be coming, not yet. No, she was doing it on purpose, trying to goad him into taking her hard and fast, and damn, it was working. Every time she tightened her muscles around him, his control eroded faster. But when she whispered into his ear, her voice low and sultry, the last shreds of his control crumbled.

"Oh Adam," she said, "I want to feel you come inside me."

He slammed into her, so hard he had to clutch her ass to keep her from falling out of his arms. Hips pistoning, inflamed by the wet slapping of their flesh and her little gasping moans, he plowed into her again and again, his cock so stiff and engorged he knew he couldn't last much longer. Her hips rammed forward to meet his pounding thrusts, and shit, she was getting wetter with every second. He tried to kiss her, but his frantic movements made him miss her lips, his mouth scraping over her chin. He shoved a hand between their bodies, found her clit, and rubbed it mercilessly.

She fastened her arms around his neck and swung her other leg up, locking her ankles behind his ass. He drove harder, faster, untamed in his need for the one woman who meant everything to him, pinching and rubbing her clit until he felt her body tighten. Her climax milked his cock, making his heart thud against his ribs, and he could wait no longer. With one powerful thrust, he exploded, throwing his head back on a hoarse shout.

Pleasure ripped through him. He pumped a second time, and with a final plunge, he was spent. Gasping for air, he hugged her close with one arm.

Between pants, she murmured, "Thanks for the hot fuck."

He would've laughed, if he could've caught his breath. Sweat slicked the bare skin of her shoulders and chest and dampened his shirt. His hair was damp with perspiration, beads of it dribbled down his face and torso. He managed to wheeze a few words. "Told you I'd deliver."

She angled her head back, smiling. With her rose-petal cheeks and swollen lips, she stunned him speechless. *So perfect.*

Her fingers toyed with his hair and danced over his scalp. "Reality is so much better than my fantasies."

He swept his mouth over her lips, then trailed little kisses down her throat. "Never came so hard in my life as I do with you."

"Ditto."

"But it shouldn't have happened like this. I had this whole scene planned out, where I seduce you slowly and it's goddamn romantic." He let his head droop, unwilling to meet her eyes. "Instead, I lost it. Took you like a rutting animal, for shit's sake. Maybe I am just a womanizing cretin."

"You got a little carried away. So did I." She grasped his chin and forced him to look up at her. "I know who you really are, underneath the Arsonist facade. I see *you*. And the man I see is good and kind and wonderful."

Her gentle expression shot guilt through him. He'd taken her up against the wall, for crying out loud. His sweet, sexy Mel. She deserved better. He shuffled backward enough her legs dropped, her high heels clacking on the floor. Her knees trembled a little. He enfolded her in his arms, cradling her like the precious treasure she was.

She wriggled her hips, working her dress back into position. "I have to go."

"You can't run away. This is your apartment."

Her quiet laughter tickled his senses. "I have to pee, silly."

"Oh." He held her for another few seconds, reluctant to give up the feel of her supple body and the toe-curling scent of…her. At last, he peeled his arms away.

Mel padded off to the bathroom.

Adam brushed his hair down with his hands, straightened his clothes, and marched to the bathroom door, barricading it. When she came out, he wouldn't let her go until he'd demonstrated how much he adored her. Forget the Arsonist. Tonight, he was Adam—no facade, no tricks, just a man.

The bathroom door swung open.

Mel's eyes widened, a tiny gasp escaping her pink lips.

Adam swooped her up in his arms and whisked her into the bedroom. He set her on her feet by the bed. She blinked up at him. He looped an arm behind her to unzip her dress, letting it fall to the floor, pooling around her feet. She wore nothing but her high heels.

"No bra?" he asked, his voice choked.

"The dress didn't leave room for one."

Goose bumps were popping out on her arms. He frisked his hands up and down her skin, intending to warm her. "Cold?"

"Not in the least." Her voice, so husky and hot, made his balls ache. "What now?"

He lifted her hand to his shirt, guiding her fingers over the top button. "Strip me."

Chapter Sixteen

Mel rubbed her bare arms, buck naked yet not embarrassed at all. How did Adam do this to her? Make her aroused and aware, of her body and his, without an ounce of guilt. A draft tickled her flesh, sensitized by hot sex and Adam's sizzling gaze on her, the eye contact somehow more thrilling than his touch. He gazed at her with more than lust, with…adoration.

He skimmed his hands down her body, over her shoulders and around her back, down her spine and back around to her sides. His fingers curved around her hips.

The memory of Adam ripping off her panties and thrusting into her again and again roared through her mind in a full-sensory experience. No man had ever ravished her before. When he'd carried her into the bedroom, plopping her down beside the bed, her heartbeat had revved up at the hope he might keep on ravishing her. Though satiated by her explosive orgasm, she craved more of him. Would she ever stop craving Adam Caras?

He stood before her, his jeans undone, his shaft hanging out, still halfway erect but without the condom. *My lord, how long can he go?* Devon had gone flaccid after one quick roll in the hay. *Don't think about Devon.* For the first time in weeks—actually, years—she had no trouble banishing thoughts of him. Taking in the totality of Adam's appearance, disheveled and flushed, she was struck by the raw, sensual beauty of him. Why had she chastised herself for fantasizing about him all these years? Why had she labeled him off limits and her desires taboo? Everything they'd done together so far had felt right, even when he shoved her up against the wall and took her with wild abandon. She'd loved it. The loss of control, the unbridled passion.

The safety of being in his arms.

Underneath his damp clothes, sweat would slick his body. She knew this for certain, because sweat clung to her skin too. A bead of it oozed down one breast to trickle over the rigid tip, its cooling effect puckering her nipple tighter. All of her skin tightened, her body readying for him again.

Adam's hands drifted onto her ass, then skated up her back. "As much as I'm enjoying you salivating over me, I need you to help me out here." He bent his head down, his breaths a whisper on her forehead. "I'm not fucking you up against a wall with our clothes on again. I need to be naked with you."

She turned her face up to his, their eyes so close their lashes skirted each other. "What would you like me to do about that?"

One of his callused hands glided around her side to cup her breast. When she leaned into his touch, he groaned. "Undress me, Mel, please, I'm begging you."

The Arsonist begging her? A surge of sexual power intoxicated her. This man wanted her, relinquished control to her, trusted her without reservation. She focused on the button of his shirt, her fingers still resting on it. Not once in her entire life had she let Adam down when he asked a favor of her. And considering his ever-hardening erection, he needed her help more than ever.

She popped the top button free.

His head came up, his eyes locked on her.

She unhooked another button. His erection blossomed and rose, until it hovered in front of her belly. She undulated her body to brush the head across her bare skin, eliciting a choked noise from him. She slipped her hands under his shirt, up his smooth flesh, still damp with sweat, just as she'd envisioned.

"Take it off," he growled.

"Yes, sir." She took hold of the lapels and ripped his shirt wide open. Buttons flew, raining down on the floor.

He glanced down at his ruined shirt. "Not what I had mind, but it works."

"Maybe you should be more specific with your requests."

"Good idea."

He shed the shirt and the fabric billowed as the garment sank to the floor. Next, he kicked off his jeans. Or tried to. His boots blocked him and he stumbled backward into the wall. Unable to stop her laughter, Mel slapped a hand over her mouth to silence it, but that only turned it into snorts and sputtering.

Adam's mouth warped into a half smirk. "Thanks for the support and understanding."

"Sorry." She clamped her teeth down on her lip to stave off the laughter and waved her hands at him. "I thought a man known as the Arsonist would be more suave."

His lips scrunched, jeans lumped around his ankles, he squinted at her. Through gritted teeth, he said, "I am suave."

Oh lord, she couldn't halt the laughter that burst out of her. She doubled over, hand over her mouth again, tears pouring down her cheeks. Adam exhaled the longest, huffiest sigh she'd ever heard. He fumbled with his boot laces, tore them loose, and kicked his boots off. They sailed across the bedroom to strike the opposite wall one by one. He dug a handful of condom packets out of his jeans pocket and tossed them onto the bedside table, then rid himself of his jeans and crawled toward her on hands and knees, hips swiveling, gaze nailed to her crotch. He licked his lips as he reached her, rising to his feet in a fluid, masculine movement.

"I don't know, Mel." He gave her ass a playful slap. "Maybe I should throw you over my knee and spank you. You have been a bad girl tonight."

She lifted her brows. "Try it, Caras, and your new nickname will be the Eunuch."

His gaze flickered over her body and a sly smile spread across his face. "You're gorgeous when you're freshly fucked."

Adam grasped her hips and hauled her against him, grinding his erection into her. Her breaths came faster, shallower, as his thumbs massaged the hollows of her hips.

She let her eyelids drift half closed, slanting into him. "Let's do that again."

"No, Mel, you're not getting off that easy." His brow furrowed, then smoothed out as he grinned. "Well, I guess you did get off easy."

Did I ever. She rested her palms on his chest, mesmerized by his face, that talented mouth, those warm, whiskey-brown eyes.

He crooked a finger under her chin, tipping it up. "This is more."

"More?" Her pulse quickened, her hands went clammy. Could she handle more? Maybe she should've considered that question before begging him to fuck her out in the hallway.

"This is more than a hot fling," he said. "A hell of a lot more."

Adam sank to his knees in front of her, running his hands down her legs, his fingers closing around her ankles. With his face right in front of her groin, she fought the impulse to wriggle away—or thrust her aching sex into his face. Instead, she held still, entranced by him.

His clever fingertips trailed around to the front of her ankles, down across the tops of her feet and back up again. He grasped one ankle and lifted, his fingertips sliding over the sole with feather-light motions. Hot currents of electricity arced up her legs, straight into her clitoris. When he performed the same teasing on her other foot, she clutched his shoulders to keep from tumbling down into a heap on the floor. She squeezed out one word. "Adam."

He flashed her a grin. "You didn't think we were done yet, did you?"

As his tongue flitted over her hip, her body relaxed into him. He nudged her thighs apart with his elbow, nuzzling her mound, and her knees buckled. With one arm behind her thighs and the other around her back, he eased her down onto the bed, laying her out on her back. The pillow cushioned her head, but every graze of the sheets against her skin sent her spiraling deeper into that mindless rapture where the world telescoped down to Adam and only Adam.

Propped on his elbows, his hands at either side of her head, he fixed his adoring gaze on her. "I'm going to make love to you."

"Yes. Hard and fast."

"No. Make love." He emphasized the words with gentle brushes of his fingertips over her cheeks. "Slow, soft, meaningful sex."

Meaningful? Panic rose in her chest, but then he stroked his fingers up her cheek, across her forehead, the gesture so sweet it warmed her heart, thawing the fear until it trickled away into the corners of her mind. An odd combination of readiness and anxiety rushed through her at the knowledge of what he meant to do. Make love to her. She swallowed, her throat tight and raw. Make love. The first sting of tears pricked at her eyes.

"Shhh," he murmured, trailing kisses over her cheek to the corner of her mouth. "It's okay, Mel. Let yourself feel it. Trust me and let go."

No words she could piece together. No voice to speak them. She shut her eyes and gave a tiny nod.

Adam kissed her lids, drawing away the tears. "You will never lose me."

The tears gone, she dared to look at him again.

His lips formed a smile of heartrending tenderness.

She took his face in her hands, pulling him down, sealing her mouth over his. They explored each other's lips with light kisses and little licks, but soon their ardor mounted, their mouths molded together and their tongues lashing. He broke away, slithering down her body, lavishing her flesh with open-mouth kisses down the center of her body, inching toward her mound.

Nothing existed except the two of them. His eyes fixated on her. His lips on her skin. The loving way he pressed his open mouth to her belly, worshiping her with every kiss. Never had she felt so treasured as when Adam touched her.

And oh God, he had touched her—more than her body, though. He'd crawled inside her heart and soul, wrapping his arms around the deepest parts of her, soothing her fears and awakening her passions. All the emotions she'd struggled to suppress for two years, maybe longer. She'd needed him for as long as she could remember. She'd loved—

She choked back a sob, tears pricking her eyes again. How long could she keep denying the truth?

Adam rose onto hands and knees, his face above hers, his expression concerned. "Are you okay? Do you want me to stop?"

Wiping at her eyes, she gazed up at the face of her best friend, her soul mate, and her heart expanded from the power of her longing for him. "Don't stop. Please, don't ever stop."

He went stone still, his jaw slack, his eyes locked on hers. "You said it."

"Said what?"

"In your office that day, when I promised I'd prove you like sex." He shook his head slowly and a brilliant smile lit his face. "I said I'd be inside you, fucking you while you begged me to never stop. And you just did. Beg me to not stop."

She stroked her hands down his face. "Not for the reason you implied. You're right, I don't want hot sex right now. I want you. My Adam."

He laughed, his grin widening. "I'm your Adam?"

"Of course you are."

He bent to brush his lips over hers. "You're my Mel."

She threaded her fingers through his hair, aching for him, more aroused than when he'd pleasured her with his mouth. This was a different sort of arousal, something far more intense and…meaningful. "Please make love to me, Adam."

Spreading her legs for him, she grasped his upper arms.

He snagged a condom packet from the table, smirking as he tore it open and sheathed his length.

Mel glanced at the six other packets on the table, her eyebrows lifting. "Someone's overconfident."

"Not overconfident." He knelt over her again, his knees between her legs. "Eternally hopeful."

She squeezed his arms lightly, loving the firmness of his muscles beneath her hands. "I am beginning to question the efficacy of my celibacy plan."

His lips tightened as he tried not to smile. "I get so hot when you use big words like efficacy."

In a way only Adam could pull off, he infused the word efficacy with sizzling innuendo.

"Although," she said, "I think I gave up that plan the first time you shoved your head between my legs."

"Can we bury that plan?"

"Definitely." She let her knees fall to the sides, bared to him even more. "I'd rather you bury your cock inside me. Now."

With his gaze tethered to hers, he penetrated her inch by inch, the rigid length of him sliding into her slick flesh until he filled her completely. She moaned from the sheer pleasure of feeling him inside her, joined with her, moving in slow thrusts. He lowered onto his elbows, his face buried in her hair, murmuring sweet things she couldn't concentrate on, lost in the bliss of him loving her. She wrapped her arms around his neck, her face pressed into his shoulder, overwhelmed by the scent of his sweat and her own arousal, the sensation of his cock gliding in and out of her, the sight of his hips rotating and his body rubbing against her clitoris with intoxicating friction.

When she locked her legs around him, his deep groan resonated through his chest and into her body, intensifying her passion until it stole her breath. His pace quickened, his shaft plunged into her harder and deeper. Every inch of him touched a part of her, his skin scraping or brushing hers with his movements, teasing her taut nipples, tormenting her clit. She clutched at him, whimpering from the power of her hunger for him. Her orgasm rose like a tidal wave on the ocean, swelling higher and higher until it broke over her with a thunderous rush, her body milking him fiercely, drawing a climax from him that pulsated deep inside her.

Adam collapsed on top of her, his body glistening with sweat, his breaths ragged. He raised his head to gaze at her with rapt wonder. "God, Mel. I've never felt anything like that. Not a wild and crazy come, but something…"

"Meaningful." She let her legs fall away from his hips as he pulled out of her body, leaving her empty and craving more than another orgasm. "You were right. It's more than sex."

He rolled to the side, tugging her along with him so they lay face to face on their sides. Tucking a lock of hair behind her ear, he grazed his lips across hers.

Overwhelmed by the love in his eyes, she had no choice but to speak the truth. "I love you, Adam."

"But?"

She lavished his mouth with all the passion in her heart, nipping and licking, forging deep and retreating, drawing a vigorous response from him. With a little moan of pleasure, she broke the kiss. "I love you, period. You are my best friend and you always will be, but I can't deny our relationship has changed. I think it changed a long time ago, but we were both too stubborn to admit it."

"Funny I was the first one to figure it out. Me, the casual-sex guy."

She caressed his cheek, enjoying the slight roughness of evening stubble. "You've been incredibly patient with me. I love you even more for that. You waited two years for me and then you took the time to help me see the truth, even though you could've had me anytime you wanted and you know it. I can't resist you."

His smile had a kind of innocence to it, making him look younger and less like the consummate seducer. "You do seem to like it when I talk dirty."

"I love it." She combed her fingers through his hair, stroking his scalp.

He slid a hand over her hip, urging her closer so his erection nudged her belly, nuzzling her neck. "Say something dirty, please."

She folded her arms around him as he rolled on top of her, pressing her down flat on her back beneath his bulk. "When I got home this afternoon, I remembered what we'd talked about on the phone. Didn't want to disappoint you, so I pictured you bending me over the coffee table to have your way with me, with my breasts smashed into the cold wood. I actually bent over the table while I was touching myself. It got me so wet, so turned on. I came hard, just like you were inside me, fucking me. Dirty enough for you?"

"Hell yeah." He snaked an arm out, blindly hunting for a condom packet on the table. "I get even hotter when you say fuck than when you say efficacy."

"I'll be sure to say it often." She nabbed a condom packet and stuffed it into his palm. "Hurry up and fuck me again."

"Tell me all about your fantasies. I want to make every one of them come true." He lifted his head to press his lips to hers for the barest kiss. "By making you come. Over and over and over."

She ran her hands up and down his back, lightly scraping her nails along his skin. "Okay. I'll describe my fantasies in great detail—and then you have to share yours with me."

"Deal."

For the next two hours, they explored their most secret dreams of each other, bringing them to life with raw lust, powerful intimacy, and a longing far beyond the carnal connection, borne of a deep and passionate bond neither of them fully understood yet. When, at last, they'd expended their last ounce of energy, they slumped onto the bed entangled in each other's arms.

Adam rested his chin onto her chest, between her breasts. "I know I talk a good game, but I'm as scared as you are this will blow up in our faces."

Her throat thick with emotion, she swept her fingers across his cheek. "I don't know what will happen, but I know you're the most important person in my life, the only one I can't do without. I won't lose you without a bloody fight."

Rolling onto his side next to her, he drew her closer to nestle against him, her cheek on his chest. "I'll fight for you too. Until my last breath."

Safe in his arms, she let her eyelids drift shut. He fell asleep first, his breaths slowing. For the first time in years, she found both security and passion in the arms of a man—not just any man, but the only one who saw into her heart and guarded it with his own. Her best friend. Her protector. Her Adam.

Nothing would wrest her away from him. Nothing.

Chapter Seventeen

A tickling sensation feathered across her cheek, rousing Mel from a dreamless slumber. She yawned and scratched at her face. The tickling moved to her forehead. She peeled her eyes open, reluctant to give up her languid serenity.

Holding a lock of her hair, Adam had fanned it out into a little brush and was skipping it along her brow.

During the night, she'd turned onto her side and he now spooned her with his hard body oddly soft against her backside. One of his muscular arms draped over the pillow above her head with his hand lying slack. That was the one tickling her with her own hair. His other arm rested on her body, stretched over her hip, his fingers manipulating the flesh of her thigh, stimulating her to full wakefulness and keen awareness of him.

She inhaled deeply, stretching, reveling in the enduring afterglow of their fevered passion.

He pressed his lips to her ear. "Morning."

An object poked her from behind. A long, hard object. She cleared her throat. "It's half past five and you have an erection? Already?"

"Uh-huh." He sounded mildly sleepy and not a bit fazed. "Happens most mornings."

"Oh." A blush heated her cheeks. After what they'd done last night, she should not be able to blush in his presence anymore.

He released her hair, letting it flutter onto her skin, and repositioned his body so she could barely feel his erection. "If it bothers you, I can go take a shower."

"I'm not bothered—in the way you mean." She rolled her hips into him, marveling at the hardness of his arousal. She slipped a hand between them to curl her fingers around his shaft. His sharp intake of breath made her smile. "You wanted to take a shower. I could join you."

"Now that's a plan I can get behind." He dipped a hand between her thighs, his palm covering her mound and her already rigid clit, while his fingers probed lower. "Here first, then the shower."

"Twice before breakfast?" She shifted her hand off his erection and reached around to grasp his ass. "My, you are a presumptuous devil."

"Have I corrupted you?"

"Mmm…" She sank her fingers into his buttock as he moved his palm in lazy circles, one finger plunging inside her. "Give me the contract and I'll sign my soul away to you."

"Don't you want anything in return?"

"No." She bent her knee, opening herself to him. "I want everything."

He pulled away, leaving her bereft and chilled by the loss of his heat and his deft fingers. Foil ripped. The bed jostled from his movements. Then his body surrounded hers once more and he eased inside her from behind, his velvet-smooth cock entering her with such torturous slowness she arched her back and shoved a hand into his hair, clenching her fingers.

"I want you forever, Mel."

Mindless once again, drowning in the bliss of desire, she could do no more than moan. He took hold of her thigh, securing it as he worked his hips, withdrawing and plowing into her aching flesh again and again. Wordless pleas spilled from her lips. He grunted with each thrust, slamming into her with a power that stunned a gasp from her, then flipped her onto her stomach and hoisted her hips off the bed as he pumped in and out, in and out, his breaths sharp and quick, his balls slapping on her ass. Her fingers punched into the pillow, clinched it so tight she heard the fabric rend. Adam's grunts grew desperate along with his thrusts. She screamed his name in the instant her climax exploded through her body, hurling her into the atmosphere, breathless, before she plummeted back down to earth. He came apart inside her, shouting her name, his voice hoarse and strained.

In that moment, as he turned her over to cradle her in his arms, she knew sex with Adam would never be just "pleasant." He would drive her half mad with need and consume her with earth-shattering releases. He would love her with his body, his mind, and his heart.

How could she not adore him in return? He was…Adam.

An hour and a half later, with two more condom wrappers scattered on the floor, they finally got dressed. Done buttoning her blouse, propped up with both hands on the bed behind her, she watched Adam zip up his pants. His hair was mussed and wet, his lips as swollen as hers from their intense kissing. Grinning, she said, "You're gorgeous when you're freshly fucked."

His lopsided smile set her pulse to racing. With one hand, he snatched up his shirt. A half-hearted frown warped his lips. He waved the shirt at her. "You ripped all the buttons off. What am I supposed to wear?"

"You could borrow one of my shirts."

True horror flashed on his face.

Laughing, she grabbed the ruined shirt. "I'll fix it, don't worry. You won't have to risk your firefighter pals seeing you in a pink crop top."

"The buttons…" Forehead wrinkled, he crouched to search the floor. He located four buttons, brandishing them in his palm. "That's all I can find."

She took the buttons. "I have spares."

He gaped at her with an adorably stricken look on his face.

"Relax." She patted his cheek. "Nothing girlie. Plain brown and black buttons, I swear."

"Thanks." He grabbed her around the waist and hoisted her up. "I'll make breakfast while you fix the shirt you destroyed."

"You didn't complain last night."

"I'm not complaining now." He dropped a quick kiss on her lips. "You can shred my clothes anytime."

Bacon sizzled in the pan, the aroma making Adam's mouth water. Nothing powered him up for the day like bacon and French toast, with loads of maple syrup. Luckily, Mel kept the ingredients on hand, because she loved a good, politically incorrect breakfast as much as he did.

And he loved her for that. Among other things.

She strolled into the living room, heading straight for the bar with his shirt slung over her arm. He took a moment to admire her—the sway of her hips, the swishing of her skirt around her knees, the pink blush of her lipstick on those lickable lips. He'd watched her get dressed, so he'd known what she was wearing today, but witnessing her in motion made his mouth water more than the bacon ever could.

It amazed him every day how she pulled off looking professional and hot as all get-out at the same time. When she bent over the bar to sniff the air steaming up from the bacon, he caught a glimpse of the valley between her breasts.

"Mmm," she said, exactly how she'd murmured earlier when he palmed her mound, right before he plunged into her luscious body. A serene smile played across her lips. "Smells delicious. Is there French toast?"

"Naturally. I know what my girl likes."

"Oh yes, you do." She tossed him his shirt. "All fixed. But if you ask me, it's a shame to cover up that body."

He wanted to throw her over the bar, hike up her skirt, and pound into her until they both screamed. Instead, he shrugged into his shirt. "Can't run around half-naked in public."

"It's not illegal or immoral, though you might cause a public disturbance, what with a throng of women swarming you."

"Does it bother you when women look at me?"

"Lust after, you mean." She climbed onto a stool. "I'm well aware of your criminal allure and I will adjust to the situation."

"No adjustment required." A spatula in hand, he slid the French toast slices off the griddle and onto plates. "I'm yours and yours alone."

She smiled with such shy sweetness, he wanted to scoop her into his arms and kiss her all day long.

Partway through their meal, a bit of syrup dribbled from her lips. He licked it away with a quick swipe of his tongue. She dunked her finger in the syrup on her plate and smeared some of it on his mouth, then lapped it up with swift, short strokes of her soft little tongue. His libido kicked into overdrive, but he knew she had to leave for work soon.

He liked sex. He liked women. But this woman drove him wild like no one else. Other women held no appeal anymore, because after making love to Mel Thompson, he couldn't go back to casual sex. Not ever. Sex with the love of his life forged a kind of passion he hadn't dreamed existed and he wanted nothing else for the rest of eternity.

While he loaded the dishwasher, Mel leaned against the counter beside him. "About this 'more' thing." She clasped her hands in front of her, biting the inside of her lip. "I think we should do it."

Her words paralyzed him. A fork slipped from his fingers to clatter on a plate. "Are you serious? That's really what you want with me?"

"Yes." She picked up the spoon, putting it in the little basket for silverware. "I love you and you love me. Let's give this relationship thing a shot."

"Not afraid anymore?"

"To be honest, I still worry this whole thing will blow up in our faces. Can't help it. This is something I can't control and you know what a Nazi I am about managing every aspect of my life."

"You're not a Nazi." He shut the dishwasher and bracketed her with his body, one hand at either side of her hips on the counter. "You won't regret this."

Mel laid her delicate hands on his chest, her eyes focusing in on his. "If Devon, or any man, had made me choose him or you, I'd have picked you. It's a deal-breaker."

Adam pulled his head back. "I was your relationship deal-breaker?"

"Of course." She fingered the collar of his shirt. "Now you're my relationship, period."

"I like the sound of that."

She ran her palm down his thigh and back up to his waistband. "You're on duty today, right? Can we get together tomorrow night?"

"Can't. I've got a…thing."

"Would this be one of your secret, helping-your-dad things?"

"Yeah." He despised keeping anything from her, especially after she'd exposed her secrets to him.

"It's okay," she said. "Probably for the best. I haven't had this much sex in such a short span of time in my entire life."

"Me neither."

Her eyebrows rose. "Really?"

"I'm not a sex machine." He tensed at the renewed motion of her hand on his thigh. "At least, I wasn't until I made love to you." He curved a hand around her nape, angling her head up. "I hope I didn't wear you out last night, or this morning."

"I'm tougher than I seem."

"Always knew that. You're an amazing woman and I'm the luckiest jerk on earth to have you with me." Her proximity had started to make his cock restless, so he backed away and took her hands in his. "Better get you to work."

"Shouldn't you call a taxi? I can drive myself."

"First, I drive you to work. Then, I call a taxi."

"Normally, I don't like orders." She hit him with a sexy smile. "But I kind of like it from you."

Despite the ever-increasing tightness in his crotch, he dragged her in for a long, lazy kiss. "Don't want to leave you one second sooner than I have to."

"You can come with me to work." She snatched her purse off the sofa end table. "But I'm driving."

"Ahhh, you kind of drive like a demon, especially when you're jazzed. Might be safer if I drive."

"My car, my rules." She gave him a overly cheerful smile. "You can close your eyes."

He shook his head. "Won't help with the swerving and screams of terror from other drivers. But I can't say no to you, so just make sure to buckle up."

Mel slapped him on the arm and sashayed out of the kitchen. He trailed her toward the entryway so he could admire her tight little ass. He'd won her, at last. No, he'd earned her—the hard way, overcoming his raging lust for her and Mel's reticence about giving in to her passion and her heart. But now that he had her, he would never let anything come between them.

The doorbell rang.

Her hand hovering over the knob, Mel scrunched her eyebrows.

Again, the doorbell rang.

She pulled the door open and her head jerked back in surprise. "Devon, what the—"

Devon McCallister barged past Mel into the entryway. He froze, eyes wide, when he came face to face with Adam.

"You," Devon said, like he'd found a wanted fugitive in Mel's bed. "What are you doing here this early in the morning?"

Adam narrowed his eyes at the little prick. "None of your business."

"He slept here," Mel said, still holding the door open. "Adam and I are involved and you have no right to show up at my home, for any reason. I told you to leave me alone."

"Involved?" Devon said, incredulous. "You can't be serious. This is some kind of weird rebound mistake."

She compressed her lips and drummed one finger on the door knob. "Just go, Devon. My life is not your concern anymore."

Devon whirled on Adam. Spittle sprayed from his lips as he snarled, "You slimy, sleazy lowlife. Taking advantage of her when she's upset about our relationship. You knew we had a chance to work things out, so you kept her from seeing me and tricked her into thinking she wants you."

Adam barred his arms over his chest, angling forward just enough to loom over the prick. "Go home."

Mel slapped a hand on Adam's chest and pushed him away. To Devon, she said, "Have you lost your ever-loving mind? It's over. No reconciliation. We are through and I have moved on." She jabbed a finger toward the doorway. "Go."

Devon glared at Adam for a moment, then spun and stomped out the door. Inches past the threshold, he turned around to stab an accusatory finger at Adam. "I won't let you get away with this. Mel loves me and you've brainwashed her or something."

Adam gave a harsh laugh. "Yeah, it couldn't be she dumped you because you fucked every piece of ass you could con into your bed. Or maybe you paid them, huh?"

"You bastard!" Devon lunged forward, seizing Mel's arm, and tried to haul her out the door. "I won't let her stay here with you."

Mel tore her arm free. "This is my apartment, you stupid son of a bitch."

Rage ripped through Adam, incinerating his self-control. He rushed at Devon, swung his arm back, and walloped his fist into the prick's jaw. Devon stumbled backward, lost his footing, and struck the floor flat on his ass in the middle of the hallway.

Palpating his jaw, Devon glowered at Adam.

Mel slammed the door.

Her hands trembled, but she seemed more angry than freaked.

Adam enfolded her in his arms and kissed the top of her head. "If that weasel harasses you again, call the cops. I mean it. Don't feel sorry for him, don't give him the benefit of the doubt. You owe him nothing."

"I'll call the cops, I promise," she said, burrowing her face into his neck. "But I really don't think he'll do that again. He lost it because he found out you and I are together. Once he cools down, he'll realize he's lost me for good and give up."

"He damn well better."

She extricated herself from his embrace, straightened her clothes, and squared her shoulders. "Time to go to work. I will not let Devon ruin my day again, or ruin my business. I've got work to do."

He smiled, admiring her strength and determination. "That's my Mel."

Mel took a quick peek out the peephole on the door. "The weasel's gone."

They walked out of her apartment hand in hand, heading out into a new day and a new chapter in their life together. More than best friends. More than lovers.

For the first time in his life, he had everything he wanted.

Chapter Eighteen

The next day, Mel sat at her desk in front of her computer and checked the clock on her phone for the umpteenth time. Ten to one. She tapped the toes of her shoes on the floor and struggled to focus on her emails—but the computer monitor kept blurring as her thoughts traveled back to the night when everything changed, when Adam made love to her and coaxed her into revealing her true feelings for him. She loved him, and the realization no longer unsettled her.

First, he freed her body. Now, he'd freed her heart.

Remembering their last time together, the night before last, her thoughts meandered back to Adam's hard body. His deft fingers. His sly tongue. Her body-wrenching, screaming orgasms. Most of all, she recalled the look on his face when he climaxed. Part wonder, part triumph, all wild ecstasy.

At lunch today, she'd see him. They had a date—technically, their first date. Ever.

Two days without him had pushed her to the brink of insanity. He starred in her porno dreams, yes, but his absence affected her in a more personal way. She missed him, badly. His smile. His affectionate teasing. How he opened doors for her. The way he'd punched Devon. Oh, she'd enjoyed that more than was seemly, but she didn't care. Then there was Adam's gentle seduction, his ravenous hunger for her, and the way their bodies seemed to fit together perfectly, their movements in sync, their responses feeding off each other. With Adam, sex became an erotic give-and-take like nothing she'd experienced before.

A figure appeared in the open doorway.

Mel started, her finger clicking the mouse button by accident, twice. The email she'd been trying to read vanished into the virtual trash can. Cursing, she retrieved the message with a few clicks of her mouse.

Adam smiled. "Didn't mean to scare you."

She leaned back in her chair. "You surprised me, that's all. You're early."

"One o'clock on the dot."

The clock on her phone confirmed it. "Oh. Lost track of time, I guess."

He strode inside, shut the door, and locked it.

"What are you doing?" she asked, excitement zinging through her, because he had that gleam in his eyes. The one that preceded voracious, uninhibited sex.

He raked his gaze over her body. "I'm plotting out exactly how to fuck you on your desk."

Molten liquid flooded her sex. Just like that, he'd gotten her primed and ready. The speed of her response to him no longer unsettled her. She reveled in it now. But this was her office and she couldn't have sex in her place of business, no matter how fiercely she wanted him. Squirming in her seat, she said, "Maybe we should talk. Catch up."

"It's been a couple days, but it feels like forever." He came around the desk to lean his taut buttocks on the edge, one knee bent. "I've been hanging around the station, playing poker and watching sports." He planted one palm on the desktop near her hands and bent toward her. "You've been working too hard and not having any fun. We're all caught up."

"I went to a movie with Kaya last night. I did have fun. So there." She stuck her tongue out.

He lunged forward to capture her tongue between his teeth. The breath caught in her throat. He sucked gently, releasing her tongue little by little. She gripped the arms of her chair, hyperaware of her breasts swelling and her nipples poking through her bra.

"Long lunch, right?" His face was inches from hers, his lips parted and oh so enticing.

"Yes. You insisted I take at least an hour, but you wouldn't say why."

"I need more than twenty minutes with you."

He grabbed her around the waist and hefted them both to their feet. Her high heels clacked on the floor. His erection stretched his jeans, big and hard, as his gaze flicked down to her stilettos. "Doesn't look like businesswoman footwear. Did you wear those for me?"

Why bother lying? Nobody, except maybe a Kardashian, wore stilettos to work. "Yes, Adam, I wore these bone-crushing shoes for you."

That devastating grin. "I appreciate it. Never told you how much I love the way your ankles look in heels."

"Did you come here to compliment my ankles?"

"Nope. I'm here for a quickie on your desk." He nibbled her earlobe, his hands groping her back.

"Why did I have to take a long lunch for a quickie?"

His lips traveled down her throat, leaving a slick trail on her skin. "Never said we'd stop after the quickie. I've had my eye on the sofa too."

At his mention of it, her gaze swerved to the sofa and visions of their naked bodies entwined on it erupted in her mind. He'd done this to her on purpose. Damn if she didn't love it. But she couldn't quite wrap her brain around what was about to happen.

"Have sex here?" she said. "We can't. My employees are right outside."

"We'll be quiet," he assured her. "Besides, knowing someone might hear us turns you on, I bet."

Oh dear lord, it did. In many of her fantasies about him, they'd get it on in a public place, out of sight but near enough others might hear. The fantasy of it had aroused her to an almost frantic degree. The reality…

Adam must've noted her stirring desire, because he looked far too pleased with himself. "See, I know what you like."

"Never questioned that."

With a leisure that had her panting, he unbuttoned her blouse and un-hooked the front of her bra. Thank God she'd had the foresight to wear a front-clasp style. His hand closed around her breast, plumping and teasing her flesh everywhere but her nipple, while his other hand braced her back. He bent to cover her nipple with his mouth, that greedy tongue coiling around her rigid tip. She arched her back, eyes half closed, and succumbed to the fire he ignited inside her. His hand on her back supported her and she knew he would never let her fall.

His tongue lashed over her nipple faster, his teeth grazed it. She bit back a moan.

Adam pulled away.

Dazed, she stared at him, unable to form a single syllable in complaint.

Her expression must've conveyed it, because he shook his head. "Not done yet."

With one sweep of his hand, he cleared off the desktop in a strip across the center. Her desk calender plummeted to the floor, along with three ma-nila folders full of paperwork. She could sort it all out later. Was this really her, thinking of putting off work? Surrendering to sex on her desk? Why yes, it was.

He moved behind her and slanted forward, pinning her between his body and the desk. His hand captured her breast again, his lips feathered over her ear. "Down on the desk."

Never in her life had she done anything so naughty, or so hot. She bent over the desk, her bare breasts mashed to the cool glass, her nipples puckering even more from the chill of it. Her high heels pushed her bottom up, curving her spine.

"You know," she said, her voice smokier than she'd imagined it could be, "this is a lot like my fantasy I told you about the other night."

"It's a little of your fantasy and a little of mine." He stroked her back with his sure hands. "Are you ready for me?"

"Yes. Please, yes."

With one hand, he shoved her skirt up—and went still. A soft chuckle rumbled in his chest. "You sure are ready. No panties, eh?"

"Can't have you tearing them to pieces again. Silk isn't cheap."

He caressed her exposed bottom. "Have you been walking around all morning without panties?"

"No." She twisted her head around to peek at him through her hair. "I took them off fifteen minutes ago."

Adam settled his body onto hers. The exquisite weight of his body, the heat and scent of him, it aroused her almost to the point of pain. He slid his hands up her arms to clasp her hands. She laced her fingers through his, just as his lips found her throat, peppering kisses down her skin.

He shifted her hands up to the desk's edge and curled her fingers over the lip. "Better hold on."

She held on, her cheek pressed to the glass. A curtain of hair spilled over her face, the tickle of it amping up her need. The distinctive sound of his jeans unzipping shot anticipation through her. When she heard a foil packet rip, she wriggled her hips.

With one foot, he kicked hers apart, spreading her before him. Cool air whispered over her exposed sex. He entered her with maddening care, drawing whimpers and gasps from her. She wanted hot, hard, fast. After fantasizing about him for two days, she was so ready she might burst if he tried to take it slow.

Snug inside her, he stopped.

"Please, Adam." She clenched the desk until her fingers ached. "Oh God, please. Fuck me hard."

"Look at me when you say that." His lips tightened against her skin, a clue he was smiling.

Opening her eyes, she pushed his head away from her neck to get a sidelong view of him. "I said, fuck me hard. Do it so hard and fast the desk jumps across the floor."

He rose up, his shaft jostling inside her. "Sounds good, with one exception. We start slow and build up to making the desk jump."

Craning her neck, she blew hair away from her mouth and said, "Quickie, remember?"

"You need to learn patience." With two quick, powerful thrusts, he had them both struggling for breath.

"No lessons." She sounded as desperate as she felt, her body trembling with pent-up need. "Do it, dammit. Do me."

She squeezed her muscles around him.

He let out a hoarse cry. With both hands, he grasped her hips. She gripped the desk, already panting. He slid out of her, inch by inch, and paused with the head of his cock nudging her opening. She gritted her teeth, shutting her eyes against the exquisite agony of waiting.

He punched into her, stunning her, forcing her to swallow a cry. His hands kept her hips steady through his frantic thrusting, but she writhed on the desk, her breasts rubbing on the glass, making a faint squeaking noise. He pounded into her with little grunts and groans, the desk wobbled, its legs grated on the floor, his jackhammering shaft propelled her toward climax, the pleasure verging on blissful torture. Nearly incoherent, she begged him to push her over the edge.

One of his hands dived under her hips, his finger ground into her clitoris.

Her orgasm convulsed her body, so sudden and blistering she mashed her face into the glass desktop to muffle her scream. He thrust faster, harder, until his own climax shuddered through him, even as her release pulsed on and on through his final thrusts, waning as he dropped onto her, limp.

His breaths blustered, blowing her hair across her cheek. He smoothed it away from her face and brushed a kiss over the corner of her mouth. "You're my heroin, Mel. One hit and I was a goner, can't get enough of you."

The weight of him shifted to the side. He grasped her hip and tugged until she rolled over, tucked against his body. They were face to face, the moment so intimate she couldn't keep from caressing his cheek and running her fingertips over his mouth. She traced the seam of his lips with one finger. "I'm addicted too."

And there, on her desk with her employees probably listening at the keyhole, she reached down to curl her fingers around the base of his cock. It was still semi-hard. She ran her hand up to the head, circling her thumb over the cap. A tiny shudder coursed through him.

She nipped his lower lip. "I work very, very hard. I deserve a long, satisfying lunch break."

"Yes you do." The breath hissed out of him as she pumped along the length of his blooming erection.

Firming up her hold, she milked him until arousal made him rock-hard again. "Sofa?"

"Hell yes," he rasped, and hoisted them both off the desk, carrying her to the sofa.

"Me on top," she said. "Please."

"Yes, ma'am." He spun around and dropped onto the sofa with her on his lap.

"I need to feel you inside me again, Adam." She positioned herself over his bobbing erection, her breasts in his face. "I want you under me so I can shred your shirt, scrape my nails down your chest, and ride you until you're dripping sweat."

For the first time ever, he was speechless.

He fished a condom packet from his pocket, handing it to her, and she ripped the foil with her teeth. The noise he made, somewhere between a growl and a gasp, had her clit throbbing. As she rolled the condom over his penis, she marveled at how their relationship—their lives—had transformed so completely in such a short time. Not only had she confessed her late-night fantasies and self-pleasuring to him, but she'd embraced a passion she hadn't recognized lay within her, reveling in the freedom of being with the man she loved more than anything.

Lowering her body onto his shaft, she took hold of his shoulders. "I love you, Adam. I love you so much."

"I love you, Mel. Forever."

Chapter Nineteen

Adam stood in his dad's garage with a hammer in one hand and a nail in the other, but he couldn't remember what the hell he was supposed to do with them.

The memory of his long "lunch" with Mel kept rushing through his mind, complete with sensations and scents and flavors—heaven almighty, the taste of her. Mel had ridden him like the hottest fantasy cowgirl in history, their bodies slapping against each other, her breasts flapping in his face until he just had to catch one in his mouth. If the desk had jumped across the floor, the sofa had launched into orbit. After they finished, he'd pointed out her employees must've heard the unmistakable sounds of wild sex emanating from their boss's office.

To his surprise and delight, she'd grinned and said, "I own the damn company. And I finally discovered the best perk of self-employment."

"What's that?"

"I can fuck my boyfriend in my office and no one can fire me."

My oh my, did that woman have passion.

They'd both come so hard he had to seal his mouth over hers to muffle both their screams. Yeah, he was man enough to admit. He'd screamed when Mel rode him to climax. The way her muscles rippled around him, pulling him deeper, crushing his willpower, her flesh slippery and hot and—

The hammer tumbled from his hand. The thump of it hitting the floor smacked him out of the memory. He was supposed to be building shelves for his dad's bedroom. Shelves. Made of wood. He should concentrate on the job, not on Mel's lithe body and her wanton cries.

"Better get a move on, or you won't finish today."

Adam glanced up at the door to the house, on the far side of the two-car garage. His father, a bottle of beer in each hand, wended his way around the lumber stacked on the floor and the workbench in front of Adam. Beyond the open garage door, he glimpsed kids racing by on their bicycles. When he and Mel had kids, he hoped they were as strong and wonderful as their breathtaking mother. He was desperate to propose to her, but she was nowhere near ready for that.

Dad offered him a beer. "Look like you need this. Mel trouble?"

"Kind of." Adam accepted the beer, twisted off the top, and took a long pull. Cold liquid slid down his throat.

"What's going on with you and Mel?" Dad eyed him with a sly look. "You sleep with her yet?"

Adam froze, his mouth a hair's breadth from the bottle's lip.

"Come on, kid." His father gulped a mouthful of beer and aimed a look of parental exasperation at him. "We're both adults. We can talk about sex."

"How many Xanaxes did you swallow with your Coors?"

"Not a one." Robert Caras shook his head. "And you're changing the subject. Is the sex no good or something?"

Adam took another swig and set the bottle on the work bench. "Dad, I love her."

"Need advice on what to do about it?"

"Your advice sucks, Dad. No offense."

The elder Caras shrugged.

Adam scrubbed his face with his hands. Man oh man, he could not talk about sex with his dad, but the pressure in his chest seemed to push the words out. "We had incredible sex, a lot of it, and I told her I love her. She said she loves me too."

"Not seeing the problem."

Adam rested his palms on the work bench and bowed his head. "She knows I'm keeping secrets from her."

"My secret, you mean."

Retrieving the hammer from the floor, Adam made a noncommittal noise.

"I'm sorry." His father settled a hand on Adam's shoulder and gave it a squeeze. "I couldn't get through all this cancer stuff without you, but I shouldn't've made you keep it secret. With this brachiosaurus thing coming up, I know I gotta tell your brothers. It's time."

"Brachiosaurus?" Adam almost laughed, but the weight in his chest blocked it. "It's brachytherapy, Dad."

"Whatever." Dad tipped his beer bottle toward his son. "Tell her."

"Are you sure? With your procedure in a couple weeks…" Adam's eyes burned, as if he might cry. He couldn't. He wouldn't. *Gotta stay strong for Dad.* "Is it the right time to tell everybody?"

"Long past time, like you've been trying to tell me." His dad shoved both hands in his pockets and hiked up his shoulders. "Besides, your mom called this morning and we had a good long talk. She convinced me it's time."

"You told your ex-wife about your cancer, but you wouldn't let me tell Mel?"

"Mel knew something was up," Dad said. "She was worried and talked to her mom about it. Then Jillian called Maggie and Maggie called me and I told her everything. Your mom's flying out tomorrow, to come and help."

"Help?" Adam couldn't hold the hammer up anymore and it thunked onto the workbench as his hand fell. His head spun a little from the convoluted game of phone tag played by his parents and Mel's mom.

"Yeah," his dad said. "Maggie and me agreed you've had too much pressure on you. It's my fault and now I'm fixing it."

"I'm okay."

"No, you ain't." His father headed for the door to the house. "Mel should know what's going on. Tell her, Adam. That's an order."

Robert Caras retreated into the house.

Adam pounded away his frustrations on the shelves, hammering in nail after nail. The shelves turned out perfect, beautiful, with clean lines and a gorgeous finish. They were nothing compared to Mel. Her lines curved in all the right places and her smooth skin had a luster like nothing else.

Go and get her.

Weariness sagged his limbs and ached in his bones. Between his shifts at the station, his odd jobs, and helping out his dad, he had no energy to spare. Even if he told Mel about his dad's cancer, he'd still tricked her with the mask stunt and she'd sense he was keeping another secret, because she knew him inside out. She'd want to know everything. She deserved to know.

If he told her about the mask thing, he might lose her. A risk he couldn't take.

The guilt of keeping it secret would eat away at him, but he'd earned the pain. He'd atone for his mistakes by making Mel happy, in whatever way she needed, for the rest of his life.

And pray it was enough.

Adam fell onto the bed beside Mel, fighting for control of his own breaths. Sweat drizzled down his chest, hot but cooling in the draft from the air conditioner. He turned partly on his side to admire the woman he'd just ravished.

Mel lay sprawled on her back, arms above her head, wrists crossed in a contented pose. Her rosy lips were parted, her breasts rising and falling, bouncing from each heavy breath. Beads of sweat dotted her skin. He bent over to lick one away on her breast, eliciting a little moan from her. The rest of the world had ceased to exist, for him at least. The rough hissing of her exhalations made him long to sample her breaths, to take a part of her into him.

Before he could do it, she yawned, shielding her mouth with one hand. Her hair cascaded down onto his arm and mouth, feathering over his skin, the scent of her strawberry shampoo flooding his senses. She rested her chin on his wrist. Her skin, soft as satin, warmed him.

Her captivating eyes beheld him with all the rapture of a woman in love. "I wouldn't change one minute of what's happened between us lately. Would you?"

"No." And he wouldn't, even if he stumbled onto a time machine and gained the power to go back and redo things. He'd smash the blasted time machine to bits, because in spite of his guilt, he would never erase these glorious days and steamy nights with her.

Mel wriggled her body until she'd maneuvered herself on top of him, with his erection caught between them. The scent of strawberries mingled with the light aroma of baby powder and the heady musk of her stirring arousal. His cock pulsed with each little wiggle of her sensuous body, as she settled in, hands folded on his chest with her chin perched atop them.

She tapped his nose with one slender finger. "Tell me what's bothering you."

"How do you know anything is?"

"Uh, let's see." She touched a finger to her chin, pretending to consider the question. "We just had amazing sex and you're still tense."

Should've known he couldn't fool her. His dad's voice replayed in his head, urging him to *tell her, that's an order.* The back of his throat hurt, a pain started in his chest, but he forced out the words. "Dad has prostate cancer."

"Oh, Adam." Tears shimmered in her eyes. She blinked them away, her gaze never wavering from him. "I'm so sorry. Is he okay? Can I do anything to help?"

"You are doing it." He traced the backs of his fingers across her cheek. "You're keeping me sane."

Her lips trembled, tears on the verge of spilling.

"Mel, it's okay. Dad's doing fine on his meds and I did a ton of research to find the best treatment for him. We both talked to an expert in California too, with Cynthia there to help us out."

"That's why she was at your apartment."

"Yeah."

She feathered her lips across his hand. "I understand now. We're together and being honest with each other, so everything worked out fine."

Being honest with each other. He forced himself not to grind his teeth. Despite his confessions, he still kept one major secret from her. Maybe he should tell her about the mask and the dance…No. She could never find out about his idiotic stunt at the club.

Her lips turned up in the sweetest little smile, her eyes brimming with compassion and love. She kissed his hand again, rubbing her cheek on his arm. "Relax, honey. I'll be with you through everything."

Of course she would. He'd never doubted that.

Unless he told her *everything*.

Mel pushed up onto her elbows again. "When does your dad start his treatments?"

"This afternoon. He's getting a procedure called brachytherapy. They inject some kind of radioactive seeds into his prostate, leave them there for a little while, then take the things out." He rubbed his eyes. "I don't completely understand it, but it sounded like the way to go. He'll need less radiation treatments after—five weeks instead of eight."

"Sounds like you picked the best option." She pecked his cheek. "You did great and your dad will be fine, so try not to get tied up in knots about this."

"What if I picked the wrong thing? What if Dad…" He couldn't finish the thought. Didn't dare.

Mel leaned in until their noses touched, her eyes fixed on his. "You're smarter than you like to think, Adam. I know you chose the right treatment."

He nodded, because he couldn't speak. Tears stung his eyes and he mopped them away with the back of his hand. Tension wound tight inside him, a coil of hot metal tangled around his heart.

She slipped her hands into his hair, nudging his head up off the pillow. Their mouths met in a tender and intimate touch, as their lips explored each other. When she deepened the kiss, it swiftly heated into a rough and frenzied joining. She peeled her lips from his with such leisure it made him groan.

"Christ, Mel," he breathed into her mouth, an instant before she pulled away. "I need you so bad. You really do keep me sane."

"I better keep doing what I've been doing, eh?"

"Absolutely. Driving me insane keeps me sane."

She took his lips between her thumb and forefinger, squeezing. In a tone of mock censure, she said, "That makes no sense."

"But it works for me," he mumbled through her fingers.

"Hmm." She slithered down his body until her hair fanned out over his groin. She pulled her bottom lip between her teeth, released it gradually, and ran her velvety pink tongue over her front teeth. "Back to it, then."

And for a short time, he forgot all about his guilt and the secret he held back from her. He lost himself in the woman he adored, the love of his life, the only one for him, the woman he intended to marry.

Under false pretenses, eh, Mr. Arsonist in a mask?

Chapter Twenty

Mel had spent the better part of the day in the hospital, slouched in an uncomfortable chair in the outpatient waiting room. She'd insisted on accompanying Adam and his dad to the hospital for the radiation procedure. Both men were clearly anxious, though both tried to hide it from each other. Adam's mom had flown in from California to offer moral support, but she would arrive with the other Caras boys, who'd gotten delayed by traffic.

The past two weeks had sped by, a whirlwind of courtship she hadn't expected, considering she and Adam had already been enjoying regular, insanely hot sex. Adam had announced he intended to woo her because he'd "heard rumors other guys do that." They'd shared the usual rituals, including romantic dinners, picnics on the beach, long walks in the park, and intimate conversations.

She was dating her best friend. And she loved it.

Now, stuck in the hospital waiting room, she kept an eye on Adam peripherally. Once his father had been wheeled into the procedure room, Adam's composure had splintered. He'd slumped in his chair and shoved both hands into his hair, as if afraid his head might roll off his neck.

At the moment, he was frowning and staring at the wall.

She leaned into him and squeezed his thigh. "He'll be okay, Adam. You did the research, you know this is the right choice for him."

"What if I'm wrong? What if I missed some important information?"

"You have got to stop second guessing yourself." She pried his hands free of his head and clasped them to her breast with one hand. "Relax, honey. He'll be out before you know it."

His features contorted with anguish. "If anything happens to him, it'll be my fault."

"No. It won't." She took his face in her hands and turned him toward her until their eyes met. "You have done everything humanly possible to find the best treatments for him. You've exhausted yourself. Let me help you carry this burden."

He made a weak attempt at a smirk. "I liked the way you expressed your sympathy last night."

Sex in the shower, during which she'd given him an erotic sponge bath. It had taken his mind off things, for sure.

Mel pulled Adam into her arms, sighing at the familiar intimacy. Why had she tried to push him away for so long? He'd been dealing with a frightening ordeal and she'd been acting like her problems engulfed the world. She would do anything to help Adam.

"Mel! Adam!"

She jerked her head up to see Jack in the doorway of the waiting room. The four other people seated in the room glanced at him with varying degrees of annoyance and confusion. Jack had twisted around to call out to someone down the hallway.

He waved his hand at the mystery person. "Come on! I found the right place." He made a disgusted face. "Toby, forget the vending machines. We'll get Sonya some snacks after we say hi to Adam and Mel. Hurry up, Rick. Where's Mom? Oh, there you are."

Adam, his face buried in her neck, had gone still but not moved to look. He'd stopped breathing, his chest no longer rising and falling against her.

"Reinforcements have arrived," she whispered into his ear, combing her fingers through his hair, gratified when he at least started breathing again.

Jack shouted another admonishment to his brother, to the consternation of several people in the waiting room, who glared at him. He trotted across the room to Mel and Adam. Giving his brother a slap on the shoulder, he took the seat beside Adam.

"Mel said Dad went in already," Jack said. To Mel, he added, "Thanks for calling with the update. Traffic was a real bitch."

Adam groaned out a sigh. "Dad went in awhile ago."

"I'm all right," a feminine voice said from the hallway and a very pregnant Sonya Caras shuffled into the room.

Her husband, Toby, kept a protective arm around her shoulders. "You should've stayed home. This is no place for a woman in your condition."

"I'm not disabled." She elbowed him without much force. "And if I stayed home alone, I'd just worry about you guys. Men are helpless without women around." She caught sight of Mel. "Aren't they, Mel?"

Before Mel could answer, Maggie, Adam's mom, walked into the room and said with a smile, "Amen to that. Caras men especially."

Everyone laughed, except Adam. He was frowning, his head bowed, shoulders hunched.

Rick bounded into the waiting room, his arms loaded with cans of pop and bags of junk food. As Toby helped Sonya sit down beside Mel, Maggie took the seat on Adam's other side.

Mel took Adam's hand and laced her fingers through his. She bent closer to whisper, "You have got to stop obsessing. Your father will be okay."

He grunted and scratched his neck.

The remainder of the boisterous Caras family started ribbing each other and laughing, but their best attempts to draw Adam out failed. He seemed determined to retreat into himself as deep as possible. Even Mel's efforts to coax a smile out of him floundered. If he didn't de-stress soon, he'd have a panic attack of his very own—like father, like son. She had one option left.

Jumping up, she tugged Adam's hand. "Come on. We're going for a walk."

He screwed up his face. "Not leaving until Dad comes out."

"It could be a couple hours yet."

Jack slugged his brother's arm. "Go on. We'll call you if anything happens."

"Go on," Maggie chimed in. "The cavalry is here, so you can take a breather."

Mel tugged Adam's hand again. He glanced at each of his brothers and his mom, then up at Mel, his lips twisted with irritated resignation.

One more tug and he relented, rising with a grumble to grasp her hand.

"That's right, man," Rick said. "You guys have a real good walk."

He infused the statement with heavy innuendo, matched by the innuendo in his smile. If she didn't love him like a brother, she would've punched him in the arm for being so presumptuous and impertinent.

Not that he was wrong about her intentions.

She ushered Adam out of the waiting room, down a maze of corridors, and out into the parking lot. He started in the direction of her car, but she pulled him back.

"This way." She nodded across the street.

His brows rose. He tracked her gaze over the parking lot and across the busy street to the motel located there. His jaw dropped. "You can't be serious, Mel."

"I am." She towed him in the direction of the motel. "You are way too stressed out and I know of one surefire way to relax you."

"Mel…"

"No arguments."

He released her hand to hook his arm around her waist, drawing her closer. "You are so hot when you're bossy."

"Then get ready to be bossed around. I may throw *you* over a desk this time."

"You know I'd love that, but—" He cleared his throat. "I'm not sure I can, uh, get up and running right now. I'm too worried about Dad."

"Oh, you leave that to me." She grinned up at him. "I've got skills."

"I'm aware of that." When they stopped at the curb, he surprised her with an open-mouth kiss full of need and desperation. Her heart ached at the emotion burning behind his every action. She loved him so much she kept having the silly impulse to gush about it, but right now, she wanted nothing more than to lose herself in him.

His hands roved her back, stoking the wildfire raging inside her. He'd learned her responses so well, so quickly, he really could set her off with one look, one smile, one feather-light kiss.

Adam hustled her across the street through a break in the traffic. They dashed into the motel office and booked a room for two hours. The place wasn't exactly the Hilton. The room was small, and shabby but clean. They barely noticed their surroundings as they tumbled through the door and pawed at each other's clothes, frantic for the bliss of skin on skin.

They didn't make it to the bed.

He boosted her onto the dresser by the door and yanked her jeans and panties down to her ankles. Her body yearned for him, her mind reeled with visions of the ecstasy to come. He gazed down at her groin, enraptured, and she couldn't help following his gaze to her glistening folds and the drops of moisture on the curly hairs of her mound. His fingers dallied over those hairs, sending little electric shocks through her, and then he delved his fingers into her folds, swirling his fingers around her clit.

"Adam," she breathed, clutching at his shoulders.

His gaze swung up to hers and the storm of emotions in them stunned her.

"I need you," he said, "and I don't think I can be gentle."

"Don't care." She wrapped her legs around him, jerking his zipper down. "I'm yours, any way you need me."

Anguish wrenched his features. "God, I love you."

She freed his erection, running her hand up and down his sleek, thick length. "I love you too."

His mouth flattened into a line as he cursed under his breath. "No condom."

"That's okay." She positioned his cock between her thighs, the head nudging her opening. "I'm on the pill. Take me hard or soft, forwards or backwards, any damn way you need to. My body is yours, Adam. My heart is yours, forever."

His eyes glimmered with moisture, but he sucked in a breath and straightened. "You're the most incredible—Shit, I don't know what I'd do without you, Mel."

"Lucky for you, you'll never have to find out."

He closed his fingers around her ankles, lifting up until her heels were braced on the edge of the dresser, her legs wide, her sex exposed. He grasped her hips and drove into her with a loud groan, his shoulders bunching as he pistoned into her again and again, hard and frantic and unrestrained. Her body unleashed a torrent of slick, molten desire that coated her skin and slicked his cock. He yanked her hips into each of his thrusts, raising her ass off the dresser and banging it backward into the wall. Soon their cries grew as loud as the smacking of the dresser.

She flung her arms around his neck, plastering her body to his as her climax ripped through her. It went on and on, wave after blistering wave of mind-numbing pleasure. He came inside her and she swore she felt the hot jet of his semen, and even as his spasms subsided, her body built toward another climax, squeezing whimpers from her. She sensed the power of this release, unlike any she'd known before, and almost feared it. He pulled out of her, rubbing her clitoris with such ferocity she had no choice but to erupt in his arms.

Her mouth fell open, a scream rising in her throat.

Adam covered her mouth with his own, plunging his tongue deep, swallowing her screams and holding onto her until the last wave finally ebbed. When she went limp against him, he stroked her hair and sprinkled kisses over her cheek and jaw.

"You are so fucking amazing," he said, circling his hands over her back. "I've never seen or felt a woman come that hard."

"Mm." Every muscle loose from the intensity of her climax, she let her head fall back to gaze up at him, her smile languid. "That was all you, honey. Nobody else could detonate me like you do."

"You do the same to me." He kissed her sweetly, smoothing hair from her face.

She turned her face into his touch, basking in the nearness of him.

He cocooned her in his arms, just holding her for a moment before he scooped her up and carried her to the bed. With his foot, he kicked the covers aside. She lifted her brows at the feel of a firm object poking her behind.

"Your fault," he said with a self-satisfied smile.

"That's one thing I'll gladly take the blame for."

He set her down on the bed, crawling over her body to lie down alongside her. "What should we do now?"

"It's your de-stressing." She walked her fingertips down his chest. "Whatever you want, I'll provide."

He studied her for a moment, his expression unreadable, his body motionless except for the engorged penis brushing her belly. At last, he frisked a palm up her thigh, over her hip and up her side, covering her breast with his palm, his fingers crooking into her flesh. "I want you, for the rest of my life."

They made love for a long time, in a drawn-out rhythm like a slow tango on a sultry night. They made love until neither of them could do anything except lie in each other's arms, thoroughly sated. Afterward, they lay face to face, simply gazing at each other.

Eventually, Mel spoke. "I used to be fun, didn't I? Before I got obsessed with work."

"You're still fun."

"But you told me recently I needed to remember how to have fun."

"Ah, that." He slid his hand up her arm and back down to her hip, his fingers plying her flesh. "You were complaining about the club. I wanted you to loosen up and enjoy your birthday, instead of fixating on work."

"What makes you think I was fixating on work while at the club?"

He tried to suppress his laugh, but it came out as a snort. "That conclusion wasn't exactly a Grand Canyon leap. You are—you were always thinking about work."

She sighed, resigned to the truth of his statement. "Not anymore. I took a long lunch for the first time ever."

"Would it be obnoxious for me to take credit for that?"

"Nope, it's all yours. You showed me the error of my ways." She settled a fingertip on his chest, lazily mapping out the lines of his muscles. "It was easier to bury myself in work than to take a hard look at my life and deal with the root of my problems. Namely, that I adore you and always have. Instead, I kept myself in relationship limbo. If you hadn't made a play for me, with all your Arsonist charms and your dirty talk, I might've languished in that limbo for a lot longer. I don't know why you didn't give up on me, but I'm so grateful you hung in there."

"I couldn't give up on you. I wouldn't."

Her fingertip stilled over his heart. Laying her palm flat, she leaned in to kiss him. "Tell me one thing, please."

"Anything you want."

"Why did you sleep around for so long?"

Groaning, he rolled onto his back, one arm stretched over his head. "Same reason you stuck with guys who didn't excite you. I tried to find a deeper connection with other women, but I never could and I assumed I just wasn't built for it. Casual sex kind of…filled the void."

"Doesn't sound very fulfilling," she said, laying a hand over his shoulder and sliding it up to his neck, her thumb on his jaw.

He shrugged. "I wasn't miserable. I like women, I like sex, and I got my emotional fulfillment someplace else." His gaze shifted to her. "From you."

"Me?"

"Yeah, you." He tucked her under his arm, her head on his chest. "I didn't need a relationship with anyone else. I had you and wish to hell it hadn't taken me so long to realize how much you mean to me."

She snuggled into him, warmed by his words and by the knowledge he trusted her enough to share his deepest secrets.

Adam's phone rang.

Mel plucked it off the table and handed it to him. He glanced at the caller ID and his body went rigid as he answered. "Hey, Toby."

Still snuggled against him, she listened to his grunts and *mm-hm*'s, until he finally said goodbye and disconnected the call.

"Dad's procedure is over and he's awake," Adam said. "Time to go."

Adam slid his arm out from under his Dad's, easing him down onto the bed. "Get some sleep. The anesthesia is still in your system, you know."

His father, eyes glassy, mumbled something.

Leaning closer, Adam asked, "What, Dad?"

The elder Caras took a long breath, then carefully whispered, "Don't let her get away."

His eyelids drifted shut and he began to snore.

Jack snickered behind Adam. "I'm amazed he stayed semi-conscious all the way home."

"He's okay. That's all that matters." Adam straightened and stretched, yawning. His dad's procedure had gone very well and the oncologist had been optimistic that a five-week course of external beam radiation would eradicate the cancer.

Mel trotted into the bedroom brandishing a pharmacy bag. She handed it to Jack. "His pain medicine is in here. Make sure he takes it if he needs it."

"Will do, captain, sir." He clapped his heels together and saluted Mel.

Adam felt a smile struggle to curl his lips, but it faded quickly. Relief sagged over him like a sack of concrete mix.

Mel rushed to his side, running her hand over his forehead, brushing stray hairs away and soothing him more than she probably realized. "You're exhausted, sweetie. I'm taking you home."

"But Dad—"

"Jack and Rick have nurse duty tonight." She cradled his face in her hands and leveled a stern look at him. "You are coming with me, Mr. Caras."

He nodded, allowing her to take his hand and lead him away as if he were a lost child. Maybe he was. He'd be lost if anything happened to his dad. He'd be lost without *her*.

As they passed Jack, his brother smirked. "You've got your own private nurse, don't ya? Make sure you give him all his medicine, Mel."

Adam was too wiped out to chastise his brother.

Mel rolled her eyes at Jack but wasted no time shepherding Adam out of his father's house and to her car parked in the driveway. A horn blared in the distance. Vehicles whizzed by so fast Adam's weary eyes had trouble resolving the blurs into shapes. He gave up trying.

Swinging the passenger door open, Mel said, "Inside. Now."

As he moved past her, dropping down into the seat, he managed a weak smile. "You really are sexy when you're bossy. I'd love a replay of the dresser thing."

She bent to plant a quick kiss on his lips. "You won't be doing anything with a dresser tonight except stuffing your clothes into it."

He watched her sashay around the car to the driver's door, admiring the view of her shapely ass in tight jeans that clung to every curve. Her T-shirt hugged her breasts. He imagined those ample mounds in his hands, the peaks pink and hard. *Stop torturing yourself. There's no way you're getting it up again today.* Sad but true. Still, he relished the thought of sleeping with Mel's nude body pressed against him, soft and warm and welcoming.

The drive lulled him, until momentum lurched him forward as she braked at a red light.

"Take it easy," he said. "This isn't a NASCAR race."

"No side seat driving." She patted his cheek. "You just sit there and look pretty, sweetheart."

Her smile was bright, in spite of the circles under her eyes. Without makeup, without a curling iron or whatever she used on her hair, she was the most beautiful woman he'd ever seen. He couldn't tear his gaze away from her, even when she floored the gas pedal, shoving him into his seatbelt.

Gripping his seat, Adam said, "Good thing I love you, because you're a maniac behind the wheel."

"Like that's a surprise." She steered the car around a corner, forcing him to grip his arm rest. "You were there when I flunked the driving test. Twice."

"I thought it was cute, how you got so flustered you bombed the test. Now I'm thinking maybe you need some remedial driver training."

"Will you be my teacher?" she asked, casting him a saucy look.

"Sure, but with me, there'll be plenty of backseat lessons."

"I'm counting on it." A car cut them off and Mel thumped her hand on the wheel, shouting, "Open your eyes, jackass!"

Adam burst out laughing. It was wild, almost hysterical laughter, a catharsis after all the stress and fear that had taken over his life lately. Amid the chaos, though, one beacon shined bright, guiding him back to himself when he'd lost every bearing.

His Mel.

Inspiration swept away his inhibitions and he twisted in his seat to face her. "I know this isn't the ideal time or place for this, but..." He let out an exasperated sigh. "I'm just gonna say this and you can feel free to tell me to go fuck myself."

"That's my job. Don't outsource it on me."

"I'm serious, dammit. I love you, I need you, you're everything to me and I want to spend the rest of my life making you happy, in any and every way possible." He glanced at the street, saw the road ahead was clear, and yanked one of her hands free of the wheel to clasp it in both of his. "Marry me, Mel. Please."

Her mouth fell open. She blinked rapidly. The car veered to the left and she corrected with a jerk of the wheel, jostling them both, but her hand stayed ensconced in his.

"Say yes," he said, "before you kill us both."

"I—Adam, this is—" Her pulse pounded in her wrist, under his fingers. "This is a shock."

"It's a yes-or-no question." He feathered his lips over her knuckles. "Will you marry me?"

"Need to think."

"You think too much. For once in your life, feel the answer."

She hauled in a ragged breath, tears brimming in her eyes. "I love you more than anything in the world and I can't imagine my life without you. Yes, of course, yes."

He whooped.

And somehow, she managed to get them to his apartment without killing anybody.

Chapter Twenty-One

Sunlight trickled in the window through the thin curtains in Adam's bedroom, but it was the feminine warmth molded to the front of his body that flowed through him like the light of a summer's day. Mel's hair tickled his face, the strawberry scent of her shampoo surrounding him. He kept his eyes closed to luxuriate in the soft sound of her breathing, the gentle rise and fall of her breasts, and the comfort of her silky flesh, dusted with fine, pale hairs. Her skin smelled of lavender, tinged with baby powder. He settled an arm over her belly.

He held his fiancée in his arms. His soon-to-be wife.

A smile tightened his lips, then widened into a grin. A few of her hairs got stuck in his mouth, but even that part of her tasted like heaven. *Wife.* There was a word nobody thought would be spoken in the same sentence as his name. Despite hoping for it, he hadn't believed he'd ever find this connection, this belonging. This love.

Mel stirred and stretched her body against him. A little moan escaped her lips as she wet them with a slow sweep of her tongue. Her buttocks pressed into him. The erection already growing between them hardened against her backside.

Her lips parted in a sensual smile. "Well, that's one way to say good morning."

"I can think of another." He nuzzled her hair, gliding his hand up to the valley between her breasts. "After we visit my dad, we've got some shopping to do."

"Shopping?" She guided his hand further south, to graze her mound.

"You need a ring." He teased her downy hairs, rewarded by the quickening of her breaths. "But first, I need to make you come so hard you'll never want anybody else."

Her laughter was low and sexy, making his cock throb. "You've already done that, repeatedly."

"Ditto." He rolled her onto her back, half covered by his body. Their eyes met and a spark lit inside him. Desire, yes. But the tug on his heart confirmed what he'd known for two years. He loved this woman without reservation, without inhibitions, without end. "I can't wait to marry you."

She feigned shock. "The Arsonist is getting hitched. Have aliens landed on the White House lawn?"

"Ha--ha." He took her mouth in a lingering kiss, absorbing every sensation, memorizing the texture of her mouth and the whisper of her breaths. "You're the only woman I want to set on fire anymore."

"I love the way you burn me." She captured his lower lip between her teeth, laving her tongue over it. "You're mine, Adam Caras. Never forget that."

"Love your possessive streak, it's a real turn-on."

"Shall we explore my possessiveness, then?"

"Mm, I've got an hour before my shift starts." He pulled her hips into him, starved for the intoxicating heat of her body around his shaft, but a thought interrupted his mental planning of how to ravish her. "Need a condom."

She put a finger to his lips. "I'm on the pill, remember?"

"I'd feel better if we take every precaution, until we're both ready for the potential consequences."

"You mean the potential of making little Adams who will become both the bane and the wet dream of every girl in Chicago."

"They might be little Mels, control freaks who organize their Play-Dough alphabetically by color." He nipped her chin, then rolled off of her. "I'll get the condom."

"Let me." She swung her deceptively slender legs off the bed. He knew how strong they were, wrapped around his hips, binding him to her while he rocked into her hot, yielding flesh. She hopped off the bed, breasts bouncing. "Which drawer?"

"Top left."

She padded to the dresser.

At the sight of her naked, those hips swaying, his body clenched with need—but the instant her fingers closed around the drawer handle, recollection exploded through him. He bolted upright. "Mel, wait."

She pulled the drawer out. And froze.

"Let me explain," he said, a cold lump congealing in his gut.

Mel stared down into the drawer, and though he couldn't see her face, he had a sick feeling he knew her expression. He'd forgotten and now…

He sprang off the bed, racing to her. "Please listen."

She lifted an object out of the drawer. Her face blank, she held the carnival mask between her thumb and forefinger. The gold edging of the black mask shimmered in the light.

"Oh God, Mel." Acid surged up into his throat. "I'm so sorry."

She took a step backward, her focus remaining on the mask in her hand. Her voice took on a deadened tone as she asked, "What is this?"

"I was—" He swallowed hard, but the constriction in his throat wouldn't lessen. "I was the guy you danced with at the club on your birthday."

She slipped the mask's elastic string over one finger, letting it dangle, seeming unable to look away from the black-and-gold object. "I don't understand. Why would you trick me like this?"

"It was a stupid, selfish mistake." He swiped a hand over his mouth, surprised by the way it shook. "I've loved you for so long, but you were with Devon. When you broke up with him and you seemed happy about it, I thought I had a chance with you. But I needed to be sure. Remember I said you weren't the only one of us afraid this thing would blow up on us? Well, I figured the one way to be sure you wanted me was to—"

"Pretend to be someone else. Deceive me."

His heart clenched at the sadness in her voice, the vacancy in her expression. He'd manipulated her—not on purpose, but his intentions hardly mattered—hiding his mistake from her because he wanted her, needed her, so much he'd do anything to keep her with him.

"I never meant to lie to you," he said. "Guess I lost my head a little, when I finally had the chance to—" He covered his eyes with one hand. "Loving you for two years, wanting you for all that time pretending to be just your best friend, it made me crazy. Not an excuse. More like an explanation. Please believe me, Mel, I never meant to hurt you."

He lowered his hand, waiting for her response, praying for a miracle he didn't deserve.

She clamped her teeth over her lips and dropped the mask on the dresser. "I know you mean that. I know you thought you had to trick me. Don't like it, but I understand you believed it was necessary. What I can't understand is why you wouldn't tell me later, when you decided to pursue me."

"I should've come clean, I see that now." He took a halting step toward her, but she backed away again. "Please, Mel, I'm so sorry. I'll do anything to make this up to you. Anything."

Her lips trembled, as if she were on the verge of tears. "I have no idea what to think about this. Don't know how I feel about it, or if I can even trust you anymore."

The back of his throat hurt, but he had no choice except to keep trying. "I've hated myself ever since that night. Maybe I did it because I am the Arsonist, a jerk who fucks and chucks women, who doesn't know how to love someone. Maybe you should leave me. But I can't stop loving you, I never will, even if you move to the other side of the world and marry some other guy."

She compressed her lips to quell a faint tremble in them and he knew she was fighting back tears.

He took her face in his hands, gently. "There is no excuse for what I did. I am so sorry."

"This is all to much."

A single tear flowed down her cheek onto his thumb. The drop was hot, like her reddened cheeks.

"I love you," he said, with all the conviction he held in his heart. "You are my best friend, my everything." He dared to skim his lips over hers, and though she didn't recoil, she didn't reciprocate his kiss either. "Please don't throw away everything we have together because of one stupid mistake."

Mel shook her head weakly. "This is all too much. I don't know if—I just don't know. I need time to think."

She fled into the bathroom.

He got dressed, guided by muscle memory, his mind as conscious as that of a zombie. By the time she emerged from the bathroom, fully dressed, he was waiting for her in the hallway. She didn't even look at him, just hurried to the front door with her head bowed and her shoulders slumped, her hair falling over her shoulders to shield her face.

One hand on the knob, she hesitated—but did not look back.

"I need to think," she said softly. "That's all I know."

She yanked the door open and rushed out. The door clicked shut.

Adam stood there for the longest time, his gaze glued to the door. Maybe he hoped she'd come back. She didn't.

Mel needed to control her life, he recognized that. Over the past few weeks, so much in her life had flown out of her hands, way up into the sky where she couldn't reach it. She'd overcome a lot of her control issues but discovering the truth about their dance must've made her feel like she was tumbling through the air, desperate for an anchor.

She needed time to think. He'd give it to her.

And keep praying.

Chapter Twenty-Two

Mel arrived home to an unwelcome visitor. Devon stood outside her apartment door, leaning against the wall with his arms crossed over his chest. She ignored him, because her frayed nerves couldn't handle his shit this morning, and unlocked the door with his gaze tracking her every movement. When she slipped inside and tried to close the door, he seized it in one hand.

"Come on, Mel," he said. "You can't be serious about the firefighter."

"If you have one iota of common sense, you'll walk away this instant."

He poked his head into the gap where he held the door open several inches. "You can't keep avoiding me. We belong together."

Eyes still burning from the tears that had streamed down her cheeks on the drive home, she straightened and gave him her best steely glare. "You are the last person I'd want consoling me. Go away. This is your last warning."

"Warning?" He grinned, chuckling. "Or what, you'll sick the fireman on me again?"

"I will call the police. This is harassment."

He pushed against the door, trying to wriggle past it. "Let's talk this through, baby. I miss you."

"Go away."

Devon reached for her.

She kicked him in the shin. When he stumbled backward, she slammed the door in his face and secured both the lock and the deadbolt.

He pounded on the door, shouting in a wildly desperate voice. "Mel, I love you. I can't live without you and I'm not leaving until you hear me out. I'll shout through the goddamn door if I have to."

Mel glanced at the table nearby, where she kept her stun gun in a drawer. No, she couldn't. Well, he wouldn't leave her alone…and it was nonlethal. Not like she'd stab him with a knife or fire a bullet into his heart. Tossing her purse on the table, she grabbed the stun gun out of the drawer.

"We're both to blame," Devon shouted. "You must've been panting for the fireman when we were still together, right? That's why you were so cold in bed."

Cold in bed? Oh, that was the last straw.

Mel unlocked the door and swung it wide. Devon all but fell across the threshold, staggering to avoid landing flat on his sorry face. She jammed the stun gun into his arm.

He jerked, his eyes bulging, and crumpled to the floor.

She closed the door, just missing his feet, and crouched beside him.

"Cut the jealous crap," she said. "No more *you belong to me* and no more stalking me with texts and voicemails and showing up unannounced. Next time, I will call the cops—but first I'll shock you with my nifty stun gun until all you can do is drool on the floor. I realize you need to control everyone except yourself, but I am not yours to command. I never was. This is your last chance to man up, get over it, and move on. Understand? Blink twice for yes."

Still unable to move, he blinked twice.

Given the brevity of the shock she'd hit him with, she guessed he'd regain motor control in a few minutes. She sat cross-legged beside him, in silence, waiting for him to recover enough she could boot him out the door. He roused gradually, moving his limbs as if afraid they might give out again, and eased into a sitting position.

"Why'd you do that?" he whined.

"Seriously? You can't figure it out?" She planted her hands on her knees, shaking her head. He'd picked the absolute wrong day to pull this crap again. "First, you cheated on me with every female east of the Mississippi. Then, when I righteously dump your ass, you start harassing me about taking you back."

When he started to speak, she silenced him with a raised hand. He pouted—honestly, he did—but clapped his mouth shut.

"You did more, though," she said, "didn't you? That stunt in my office, with the mariachis, cost me a big contract."

Over the past couple weeks, she'd landed two even better ones. But he didn't need to know that.

Devon stared at her blankly for a long moment. At last, he scrubbed his face with both hands.

"I'm sorry," he said, and for once, his expression matched his words. "I knew I was overdoing it but I couldn't stop. You were the best thing and I had to get you back." He massaged his arm, where she'd hit him with the stun gun. "I could have you arrested for assault, you know. You and your boy toy."

"My boy toy's father used to be a cop, moron. A highly decorated one. Two of his sons are firefighters. Plus, my entire staff can testify to your harassment. Whose side do you think the police will take?"

Devon pushed up onto his knees and shakily got to his feet. "I just want you back. I'll do anything you ask if you'll forgive me."

"Okay." She stood, regarding him with what must've been a devious gleam in her eye. "You can have my forgiveness, and I won't call the cops on you, on one condition."

He eyed her warily. "What is it?"

"Leave me and Adam alone, forever."

Devon scowled.

Mel grabbed her purse, extracting her phone. "Guess I have to make a call."

"Wait." He raised both hands, as if surrendering. "Okay, I'll do it. Besides, there have to be better women out there for me, ones who appreciate what I have to offer."

"Goodbye, Devon." She opened the door.

He left without saying a word or looking at her again.

As she closed the door behind him, her thoughts spiraled back to the moment in Adam's apartment when she'd discovered the mask. He'd been so penitent, so frantic to explain, and so sincere in his apology. Maybe she'd overreacted. Compared to Devon's antics, Adam's mask trick seemed trivial.

She wandered to the sofa and collapsed onto it, not bothering to shed her shoes.

Devon had refused to leave her alone, demanding she forgive him. Adam had apologized but let her walk away. He loved her enough to give her space.

The look on his face when she left, it had torn at her heart. He honestly believed he didn't deserve her. Add in her need to control everything in her life, including her emotions…How many times had she sworn to stay celibate? She let him pleasure her, only to proclaim it meant nothing. No wonder Adam resorted to hiding behind a mask. He'd been right to worry about her reaction to the idea of a romance with him.

She needed to talk to Adam. Since he was on duty, she called his cell. Voicemail picked up. She left a brief message asking him to call back.

Turning on the TV, she slumped into the sofa and braced her feet on the coffee table. Her eyes, though aimed at the TV, blurred out of focus and then back in, only to blur out again. Voices from the show beat on her eardrums, the words indecipherable. She flipped channels on the TV, but nothing caught her interest. Although it was Saturday, she normally would've headed to the office. Today, she had no stomach for work. It seemed irrelevant when she might've ruined the only good relationship she'd ever had, all because she'd gotten overwhelmed. Control freaks did not handle surprises well.

To pass the time while she waited for Adam, she did her laundry, even ironing her sheets just to waste more time. She washed the dishes. She cleaned the windows. The phone didn't ring.

When would Adam call?

Returning to the sofa, she curled into the cushions with her legs wedged under her. The TV was still playing, so she gazed at it without seeing anything on the screen.

The phone rang.

Mel snatched it off the table and answered with an overeager hello.

"Have you seen the news?" Kaya asked.

"No." Mel blinked until the screen came into focus. "I'm watching one of those Alaska reality shows."

"Switch to the news."

Mel absently flipped to a local channel. A woman reporter stood in front of a four-story building. Flames leaped from the windows, smoke swirling up into the sky. Behind the reporter, a fire engine squatted at the curb in front of the building. Firefighters manhandled a hose to get a better angle on the fire, a massive geyser of water erupting from the hose. The reporter described the situation in an excited tone.

"It's a fire," Mel said. "Why do I have to watch the—"

"Aren't those Adam's guys?"

The camera zoomed in on two of the firefighters working the hose. Mel froze, her gaze nailed to the familiar faces displayed on the screen. "Brett and Trevor."

"A few moments ago," the reporter said, "an injured firefighter was taken away in an ambulance. His condition is unknown at this time."

The flames. White-hot. Consuming the building and everything in it.

Kaya's voice was hushed in her ear. "You don't think..."

"It's not Adam." It was more of a prayer than a certainty. Mel's stomach churned, with an anxiety she could neither explain nor dismiss. *Adam's okay, he knows what he's doing, it's not him.*

An explosion rocked the building. The structure shuddered and the top floor pancaked down into the one below. Debris showered the street.

Mel jerked, hiccuping out a breath. Time slowed to a crawl. She dropped to her knees, inches from the TV. *Please, God, no-no-no-no.*

A beep sounded in her ear. Mel said, "Hold on, got another call."

She jumped to the new caller.

"Mel, it's Bob. Adam's been hurt, don't know how bad."

The phone tumbled from her hand, clattering to the floor.

Chapter Twenty-Three

el sprinted down the hospital hallway, dodging nurses and order-lies pushing carts. She bumped into a doctor, mumbled an apology, and barreled onward. When she reached the emergency department, Adam's family was already in the waiting area. She stopped too fast and stumbled, but Jack caught her.

His smile was close-mouthed but genuine. He let go of her, jerking his hands away as if she were too hot. "Whoa, I better not hold Adam's girl that close."

Gasping for oxygen, her heart thudding, she struggled to speak. "How—is he?"

"Alive and kicking." Jack patted her arm. "Alive and bitching's more like it, but you know Adam." Jack waved toward a room closed off with a curtain. "He's been waiting for you."

Toby, Sonya, and Maggie occupied chairs nearby. Rick stood near the wall, watching his father pace in front of Adam's room.

"He's really okay?" Mel asked. *Please, please, please.*

"Yeah," Jack said. "Smoke inhalation and a few cracked ribs."

Thank you, God. Relief flooded through her, buckling her knees. Jack steadied her until she could stand on her own and she waved him away with a grateful smile.

Robert flashed her an Adam-like smirk. "Kid's asleep, but he wanted you to wake him up when you got here. Kept ordering me to go home and rest." The elder Caras snorted. "Like I'm doing that. Even with a sore throat and his chest bandaged up, Adam's bossing me around."

Mel glanced from one Caras to another, biting her lip, her gaze flitting back to the curtained-off room.

Robert crooked a finger at her. "Come on, kid."

She shuffled to him. Her throat had gone dry, her mouth cottony, her palms sweaty.

He drew back the curtain. "Go on in."

Adam reclined on a bed raised into a half-sitting position. His cheeks had color, and though his eyes were shut, his breathing was regular.

Bob placed a hand on her back and gave her a gentle shove.

Mel staggered into the room. The curtain fell closed with a rustling sound. Though machines beeped and whirred in other rooms nearby, though patients coughed and their beds creaked as they moved, she paid no attention to the hospital noises. The adrenaline that had kept her upright and coherent on the fifteen-minute cab ride over here had drained out of her the instant she saw Adam. Every muscle went weak and her knees trembled, her hands too.

She tiptoed to the bed. He looked...peaceful. Healthy. *Alive.* She perched one hip on the bed's edge, sneaking her hand around his, where it lay slack on the sheet covering him from the waist down. She stroked her thumb over the back of his hand.

"Kiss him or something." Bob had poked his head around the curtain to utter the command.

She shooed him away with a wave of her hand. Once he'd gone, she leaned over Adam. Her mouth hovered millimeters from his and even the odor of disinfectant and smoke couldn't overpower his natural, masculine scent. She breathed it in, eyes half shut. God, she could've lost him today, without him ever knowing how much she needed him and yearned to make this work between them, without ever hearing her apology.

"When do I get that kiss?"

Adam's raspy voice roused her and she met his bloodshot gaze. "You're awake."

"Huh. Guess I am." His lips parted in a sly, if drowsy, smile. "Figured that out, did ya? Always knew you were smart."

Her eyes burned, tears threatened. "Thought I'd lost you."

"Not so easy to get rid of."

Their lips lingered so close his breaths mingled with hers. She caressed his face, running her hand from his stubbly cheek up to his forehead and down to his jawline. His skin felt warm on hers. "Please don't ever scare me like that again."

He lifted one eyebrow. "Thought you hated me."

She shook her head and their lips grazed each other. His were a bit chapped, but still, even the light contact sent a thrill rippling through her. "I love you, Adam. I could never hate you."

His lips curved in a shaky smile. "But after you found the mask and I admitted what I'd done, you ran away."

"I know, I overreacted." She exhaled, her breath reflecting off his face and back onto hers. The heat of his skin so near hers made her long for the feel of their bodies molded to each other. "The mask shocked and confused me. I freaked out. I'm sorry."

"No apology, please." His hands settled on her back, tentative but warm and firm. His body had gone tense and his gaze was intent on her. "It was all my fault."

She cupped his face in both hands, sliding them up into his hair and back down. "When I saw the fire on TV and Kaya said she'd seen you taken away in an ambulance, I couldn't breathe. I had the horrible, sickening feeling I'd lost you and you'd never even know I'm sorry for freaking out. Then your dad called to tell me you were in the hospital and it took all my strength to keep from breaking down. I was terrified of what I'd find when I got here."

His arms came around her, so strong and yet gentle, binding her to him. "When I was in that building, for a minute I thought I wouldn't make it out. Then I remembered how I promised you'd never lose me and I knew I had to make it out, whatever it took." He tugged her tighter against him, wincing slightly. "I had to come back to you."

"Thank God you did." She skated her thumbs across his mouth, against lips still supple despite being chapped. "I don't want to live without you, Adam. You made a mistake, but the mask thing wasn't meant to hurt me. I understand now you were scared, because you've never had a real relationship before and I wasn't exactly an easy catch. I clung to my celibacy plan, despite all the things we did together, and kept telling you I wanted friendship only."

"I didn't mind waiting."

She moved her fingers to his cheek. "I think I knew, deep down on a subconscious level, it was you that night. The man in the mask. I thought about it the next morning, but I couldn't let myself believe it. Now I realize I never would've danced that way with anyone else."

"Me either," he said. At her surprised look, he added, "I've only ever danced with you."

"Really? I like that." She paused, circling her fingers on his cheek. "Look, we both made mistakes and we need to put it all behind us. Start fresh."

"Does that mean I have to woo you again?"

She smiled, shaking her head. "By starting fresh I mean throwing out all our emotional baggage. You deserve me and I deserve you. Nothing else matters."

"Does this mean we're…"

"Getting back together, if you'll have me." She kissed the tip of his nose. "Will you marry me, Adam Caras?"

He grinned. "Yes. Absolutely, no doubt about it, yes-yes-yes."

She slanted her mouth over his, holding his face possessively, forging deep to savor the taste and heated softness of him. Their tongues tangled, hungrier than ever for the intimacy of the contact, feeding off each other's passion. His hands groped her back, her fingers stroked his face, she moaned into his mouth. When they separated, neither of them could stop grinning.

The curtain slid open and a nurse entered the room. Her brows rose when she spotted them—two flushed people breathing hard, caught in an intimate embrace—but she simply said, "You're being released, Mr. Caras."

"Good," Adam replied, still grinning. "I have to buy my fiancée a ring."

Epilogue

Nine Months Later

Mel reclined in a lounge chair, her legs outstretched and her hands clasped over her very pregnant belly. A warm spring breeze wafted over her, carrying with it the scent of the roses that climbed a trellis fifteen feet away on the side of the little house. Their house. The one where she and Adam would raise their children, beginning with this one.

Running her hands over her belly, she whispered to her unborn child. "You are a very lucky baby, you know? Look at all these people who are going to love you."

She surveyed the backyard party with a smile. Bob Caras manned the barbecue grill, with Jack and Rick hanging around him, cracking jokes and passing him buns to drop on the grill while Kaya rolled her eyes at their goofy humor. Kaya had blossomed in her new position of vice president at Claddagh Web Design, with her own office and her own executive assistant.

Since learning his cancer had gone into total remission, and getting off the hormone therapy, Bob had become his old self again—happy, but slightly grumpy. Toby and Sonya, their baby boy in her arms, loitered near the rose trellis with Adam's mom and Mel's mom. Maggie had moved back to Chicago, and though no reconciliation was likely with her ex-husband, the pair had become good friends. Adam and his brothers loved having their mom around again, though none of them would admit it. Wouldn't be manly, of course.

Mel's smile deepened when she spotted Adam laughing with Brett and Trevor. Her husband had mellowed out in some ways, settling in to their new life as expectant parents, but he'd kept his intensity in the bedroom. Though their love life had slowed down of late, given she was four weeks from her due date, they still found ways to enjoy erotic moments. Adam relished every chance to make her blush with his naughty talk, and she'd gotten pretty darn good at spicy-sexy talk as well. Despite his wicked side, or maybe because of it, she knew he'd make a wonderful father, the kind who hugged his babies, horsed around with them, and made them laugh at his antics.

Adam wandered across the yard toward her, a bowl of chips in one hand. While she admired the view of him, he swept his gaze over the gang in the backyard, until his eyes found her. He trotted to his brothers, handing off the bowl, and hurried to Mel, flopping onto the lounge chair beside hers.

"Hope you're not getting too hot out here," he said, aiming a suggestive smile at her. "The sun can be scorching, you know."

"Not as scorching as you." She rested a hand on his thigh, massaging the flesh exposed by his shorts.

"Don't get me too worked up," he replied, pressing his hand atop hers. "We can't do anything about it for a good while."

"Are you sorry we decided to have a baby? I mean, you must miss all the sex."

His smile softened as he leaned in to kiss her cheek. "I'd give up sex for the rest of my life if it means having adorable little girls like you bouncing around the house."

She raised her hand to thread her fingers into his hair. "With your DNA in there, she'll probably be a heart-breaker too."

"Her brothers will look out for her."

"Brothers?" Mel pulled her head back, squinting at him. "How many babies are you planning on us having?"

He shrugged. "Couple dozen?"

"Dozen!" She slapped a hand over her mouth to stifle her laughter. "I hope you're saving money for adoption fees, because I am not giving birth to two dozen kids."

"I'll settle for two or three."

"That's doable."

Sliding one hand up her cheek, into her hair, he tilted her head back for a deep kiss. When they came up for air, Jack and Rick had crept closer, ten feet from the feet of their lounge chairs.

Jack smirked. "The way you two go at it, you'll need a bigger house for all the babies you'll be making."

"We agreed on two or three," Adam said, relaxing into his seat, casting a playful smile at Mel. "But I think I can seduce my wife into giving me a few more."

"Hmm," Mel said, moving to sit on his lap, looping her arms around his neck. "Well, you did seduce me into falling in love with you and marrying you, so I imagine you could convince me to do almost anything."

Adam folded his arms around her waist. "Ditto, babe. You command, I obey."

She glanced at his brothers. "I think it's finally time to announce the bad news to the world, honey."

"What bad news?"

"The Arsonist has been caught." She wagged a finger at him. "And you've been very naughty, so I'm giving you a life sentence—of total devotion and wickedly hot sex."

He grinned. "That's one sentence I'm happy to serve."

Anna Durand is a bestselling, multi-award-winning author of contemporary and paranormal romance. Her books have earned bestseller status on every major retailer and wonderful reviews from readers around the world. But that's the boring spiel. Here are the really cool things you want to know about Anna!

Born on Lackland Air Force Base in Texas, Anna grew up moving here, there, and everywhere thanks to her dad's job as an instructor pilot. She's lived in Texas (twice), Mississippi, California (twice), Michigan (twice), and Alaska—and now Ohio.

As for her writing, Anna has always made up stories in her head, but she didn't write them down until her teen years. Those first awful books went into the trash can a few years later, though she learned a lot from those stories. Eventually, she would pen her first romance novel, the paranormal romance *Willpower*, and she's never looked back since.

Want even more details about Anna? Get access to her extended bio when you subscribe to her newsletter and download the free bonus ebook, *Hot Scots Confidential*. You'll also get hot deleted scenes, character interviews, fun facts, and more! Plus you'll receive the short story *Tempted by a Kiss* and mutliple bonus chapters in both ebook and audiobook formats.

Visit AnnaDurand.com to sign up.